FRESHERS

Kevin Sampson

JONATHAN CAPE
LONDON

Published by Jonathan Cape 2003

2 4 6 8 10 9 7 5 3 1

First published in Great Britain in 2003 by
Jonathan Cape
Random House, 20 Vauxhall Bridge Road,
London SW1V 2SA

Random House Australia (Pty) Limited
20 Alfred Street, Milsons Point, Sydney,
New South Wales 2061, Australia

Random House New Zealand Limited
18 Poland Road, Glenfield,
Auckland 10, New Zealand

Random House South Africa (Pty) Limited
Endulini, 5A Jubilee Road, Parktown 2193, South Africa

The Random House Group Limited Reg. No. 954009
www.randomhouse.co.uk

A CIP catalogue record for this book
is available from the British Library

ISBN 0-224-06225-5

Papers used by The Random House Group are natural,
recyclable products made from wood grown in sustainable forests;
the manufacturing processes conform to the environmental
regulations of the country of origin

Typeset by
Palimpsest Book Production Limited,
Polmont, Stirlingshire

Printed and bound in Great Britain by
Mackays of Chatham PLC, Chatham, Kent

For Joe and Anna

With almighty thanks to these stalwarts for enduring my petty and pedantic questions. You are saints, one and all: Professor Neil Roberts, University of Sheffield; Olie Clay; Tristan Moriarty; Clare Milligan; Sarah Murphy; Rachel Garman; Ian from QM; and the mighty Tanner Broon.

'At seventeen you are not serious.'
– Arthur Rimbaud

'*I* fucking am!'
– Kit Hannah

1. First Semester

Week 0: Day 1
Weather: Drizzle
Soundtrack: Autechre – *Chiastic Slide*

I should've gone for all or nothing. This belated change of heart has not so much backfired as left me beached. I'm on a bed, in a small room, in a vast hall of residence, totally alone. I have no notion at all of what I will do next. I can't even say I'm unhappy. I'm just numb, empty, flat. If I feel anything it's the desperate gnawing dread of loneliness. For the first time in my life I feel utterly alone and rudderless. My life choices at this exact point in time consist of unpacking or not unpacking. I truly do not know which way to turn, so I just lie here and wait for something to happen. I'm lying here on top of the bed, cold but too listless to climb under the sheets, watching the rain run down my window pane.

My original plan was to miss freshers' week entirely. I was going to just turn up next Monday, go to school, do the work. I want to make friends, course I do, but something about freshers' week made me tense up the more I was forced to think about it. All I could envisage was hordes of people fiercely befriending one another out of nothing more than the terror of getting left behind. I'm not anti-social, me, but the idea of crowds, of mass participation, of organised fun . . . I don't know. I really can't be doing with it.

The more that Mum went on about it, the more I knew I was making the right decision. All summer she'd been going on about 'uni' and rag japes, like that's all there is to it. But the closer it all got, the more she seemed taken over by the whole thing of freshers' week. She went on and on and on about it, not even insinuating but flagrantly lecturing me about all the amazing 'characters' I'd meet from all over the country, from all walks of life and, frankly, about the endless parade of women I'd pull. She was only being Mum, but her increasing obsession with freshers' week began to get to me. This low-level throb would burn in my head every time she mentioned it, every step closer it came.

All those people, each with the power to accept or reject me – that's what freshers' week seemed to be about. I wouldn't have the chance to stand back and evaluate things, get a good sense of what a person was all about. It was going to have to be all yes, yes, yes, now, now, now, if you didn't want to get left behind in the stampede for conviviality. What if you make friends with the guy that lives next door then find he's a complete twat, though? You're stuck with him then, aren't you?

So I was all for bodyswerving it and, in doing so, sort of defining myself, setting myself apart. I was eyes wide open to the consequences, the prospect that everybody'd be chummed up and paired off by the time I got there – and I was fine with it. It was all settled in my mind. I'd go away to Sheffield, turn up to lectures and take it from there. I was going to miss freshers' week and I was absolutely fine with it. And once the decision was made I felt an instant and exhilarating relief. All that skull buzz seeped away and for the first time since I got my results I felt ready for it. I felt good.

But I didn't, did I? I didn't miss freshers' week at all – not all of it, at least. I caved into Mum's hourly onslaught – tales of what a blast Willie Wilson was having, all the friends he'd made already, how he'd spent the whole day in bed after the Broomhill Crush then got up for the Tapton Freshers' Ball and done it all over again.

That was what did it for me. Not that she was gradually selling me this wet dream of a careless student wonderland – just that *she* was selling it. Quite a lot of people I know are quite OK with all that. They get on great with their mums, tell them everything. Not me, I don't. I just couldn't be doing with letting her in on my life like that. What's that all about, your mother putting her head round the door and asking you things, really intimate things that you don't even want to think about yourself?

'You cop off last night then, son? Get your hole, did you?'

Spooky, is what it is – weird and, I don't know . . . *wrong*. Not that she'd ever ask me that, like, though from the way she's been carrying on I really, truly do not know any more. And I don't even *know* fucking Willie Wilson, either! He went to our school, fair dos, but I didn't *know* him. But no, that doesn't matter – just cos we're both going to Sheffield (doing completely, radically different courses incidentally) our two mothers are suddenly in cahoots, plotting out the grim jollitude that's ours to be had at lewd and luscious 'uni'.

I was holding out, though. I had a plan and I was sticking to it. It was fine while Erk was still around. He thinks the same as me. We can spend hours, mornings, days, me and Erk, just slumped in his room or mine, saying nothing. When we do speak, we'll be ripping it all to bits. He's my one true friend, Erk. He's like me. When it all comes down to it, he doesn't really want to go to college at all. True, he didn't get his grades, but he was never that set on university anyway. I was stunned when I called round and his mum told me he'd gone to Aston. *Aston*, for crying out loud! To do *metallurgy*! He won't last a month. But I felt exposed without him. Felt like it was just a matter of time, after that.

And it was. It was. I was out with Mum down Golden Square, giving in to her will, to her *need* to buy me some new jeans and a warm jacket to go away in. She wanted to do that, badly wanted to, and in all honesty I was happy just to let her have her way. She's not one of these mums that'll try and buy you clobber from Matalan and pretend she doesn't know the difference. She's always been sound about clothes. I think that's where I get it from. I'm not saying I love being out with her or anything. I'm not one of these that's trying to make out they've got loads in common with their old girl and she's more like a mate than a ma. Fuck that. What I will say about her is she's dead realistic. She *knows* a good parka is going to set her back a ton at least, and she's all right with that. She knows the score. Other than that, I'd have to say that shopping with her can be a bit of a nightmare.

The real nightmare came when we bumped into Willie's ma outside HMV. She looks about sixty by the way, Willie Wilson's mother, she even *talks* like an old lady. She kept flashing me these knowing little looks, as though I was pathetic, a real little pansy by not being over there in Sheffield already, drinking fifteen pints a night and boning loads of girls. She was looking at me dead sly, like she was reading my mind, seeing me for the coward I am, a mummy's boy, a little Safe Eddie. And Mum was having it, too. She was going along with all that.

'I know, I know – I don't think Kit knows what he's missing. But you know what they're like. Once their mind's made up . . .'

And she rolls her eyes and gives Mrs Wilson a bit of a 'what can you do with them?' look and starts into all this crap about girls and safe sex and condoms. Your own mother, for fuck's sake, talking openly about johnnies with someone else's ma! Calling them 'condoms', she was – horror show!

Then it started getting to be like that all the time – and I was beginning to hate her for it, to be quite honest. Seriously, I was starting to feel abused. She was just coming into my room and sitting on my bed and looking at me with that awful, twinkling expression. I really don't believe it's a parent's place to twinkle at their children. They should be discouraging all that. Sex, drugs, drinking, staying out – they should at least adopt a tired and weary resignation to it all instead of all this winking familiarity. Not her. Oh no. She gives me this big, insider's smile and goes: 'Guess how many Willie sank in the Dox last night?'

I just gave her nothing back whatsoever. I was blazing. *Sank*, for fuck's sake! How many mothers say that to their only son, in all good conscience? And the idea of Willie's mother, that stale, sturdy old cow with her mean, tight perm, getting on the phone to her and besting her like that. And my lovely, simple mum not having a clue that it was all a competition to Willie's loveless mother. She wasn't phoning Mum to share intimacies with her. She was phoning to crow and boast and compare and Mum was taking her shit and swallowing it whole.

But it wasn't that that did it, either. It wasn't that at all. It wasn't Willie Wilson's ma and it wasn't all this insinuating, twinkling crap about the Dox. And God, I love her, I do. I didn't want to stop her fun, kill it all stone dead. She was loving it all, loving the whole thing of trying to be a part of my life. And more than anything, she was trying to tell me that she knew what big, big times were just around the corner for me and that she was just . . . dead *excited* for me. That's all she was doing – just being a mum, full of it all and want-ing to enjoy it with me. I was on the cusp of leaving home, leaving her, not needing her any more and, far from getting all maudlin about it, she was made up for me. She was buzzing on it. But me – I really did not, do not, want any of it. I didn't want it from her, from my *mum*. I didn't want to just blank her out – I just wish she hadn't put me in that posi-tion. I knew what I had to do, though. I knew I'd have to do it for her, for Mum. Not before I'd played it out I wouldn't, though.

'Docks? Didn't know Sheffield *had* docks.'

That just made her worse. Her eyes went all sparkly with tease and affection.

'That's what they all call it, duh! The Dox.'

'Who's *they all*?'

'All the studes. The freshers.'

That word. How I fucking hate it. She just carried on,

7

oblivious to the pulsing of my temples. If only she knew what I was thinking, what I was about to do for her, perhaps she wouldn't have been so dogged. But dogged she is. She's relentless.

'You won't be asking me this time next week what the Dox is!'

I hung my head and said nothing. She was starting to get the message, but still she soldiered on as though, once I'd heard her out it'd be game over. I'd dance with delight and hug her and, there and then, start randomly hurling clothes into a holdall, shouting: 'Get me there, now! How soon can I *be* there!'

'It's your *local*, Kit! The Fox and Duck. Well, there's *millions* of locals, but everyone says that the Dox . . .'

And that was the moment I gave in. That was what did it. I never heard the rest. That sentence, which had me gaping at her mouth as it let the words out, finally persuaded me to just go, now, go and get it over with as soon as possible. In fact, I can refine the moment to one word. *Everyone.* I got as far as her saying 'everyone' and the drilling came back in my head. All I could see was the pleading in her eyes, and I could see that it would not take much more for that pleading to turn to embarrassment. So I did it for her. By getting up off my bed and looking her in the eye and saying let's go, I gave my mum what she wanted. I let her in.

The drive across the Snake Pass was one of silence, and sadness. The last time I cut through these moors and hills, when I came for my interview, I was overcome by the unyielding beauty all around me. The streams, the rocks, the deep and mournful pine-flanked reservoirs seemed to reflect the discord in my soul. Then, as now, I was struck by a similarly unyielding truth. The truth is that I'm terrified by all this. I know, I know, I *know* that I want to have this experience, to have been away to university, to make it on my own — but it scares me. That's the truth. That's the real reason I've put off coming here. It's nothing to do with defining myself as Me. It's cos I'm scared.

The growing nausea that's been draining through my guts since damp and dismal Glossop knocks me sideways on first sight of Sheffield. There's no preparing for it, no way of being ready for the crude reality of this stripped and savage metropolis. One minute I'm daydreaming as moorland sheep chomp at wet and springy verges, close enough to touch. The next thing there, below me, massive and white and chilling is the sprawl of the city. Six, eight, ten priapic concrete tower blocks lurch into view. Twelve blocks, sixteen – and cars, lorries, people, loads of them, all down there below. Fuck, but I don't like it. I don't like it here.

Now I'm laid out here in my Ranmoor cell, surrounded by the sounds of merriment and it's already too late. I know nobody. They all met yesterday and the day before. I can hear them laughing and making plans and diving in and out of each other's rooms, careless and coltish and fresh. I felt a brief elation as Mum and Dad drove away. I won that little battle, at least. I just wanted them to let me out, let me get on with it – I wouldn't even let them help me carry my stuff in, with so many people hanging around the main entrance. Dad, who hadn't tried to break into my thoughts at all on the drive over, just turned to Mum and said it. He put it into words.

'Come on, pet. He wants to do this on his own. Let him be.'

Be what, though? Dad put his hand on my shoulder briefly and got back in the car. Mum tried for a big, long hug, but I got free, pecked her on the cheek and picked up my bags. I'd long imagined that the moment they got back in the car and drove away, that'd be the moment I went to pieces. It wasn't like that. As Mum fought back her tears and made a 'phone' gesture out of the window, I found a strange surge of power run through me. It lasted as long as it took me to glance up at all those windows with lights on already, rooms

9

where people all know each other, know the ropes. Standing there in the Ranmoor car park, I was transfixed. I could see posters on walls, people ironing clothes and making tea, faces lit up by the macabre glow of computer screens, communing with the ether.

What stunned me most was the football scarves hanging from windows. Wigan Athletic. Nottingham Forest. It smashed me, that. It crushed what there was of that ego surge, to know that here, just there, were people so confident in themselves that they could fly their convictions from the mast. I could *never* do that. Even if you asked me a dozen times what my favourite album is, I wouldn't tell you until the thirteenth time of asking. Even then, I'd probably lie. I wouldn't really want you to know.

I found my own way to G Block, passing door after door festooned with gay and desperate stick-on notes.

Mally's Pit. No need to knock – just pile in!

Dumbledore's Den. Come with smiles (beer and spliff gladly welcome, too!)

Another one said:

John Dowie

I let myself into my cell, happy that I hadn't been waylaid or quizzed by obliging fellow residents, yet drenched with a dull despair that now, truly, I am on my own. Out there, beyond that door, young people are living their lives. They're doing it, doing all the things they longed to do when they came away to 'uni'. I, Kit Hannah, am hiding from it all.

I drag myself to my feet and move a couple of things around. I unpack the toilet tissue and hide it on my wardrobe floor, as though I'm being watched. I stand facing the wall and when I come to (seconds? minutes later?) I'm still just standing there, looking at the wall. The room is tiny and bare. It needs posters, it needs CDs lining the walls, it needs *things*, but I can't find the spark to do any of it. All I can think about is: who the fuck *are* all those people out there? I find myself pushing my ear to the wall. This is simply not me, but it's what I'm doing. I'm listening for signs of life in the adjoining room. My own little cell is at the end of the corridor, right by the exit stairs and the bridge to the next block, so I only have a neighbour on one side, thank fuck. I sit myself up and take a deep breath. I know that never, never, never in a million years will I stride out and knock on some stranger's door and introduce myself. But maybe somebody will come to me. I stick on Autechre to let them know I'm here, but I don't crank the volume past 3 in case anyone's working. I leave the door open a crack, just a crack, enough to encourage jaunty corridor mates to push their way in and envelop me with their bonhomie. I unpack my computer as loudly as possible and sit there, staring at the screen, a fixed and friendly grin on my face lest any passer-by should spy me. Nobody knocks.

I return to my bed and lie with my arms crossed behind my head. The deviant snag and pull of *Chiastic Slide* is over too soon but I don't get up to put more music on. I stay there and listen to the air. I can hear the air, have always been able to hear it. If I concentrate on one small space in front of my eyeline I can see the multitude of particles colliding, can hear them too, hear them tingle and thrill as they oscillate through time. All the noise of the corridor has died down, now. Distantly, possibly outside in the gardens, I hear a voice, South Wales, male, asking, rather shouting, about dinner. He wants to know whether somebody is going over for dinner. Another voice, one from the universal South-East, replies that she'll be along in a mo. She adds, apologetically, that she hasn't called her folks since Sunday. I can tell from her voice that only good resides within this girl. I see her life laid out behind and in front of her, and it's all good, all happy, all to plan. If I'm to bump into someone now and have to make conversation, make an impression on them, then that's the sort of person I want to meet. She's good and she could only make me feel good, too. Yet the idea that people have been here since Sunday lays me low with inadequacy. It's already too late to meet anyone, of any sort. Why did I not stick to my plan? Come then, or come not at all.

There's a general increase in noise, an opening and slamming of doors, a shuffling of feet, all coming together for food. I realise I'm hungry, but I can't bring myself to go across for the meal. To walk into that cavernous dining hall; to see puzzled heads turn as familiar inmates strain to recognise the incomer; to queue up in silence, unknown, unwanted; and to take my tray to whatever remote spot of solitude I can find at the furthest and least populous table would be too much, right now. I can slip out of the side door instead, walk into Broomhill, treat myself to a nice Chinese, maybe stock up on water, orange juice and Maltesers. That's what I'll do.

But no sooner does the idea suggest itself than it drags me deeper into this bog of despondency. I hate the functionality of it, hate the *responsibility* of such a thought, but I can't help considering how much Mum and Dad are paying for these meals. Between them they're over the earning threshold that condemns me to only 75 per cent of the full loan, but was Mum fazed by it? Was she fuck! She'd been planning and trimming and tucking away for this since Maddy went away to Florida. Did she tell me I'd jolly well have to find a job to make up the difference? No. Did she tell me they'd do their best, they'd give me as much towards the shortfall as possible? No, they didn't. They found the dough. They came up with the readies, and a little bit more. I'm fine, I'm sorted and it's all down to Mum's tenacity. If I don't walk over there, find a place and eat the meals she's paid for then I'm nothing. I'm nothing. I may as well go back to fucking Twiss

Green, Nowheresville, and lie on my own sad bed there.

I check myself out in the mirror. I stand on the bed to make sure my arse is framed to its best in these new cords. If I'm going to walk through a roomful of people, it's important that the arse looks all right. When you're a titch, which I most certainly am, you have to play to your strengths. A snug new pair of cords are one of the things I wear well. My clothes, the clothes I picked out this morning with painstaking indecision, look good. Everything I have on defines me as me. I'm not looking to stand out – but I look good. There's nothing sloppy or by accident about me, nothing that others can see but I don't know about. Those who know will pick out the things that matter and those who don't, won't. I take a deep breath, note that I am fucking shitting myself and exit the room.

I try to force some bump and swagger into my walk, but everybody's too busy acting at ease to notice. The canteen is nothing like as bad as I've been imagining. The most intimidating thing about it, I find, is the smell. There's an alien, cloying scent of floor polish and vegetable oil and well-tried routine in the atmosphere, a sense that everything that everybody is doing in this vast room has been done a thousand times before and will be done again, because that's what works. I know intrinsically that the smell that overpowers me now is one that has dismayed many a new kid on the block. It's not that it's an unpleasant aroma, just one that I immediately associate with knuckling down and fitting in. I have to fight to maintain a semblance of self-possession.

I queue up and look around. There are plenty enough people sat on their own, avidly staring at their freshers' handbooks or otherwise studiously trying to avoid any kind of eye contact that finds them out as friendless. If I want to push it here, I can put on a brave smile, find someone who looks OK and I guarantee they will gobble up the offer of camaraderie like crazy. But I don't. Now that I know that everyone else is in the same boat – apart from those odd little knots of chums who are talking too loud and bigging themselves up as wags par excellence – it's easier to sit through the meal in silence.

To the far side of the hall some highly self-conscious, self-consciously jaunty students are whacking together a sound system. My heart sinks as I read the bunting – RANMOOR FRESHERS' BALL, and tonight, no less – and I find myself a spot on the table nearest the exit. The food's OK. The veggie option is a quite tasty shepherd's pie. I'm enjoying it, already three-quarters lost in my own thoughts, when a good-looking woman hovers over me and asks if it's OK to join me. With her is a fool. There can be no other explanation for his fanatical smiling. Throughout our three-minute exchange he grins like a simpleton, while the woman does all the talking.

'Hi there! I'm Julia, Julia Forte, Welfare Officer for these halls – though that sounds *far* too grave and far too much like a real, grown-up job for a big kid like me. Now, tell me, who are you and why haven't I seen you yet? Did you come to Registration?'

Her intention is reassurance and inclusion. She alienates me immediately with yet more implications that I've Missed Out. I manage to persuade her that I'm fine, I'm settling in wonderfully and that I wouldn't miss the Ranmoor Hop tonight for anything. She eyes me carefully and slips me three light blue vouchers, each good for a pint of beer at the Nightingale Bar. It's at this point that the simpering sidekick makes his move.

'Yeah, and like, I'm Matthew and I love Jesus yeah, and Jesus loves *you*. And like, listen, yeah . . .'

He makes what appears to be an attempt to hold both my hands. I resist his gesture emphatically, causing him to stagger backwards. It doesn't stop his sermon.

'. . . none of this shit is easy, yeah? If it ever, *ever* gets too much for you . . .' He sighs passionately and drawls his words

14

with real, candid drama. 'Just fucking *knock*, yeah? Just knock.'

He eyeballs me for three agonising seconds, palms me a card with his room number, email and mobile-phone details, and the pair of them are off. Swearing Christians. Too much, man.

If any of these students here saw me heading towards them in the street, they'd have me down as a townie. I'm not. I wouldn't be seen dead in Stone Island or Henri Lloyd and I would never, never, *never* wear a Burberry baseball cap. I'd never wear *any* baseball cap. The thing with me is, I'm what might best be described as petite. I'm five foot six, just, and there's only certain things look good on me. I wear a lot of black and navy-blue and grey attire, but close-fitting – I hate baggy clothing. I hate suits, hate football shirts, hate anything with a band's name or a slogan. I wear things like needlecords, Clarks shoes, Farhi and Smedley pullovers, parkas. I'm fond of a crisp denim jacket, whatever the weather.

Standing here at the very end of the bar, four whole steps from the stairs and, consequently, the exit, I must stand out massively. Well, not massively if I'm strictly honest about it – I'm small. But I know I don't *look* like a student. There's loads of lads in those Italia tracky tops, loads of girls in Miss Sixty flares. They do – they all *look* like students. Even the things about myself I can't adjust seem different, somehow. I don't think I've got a studenty face or studenty features. I've got hair and eyes so dark they're just about black, and cheekbones that could've been moulded from plaster of Paris. My hair's always cropped number five on top, two at the sides, and only accentuates the narrow slit of my eyes. I've grown up being told I'm pretty. Right up till I was about six, people didn't know if I was a boy or a girl. Way, way back in the family there's Formosan on Mum's side. That's what she's always said, *Formosan*. Her great-grandparents weren't from Taiwan inci- dentally, they were from Formosa. I love her for that now, just as I loved her slant, flashing eyes and her perfect, porcelain skin when I was a boy.

I've been here for exactly twelve minutes. I have my back, or rather my arse, to the room, feigning nonchalance as I watch the bar clock and drink steadily. I've very nearly finished my second pint. Nobody has been actively unfriendly – two girls and one lad have smiled at me, indeed – but I haven't exactly been welcomed into the heaving family bosom of Ranmoor, either. I can see Julia and that mad Christian loon over by the windows, dragging reluctant souls together. Frankly, I'd consider it a false start to meet somebody that way. It just wouldn't be right.

But I'm fine, here. It could be that the two swift pints of Ruddles have smoothed away those anxious edges, but I'm quite happy to stand here and let fate be the winner. I've made my plan. I have another beer voucher courtesy of Forte, J., Welfare Officer. I shall calmly exchange same for one more pint of Ruddles which I shall drink at a less hurried pace this time, giving those around me time to make my acquaintance. But if no such fellows are forthcoming, I'm quite drunk enough – or I will be in half an hour – to toddle back to my room and snooze away my first night untroubled by the howl of loneliness that dogged those first few hours here. As a significant concession to friend-getting protocol, however, I turn away from the bar and face the bustling lounge. I wouldn't exactly say I'm smiling, but my face is open to offers.

The drink helps me feel aloof. Something from within protects me, seals me from those earlier fears and insecurities and makes me able to contemplate the room with a calm and appraising eye, and with authority and distance, too. I feel like I'm in the place where everyone else wants to be. I watch them all drink, watch them gather in groups and circles, hear them boast and thrust about this and that – boys in boy gangs talking loudly of girls they've had, girls in boy gangs talking of football teams they love and hate, all of them yattering about gap years, about Thailand, about the courses they're going to do . . . and I'm fine with it. I don't feel too bad at all. None of them is any worse than the next one. No one here is a threat to me. It's going to be fine. I still don't feel as though I can just barge over, sidle into a group and, like, intro*duce* myself, but I know intuitively that if I do, when I do, it's all going to be OK. I drain my pint and decide to retire.

A hand, quite a large hand, grabs me and yanks me back to the bar. I hadn't even noticed her standing there in the corner, but fuck knows how I missed her. She's huge, this girl. She's a giant – though a giant in perfect, perfectly enormous proportion. She's well over six foot, a good six-three, at least – and her hands, eyes, breasts, feet are all outsize, too. There is no fat, no spare about her, yet she's *large*. I think she might be beautiful, but I can't be sure.

'You ain't going nowhere, kidder.'

Her voice is quite deep, bit slurry, bit pissed, but it's a nice voice. She's sort of happy-sounding, like the girl outside my window before – well spoken without being austere. She's not posh, as such – just *nice*. She pulls me back to the bar. I try to smile, but I bet I look traumatised.

'I've been watching you . . .'

'Oh aye?'

I wish I could think of something witty to say. I can, most of the time – but it's usually a good few hours after the moment has passed. She doesn't seem to notice my discomfiture.

'You want to know something?'

That one's a bit easier.

'I do, you know. I really want to know something.'

She smiles with her eyes. She's lovely. She's a whole foot taller than me.

'You're me, you are.'

17

Now that's a tricky one, that is. I'd defy most people to come back with a winner from that one.

'So let's see, then. Does that mean that when you buy me a drink it doesn't matter cos it's me that's paying for it?'

It takes her a moment, but it's worth it. The smile is just the best. Her whole face opens up, her eyes sparkle and she leans her head right back and submits to laughter, actively seems to give herself over to hilarity. When she's stopped cackling she offers her hand, her long, clammy hand, and shakes.

'Jinty. What you drinking?'

'Kit. Ruddles please.'

She inclines her head, acknowledging the order. I like her. I think I know her, already. I think about it, think fuck it and I go for it.

'Twat of a name, by the way.'

More delightful peals of giggly laughter.

'Tell me about it! Better than Virginia, though.'

We end up slumped against the wall, thick as thieves, watching the dancing fools give it all they've got. No one is spared.

'The ones that get me are these, you know, porky lasses that squeeze themselves into little tops that say *Babe* . . .'

'Lads who err on the side of heft wearing Brazil shirts.'

'. . . these little girls' tops on, you know, well-made girls that say *Sex Kitten* . . .'

'Or *Cute* . . .'

'Exactly. Little midriff tops and these big ale guts sticking out. Shameless, really. If they really *have* to wear stuff like that, it should say . . .'

'*Dog.*'

She stops and stares at me. Shit! I really wish I hadn't said it. But then she guffaws again and hugs me. She radiates naughty good humour.

'You really *are* me, aren't you? I could tell just by looking at you, from the way you were leaning back there, taking it

18

all in, looking at everyone else . . . You're horrible, aren't you? You're nasty!'

'Am not!'

'Are too!'

I eye her with drunken sincerity.

'Jinty. I think I'm going to pass out.'

'Oh no you don't. Come on.' She drags me to my feet. 'Reefs are 99p all night down at Bar One.'

'Bar One? That's the Union, innit? That's *miles* away!'

'So? Nothing ventured, hey?'

'Ah, no. Not tonight, hey?'

'Come on!'

'No. No. No, no, no, no, no.'

'Yes.'

'All right then.'

Bar One gets off rather lightly. We tune into a gaggle of excitable newberters trilling on about Glastonbury. I turn to Jinty.

'How can anyone even pretend to like Polyphonic Spree?'

'I know. Insanity. Utter insanity.'

She drifts off, smiling to herself. 'What's that other lot? *Always* turn up, *every* fucking festival? Bore the arse off every poor bastard in the field, but you *have* to say they're amazing! Fuck are they called, Kit?'

And I know. I know straight away who she means. 'That'll be Ladysmith Black Mambazo, madam!'

'*That's* them! Bastards!'

I love her for that. I really do. We swig on alcopops and look for more sport. I point out to Jinty the girls who comically clutch their bosoms and sing with their eyes to the ceiling when Britney goes: '*Oh so typically me!*'

And Jinty points out the lads on the periphery of the bar who nudge each other so hard whenever a good-looking girl passes by that they can only be virgins. But by and large we just sit there, drinking, and find out all there is to know about each other – all that we choose to reveal at least, anyway. When we get back to Ranmoor I don't get any 'kiss me' vibes off her whatsoever. There's no way I'd make a mess of such a great and unexpected first date anyway, but this is unambiguous. She wants me as a pal. By the time I've grappled with my shoe, got it stuck in the leg of my cords and fallen backwards into bed, the room is spinning with girls in slogan T-shirts dancing to Britney, smiling stoically. I know I haven't been as nice as I might. I know I could have tried harder to fit in. But I have a friend.

Week 0: Day 2
Weather: Pale Sunshine
Soundtrack: Lemon Jelly – 'Nice Weather for Ducks'

Fuck, does my head hurt. And fuck, do I feel good. I spring out of bed, something I haven't done for a long, long time, and heave the stiff window open. Shafts of sunshine backlight the yellowing leaves of the little tree outside. I don't know what kind of tree it is. It seems perfectly symmetrical, seems to hold out its branches in all directions, saying: 'This is how it is.'

The sun isn't exactly singeing the carpet, but it's out there, it's up there, I can sense it. The patches of wet on the paving outside are drying around shapes of scuffed leaves. There's the smell of ciggies from people smoking as they pass outside, and life seems good and slow. There's no hurry today, nothing to chase after.

I rattle through my CDs. I know what tune I want on. I look for the vibrant technicolor of the Lemon Jelly CD and bang it straight on to track five. The subtle inanity of the lyric matches my mood perfectly.

'*All the ducks are swimming in the water, tra-la-la lala-la!*'

Genius! I graze the booklet for a moment, case that queer picture of the kids staring at, what? A dead bird? An insect running round in circles with no wings? Then the hazy summer guitar comes in and I feel good all over again and I check the time and I'm fine. I brush my pegs hard, poke my head around the door to check the corridor, make sure no one's coming. With towel and full kit, I patter down to the shower room and set to work.

I give myself a good all-over scrub and, heavy as my knob is in my hand, I resist the urge to kill it. Someone comes into one of the other cubicles, shouts 'Hi!' I shout 'Hello' back. I crank off the taps and start to dry and dress myself in a hurry. There's something not quite right about conversations with people you don't know and can't see and besides, I don't want to be late. Nonetheless, I shout 'See you' as I'm leaving. No need to be ignorant, I think – specially as I'm dressed now and the escape route is clear. The dining room is almost empty when I amble through. I see her straight away. My spirits are crushed. She's sitting there, laughing. She's throwing her head back and laughing passionately, fully, like she was last night. The sight of her tears me in half. Her pale and beautiful face is creased with merriment. Her red lips are dragged right back into a smile that's almost painful and her eyes, when she opens them again, are shockingly blue. Her head, framed by that shaggy vermilion bob, returns to landing position but still her shoulders heave gently with mirth. Jinty is sitting there, laughing, with two lads. I hate them both at first sight. I hate them hard. But, as nobody has seen me yet, I pick up the gait of my walk and bounce over to them. She gives a good impression of being pleased to see me.

'Kitty, darling . . .'

I try to come across as someone with a terrific sense of humour, self-deprecation a speciality. I wince and hold my hands up, as though surrendering to pain.

'Please, please, no more diminutives, I beg of you. I'm wee enough as things stand. Just Kit, if you will. Kit is fine.' I try to look as amiable as possible, awaiting introductions.

'Kit, this is Simon . . .'

Hate that name. A freak, let's face it, a bony freak with a long, sharp head, mad, mean, round little specs and crazy facial-hair arrangements holds out his limp hand like he's waiting for change. To be precise, he holds out his fingers. The rest of it is hidden in the sleeves of his Quiksilver hoody, which he's pulled right down over his hands and wrists. I shake and smile.

'All right, Simon.'

I'm on best behaviour, here. No overfamiliarity, no 'Si' or 'Simes', it's just warmth and sincerity all the way, from me. Simon's eyeballs, I notice, are tiny and they gleam behind his glasses. He looks all right, though. For such a skinny, angular, scared-looking lad he's got a nice way about him.

'And this is Ben.'

Ben has wet teeth. He has a space between each tooth, and each tooth is moist. He wears earrings. He has approximately fifteen to twenty earrings in his left ear and he hasn't washed his hair for many, many moons. There's something sly about him. Surely it can't be him that's making Jinty chuckle.

'Hi there, Ben.'

We shake. His hand is soft and strangely warm.

'These two reprobates are from my . . .'

She turns to the boys for help. I *hate* her calling these two dunces 'reprobates'. Every little thing about them gives off a smell of mundanity that no amount of earrings and funky sideburns can disguise. Reprobates they are not.

'What *is* it that we inhabit, precisely? Wings? Annexes?'

She sounds posher than she was last night. Maybe it's just me.

'Dunno. It's blocks, innit?'

'Sounds a bit like prison, dunnit?'

Ben has a Frank Skinner accent, more or less. Skinner, perversely, is in possession of moist teeth also.

'Well, it *is* prison, isn't it?'

I just blurt it out, almost surprised to hear my own voice. It's not even funny. It's a comment that marks me down as a dullard and I'm kicking myself for being so needy and nervous that I had to say something, anything, just to have joined in. It's not me, that. I look around, aware of myself now they're all looking up at me. There's a bit of a silence.

'Brekkie worth bothering with, then?'

'Not bad, as it goes,' says Simon.

'Had worse,' offers Ben.

I find myself thinking it's high time I made a mission statement – something that tells the world a little bit more about myself.

'Much on offer for the loony vegetarian element?'

Jinty wrinkles her nose up.

'Eggs. If you like them emulsified and dripping in oil.'

I smile in a way I like to imagine is endearing, and go and sit down next to her.

'Think I'll leave it. Anyone need a cuppa?'

More wheedling, needy plea-bargaining in my voice, but only I seem to notice it. Simon gets up. He cranks his arm back and scratches between his shoulder blades.

'No ta, mate. I'm done.'

He's got a slow, doped-out voice with a distant hint of a local accent somewhere in the mix. He seems to be addressing me more than the other two.

'Gonna catch up on my mails, and I said I'd help some dude from home find digs.' He makes a steering gesture as he drawls.

'Drive him round a bit?' I almost beam approval at him in my eagerness to be liked. 'Nice one. You've got a car then, hey?'

Yet again I'm cringing almost before the words have taken flight. A sneaky look passes over Ben, who gets up too.

'I'm away myself. Got to meet a dealer.'

No one asks him what manner of dealer he might be meeting. This doesn't stop him from telling us.

'Bit of skunk.' He makes a casual circle of perfection with his thumb and forefinger. 'Laters.'

He winks and pads off surprisingly quietly for a lad of his width. This leaves me sitting there with Jinty, who doesn't waste a second. She takes my hand, and I know I'm dead.

'Look, Kit, honey. Last night. I got *reaaaalllly* pissed.'

'And?'

I'm going for the cool defensive. Whatever she comes up with, I'm going to knock it back.

'And, I think I might have given you the wrong impression.'

'You gave me the impression that you are a) quite long, b) fond of drink, and c) very funny.' I look at her full-on. I have a stab at a funny-bereft voice. 'Don't crush me, Jinty. Please. Please don't tell me the drinking was all an act . . .'

She waits patiently for me to stop pretending to sob and takes up where she left off.

'I just feel a bit awkward, that's all. Bit exposed. I felt *very* weird about meeting you here this morning.'

'Weird how?'

'Like, I dunno. Like I'd got you here on false pretences.'

I look right into her eyes.

'Jinty. What the *fuck* are you on about?'

She sighs out loud, long and wearisome.

'Look. Last night . . .'

'Yeeees?'

'I mean, I was standing there at the bar and I *so* felt like I'd made this terrible, awful mistake and I didn't fit in and. . .' She flaps her hand at thin air. 'Oh, fuck – you know, Kit!'

I nod. She continues.

'I just . . . I didn't *like* it here and I didn't like anybody I

24

saw, didn't like the *look* of anyone. They all seem so young and . . . and . . . easily fucking pleased. You know?'

I nod again. I don't feel I should be saying anything, yet.

'And I think you've responded to a side of me . . . I mean, I think I've *made* you like a version of me that . . .' She looks away, tongue-tied. 'Fuck! You know what I'm trying to say. I don't want you thinking . . .'

I try to make this easy-peasy for her.

'Erm, 'scuse me? Can you just wind on to the bit where I asked you out? Did I miss something? I thought we both went to bed on our own last night?'

'We did.'

'So? What's with the big finishing speech?'

'Just . . . *listen*, will you?'

I make a big thing of sliding right down low in my chair to listen.

'It's nothing. You'll probably think I'm mad. But, Kit . . .' She sighs again. 'If you think we've built this big, impregnable friendship based on sitting back and taking the piss out of every poor wretch who stumbles into our viewfinder . . .'

She's right. I do. That's exactly what I think we've got and it's *exactly* what I love about her. I have to deny it as vehemently as humanly possible.

'Jinty, hon – I've got to stop you right there. I want us to be mates, right? And the way you're going, you're going to end up so embarrassed that you'll spend the next three years jumping into doorways and diving into wheelie bins whenever you see me coming . . .' I take her hand and fix her with as much sincerity as I can muster. 'I had a great time last night. I don't remember too much about it but I know I was dead nervous and you were dead nice to me.'

She's starting to look a tad embarrassed. I'm winning here.

'Now – I'm gonna fuck off down the Union and see what that's all about. You gonna come with me or you going to sit there and analyse those dinner ladies until you've unearthed some deep-seated hatred of youth that keeps them here year after year, spitting in our porridge?'

She hugs me. Not a love hug or anything – more of a kind of thank-you thing.

'Fuck, Kit – I feel such an idiot. Thanks, darling! I just want to . . . you know?'

'Fit in?'

'Yah. More or less, you know. I'm a nice girl, me. I want to enjoy it all, you know?'

My heart is heavy and the weak sun has gone as we head out of Ranmoor and on down Fulwood Road.

The building in which I sit is known to certain students as the Onion. That's what my mother would call it, given any encouragement at all. Fuck, but she would love for me to call her up every other day with tales of derring-do in the Onion. And fuck, but I miss her, for all her smothering, clinging, interfering mummery. I wouldn't be here, I don't think, if not for her. She's a tenacious wee thing, tiny like me, but nothing daunts her. She doesn't care. Dad's a good, good man, a real Steady Eddie job-for-life-type fella. He's grafted hard and without complaint in the brewery all these years, but it's Mum who's made the difference. She wants the best for us all and she's done her best to get it. It's her who's pushed for holidays in Corsica and Madeira instead of the Canaries, her who travelled the extra four miles by bus before she could drive, so she could shop at Sainsbury's instead of Netto, and her who stood over us all while we did our homework. Education was her credo, not Dad's. Shy, handsome, hard-working Dad is still completely in awe of his little Orford terrier. He'd be lost without her. Yet without him, with a different, watchful, possessive sort of partner, she would never have been able to push on herself. She could never have done the night school in basic accountancy. She could never have gone on to complete her degree. And she would not now have her own high-street book-keeping and tax-advice business Account Ability. Me, Dad, Madeleine and Emma – we're mad about Mum.

And I love her honesty – she really does not give a toss about what anyone thinks, Mum. She *knows* who she is, absolutely – she knows the neighbours are laughing behind their hand at her lofty pretensions. She knows she's got as far as she's ever going to get and that's why, for as long as I can remember, she's thrown these little clues and tempters in front of me and the girls. That's the way it happens, truthfully – it's like she's actually leaving a trail of good things in front of us in the hope that we'll stop and sniff at them, like the smell and take the bait in full. Like, her book club will recommend *The Corrections* and she's smart enough to know it's one of these important books, important that you have an opinion on it. So she'll order it for *me*, won't she? She'll just get stuck into the next Kathy Reichs. So long as someone in the family has read the highly regarded novel *The Corrections*, then she's done her job. The *Onion*, for fuck's sake!

I don't smoke, but I couldn't half do with one now. I'm sat, more or less, in the same spot Jinty and I sat last night, waiting for her. She's late. Everyone in here seems older, and their ease with the whole business of being a student having a drink at lunchtime is effortless. They slouch and loll and gossip. The buzz of their noisy chit-chat is starting to agitate me. Will I ever be so at ease? Will a timid little new boy sit and stare at me and Jinty, laughing and joking and laughing, this time next year? They laugh and spread themselves out and colonise the games arcade at the back of the bar. Me, I'm right at the front, perched at the first little two-seater by the pillar as you come down the stairs. I know that nobody has even noticed me sitting there, eager and watchful, but it feels like every eye is on me, waiting for me to give myself away. A ciggy, at least, would give me something to do with my hands and, no matter what anybody says, it does look good, narrowing your eyes and pulling on a cig – especially for a lone drinker. I glance at my watch. I'll give her another ten minutes.

To my unexpected relief and pleasure, Ben comes shuffling towards me with two pints, spilling hardly a drop. For a chap of his latitude he's surprisingly nimble on his feet.

'Awright? Just seen her. She'll be along in a mo. Said you drink bitter. Hope that's right.'

'Cheers.'

'Gonna need a bigger table 'n this.'

He's fearless. He spies a corner with bench seating and, although there's a couple occupying the corner bit, he strides right over, pushes their coats to one side and plonks himself down. I pull up a little tuffet. Ben looks around surreptitiously. I'm quite happy to fulfil my role here. I know he wants me to notice.

'Everything OK there, mate?'

He jerks back round as though snapping out of a reverie.

'Oh. Yeah. Irie, mon. No . . . I was checking, making sure AK ain't in here.'

He gives me less than two seconds to ask the next question. I don't quite get it out in time.

'AK 47 being me bagman. He don't like me dealing in here under his nose.'

'*Dealing?*' I summon every nuance of disinterest available to the man who wants to know more. 'You've only been here a day!'

He glances around again, with the effect that he's talking to five empty glasses balanced on the ledge behind. 'Got here Saturday, mate, but you can't waste no time in this game. AK's laying a bit on for now, just until my own contacts come online. Know what I'm saying?'

No, I don't – but I nod and hope he'll tell me. I find myself in the shameful position of being impressed by a dickhead. He turns round and talks to my face for the first time.

'Like, when I was in Morocco, yeah?'

28

'You've been to Morocco?'

He nods modestly and carries on talking in that quiet monotone.

'Sure. Went out to the kif country, made some contacts. Way I see it is, we're all getting ripped badly on the smoke, yeah?'

My cue to nod.

'So, right, if the likes of myself can get right in there, get to the source, sort out a price, then the benefit's going to be felt where it counts. Yeah?'

'So this gear, right – the stuff you're getting from Morocco. I mean – how will you, like . . . how does it *get* here?'

He taps his nose.

'It gets here. That's all you need to know. 'Nother pint?'

I jump up automatically, alerted to his empty-glass crisis, but Ben will have none of it. He pulls out a substantial wad and sits me back down.

'Had a good morning, Kit matey. Had a *very* good morning. Know what I'm saying?'

It's hard to resist a man who buys me drink after drink, but Ben is a graft. As he scuffs off back to the bar I give serious consideration to my options, of which legging it, now, is an attractive one. But all of that's forgotten when Jinty flies in, all legs and apologies.

'Ben find you? God, it's gone cold out there! Sorry . . .'

She looks fantastic in faded jeans. They're really tight and they show off her incredible, never-ending legs. Her feet turn in on themselves slightly as she hurries over. Her pale face has been blushed pink by the fresh autumn wind. She plonks herself down and pulls off her mittens, smiling. Again, there can be no ambiguity. She really is pleased to see me. She shifts me sideways with her arse. It feels nice.

'Budge up.'

I move along, sorry that our hips can't stay close. It's great, though. It's great being here, with her.

'Aren't you gonna buy me a drink, then?'

'Yes, yes and yes. Two questions. What d'you want? And did you know Ben's wanted by Interpol?'

She smiles and checks around, makes sure he's not within earshot. She pulls that kind of 'Ah – sweet!' face that people reserve for small babies and koala bears.

'What's that mean?' I say, doing my level best to replicate the facial expression. She checks around again.

'He's very, you know – *eager*, isn't he?'

'Eager to flash his cash.'

'That's what I mean. He's keen to impress.'

Now it's my turn to check around the bar.

'He's *your* bloody mate!'

'He's not a *mate*!'

'You're the one that brought him here!'

She makes a spoilt-kid face and mimics me. '*You're the one* . . .' She drops her eyeline slightly, looks a bit shamefaced then comes back up with a gorgeous smile. It's a smile she knows is calculating, I know is calculating and we both know I won't even try to resist. She leans over and kisses me gently. 'Stella and lime?'

I wince and stand up to fetch it for her. The bar's still busy and, with my lack of height, it takes a while to get served. I order another one each for Ben and me, while I'm up there. When I get back, Ben is boring the arse off Jinty. Her role in the conversation is to nod her head. I plonk the three pints down. It's a key moment in that it momentarily silences Ben. I seize the opportunity to change the subject.

'So? Any of these society thingies any good?'

'Fuck that!' spews Ben. 'Fucking students!'

Jinty rolls her eyes at me. 'We *are* students,' she pleads at him.

'*I'm* not!'

I fiddle with my pint. I'm embarrassed for him.

'Well, I am, like – but you know what I mean. Twats.'

The afternoon idles by. We find out little things about one another. I already know Jinty's doing psychology, but I didn't know she wants to work with kids. I think that's so ace. She wants to work as a behavioural therapist for fucked-up kids. Who would've thought it? Ben seems genuinely interested in my American-studies course. I'm not one of these pricks that sits around saying he's come to uni cos it's a doss, me. I'm quite looking forward to getting stuck into the work, truth be told – specially the Introduction to Cinema module. I know I'm going to learn loads, get loads out of it – but I do have to confess that one of the real attractions of doing this is the year-three exchange at an American university. That, I don't mind saying, is of spectacular personal appeal. I don't mind where it is. California would be nice but Wyoming or Tennessee would equally be just fine. I mean it, I don't care where I go, but I'm going to America – that is for sure. For the longest time I've had this understanding – more than that, actually, it's more than a feeling, it's a certainty. I know that that's where it's going to happen, just as I'm certain it won't happen here in Sheffield. In the United States of America I will definitely meet the sort of girls who can help me.

I think I've sold the course too well, though. The replete Ben, who I can't help liking more, the more we sup, is determined to try and swap courses first thing tomorrow. I don't know if that's possible. I truly do hope not. I can take him in small doses but I could not hack him on a full-time basis. No way.

Ben's voice is getting louder, his stories more outlandish.

'Shoulda seen the customs at Dover when I goes para-gliding right over them with six keys of coke strapped to either side of me!'

I yawn. I don't mean to be rude, but last night is starting to catch up on me. The only other measure of how long we've been in here is the stack of plastic pint glasses on the table and the ever thinning maul at the bar. There's hardly anybody left by the time we get up to go. We're all a bit tipsy. Ben and I both put our arms around Jinty as we make our way up the stairs. It's innocent, although I like the feel of her waist in my hand and for a moment, just for a moment, I stroke her ribs gently with my three middle fingers. Then I close my fingers in on themselves like it never happened.

Outside, the chill and the bluey dark of the early evening make me tingle. I feel as though I'm on the verge of something big and good. It's like that thrill of Christmas you get when you're a kid. I don't get excited like that any more. I don't get excited. Even when my results came through in the summer, I greeted the news with little more than ennui. I knew I'd get my grades. Even if I hadn't got them, my dejection would have equalled my excitement – that is, nil. I tend just to take things as they come, accept them for what they are. I've always found that when you try to bend things your way, when you try to change the way things are, you only end up disappointed. But here, now, stumbling along from bus stop to bus stop with these two, I just feel warm and content. It's five in the evening, the air is cold, and the night holds possibilities. We keep looking behind us for a 60 or a 52, any bus that'll take us up the hill and out of this bitter, biting wind. Nothing in sight, so we push on to the next bus stop, chattering about our favourite things. Ourselves. Through the windows of the Yorkstone houses we pass, kids are sprawled out by the fire doing their homework and eating toast. For them, the day is over. They're working towards another day. For me, right now, the moment is upon me.

A knock at the door. Unusual – we said we'd meet in the Nightingale, and not until seven thirty at that. It's not even a knock as such – more of an apologetic tap, a tap that doesn't *really* want to be acknowledged. It's the tapping equivalent of a phone call you don't want to make – so you let it ring four times then put the phone down, conning yourself you've made the call. Whoever is out there doesn't *really* want me to answer. They're just telling themselves that they've made an effort to socialise and it's not their fault no one was in. This makes me warm to the mystery tapper immensely.

'Enter, tappist!'

What a character I am! How very full of personality! By golly, but if there's a kid at this university more brimful of cheer and spunk than me then I'd like to meet 'em!

'Come in!'

No one comes. I bound off the bed and leap for the door, face already distorted into a terrible, glinting, welcoming smile. I wrench the door open. I wish I hadn't. The face that greets me is one I can never like. This boy is standing there with very *brushed* hair. It's that nondescript, almost centre-parting style favoured by the likes of Rob Lowe in the high-school movies of John Hughes. It's a hairstyle that tends to be accompanied by unthreatening good looks, perfect teeth and shirt cuffs pulled up just above the wrist as a mark of individuality. The lad in front of me looks like Tom Cruise on steroids, is wearing a rugby shirt and on his rugby shirt is a large badge that says 'Lend Us A Quid'. There's worse. His highly ironed rugby shirt is *tucked into* ironed jeans with creases which, in turn, are pulled tight by a belt. This bodes badly enough. I can't really be doing with belts and tucking in and the like anyway, but he's wearing a fucking *Boy Scout's* belt. It has a polished clasp positioned directly above his zipper and it says 'Be Prepared'. It's looking bad. All the signs are that this fellow is a prick. He is leaning on the door jamb in a very nonchalant way. No bad thing has ever troubled his taut brow. He's looking at the floor rather than me, and his tone is weary if not a little belligerent.

'Just moved in next door. Thought I better say hello.'

I look at his badge and his over-developed wrists. What I want to say is: 'You've said hello, now fuck right off and do some more press-ups, you knob!'

What I actually say is: 'Great! Thanks! Come on in!'

And when he doesn't move and continues leaning on the door jamb and staring at my feet, I hold out my hand and say: 'Kit! Aulroon! Welcome to G Block!'

Aulroon is an Erk-ism. It's a measure of my desperation that I've blurted it out. 'Like me!' I'm saying. 'Fear not! I'm a character! I have funny little sayings!' I could shoot myself. Grovelling to a beefhead like this – I could top myself. He runs his eyes over me like he's considering a purchase.

'Adrian Hewitt. Adie.'

Hate that name, Adrian. Adie's even worse. I expect him to break my hand with his grip, but he's limp and squalid. He takes one step into the room. He nods to the tranquil scream flowing from my speakers.

'Who's this?'

'Sigur Rós.'

He thinks about it, long and hard. You can hear his clunking mind grope for something to say.

'Quite nice, actually.'

He just stands there. I think he's shaking his head to the music, but he might be building himself up to make conversation. I give him a helping hand.

'You just got here, then?'

'S'afternoon.'

He's quite a toff.

'Come far?'

'Kent.'

'Wow! Quite a jog, hey?'

'Yah. Just wanted to get as far away from the parents as possible.'

'Know the feeling.'

I don't know why I'm making such an effort. I don't like him. I don't like anything about him. I can tell he's aggressive and competitive and selfish. That's what comes through more than anything – he's selfish.

34

'Listen. There's a few of us meeting up over in the bar in a minute. Fancy it?'

He shrugs. 'Few beers, eh?'

Oh no, no, no, no, *no*! Please, no – let me not be dwelling next to someone who says, 'A few beers.'

'Yeah, you know . . .' I try to come across like a game and worldly in-crowder – one who knows what's happening, and one who gets invited there. 'Just a couple of us, like, nothing too mad.'

He weighs up the offer with a jutting bottom lip.

'Sure. Why not.'

What an arrogant dick! I should just tell him to leave it if he's got better things to do. But I don't, of course. I'm all over him, gushing like a Girl Guide.

'Great! I'll give you a knock about seven thirty, then.'

And then he does something *really* disgraceful. Having stood there for five minutes with not a flicker of emotion on his spotless face, he trudges out of the room, lingers in the doorway and salutes. He fucking *salutes*!

'At ease!' he says.

I manage to keep the smile flickering just long enough to wave him off and get the door shut. I flop on to the bed and marvel at the inane diversity of mankind.

Week 0: Day 3
Weather: Ice-Cold Wind
Soundtrack: Squarepusher – 'Jacques Mal Chance'

Last night was fine, wasn't it? I don't *think* anything especially bad happened. Yet today I awaken with the chill winds of dread howling through my soul. I lie there, face down in the pillow and track back through all the major incidents. Nothing. Nothing to make me feel like this. I pull the duvet up around my shoulders and shrink down, down into the warmth of my bed. I'm so low, so miserably low it's debilitating. I can't be bothered thinking about it. It's there – I sense it, whatever it is. It's there waiting to be found out, if I want to look a little closer. But I don't. I don't want to know any more. I already know enough.

It wasn't as though we were having a brilliant time. It was OK, considering who was there. We'd gone from the Fox and Duck to the Notty House and ended up in the Broomhill Tavern. Ben was telling us about how he'd nearly got taken prisoner by the Taliban when he was hitching in Kathmandu and I was only too glad to go up to the bar and get my round in. I didn't want to fuck things up with Ben so soon after getting to know him – it's not as if I've got loads of spell-binding tales to amuse folk with myself, anyway. But he was getting far too big an audience and people were lapping his shit up, truly they were. I didn't feel like challenging his wild fables myself, but I wasn't going to just sit there, taking it. How's he ever going to stop the porkies if people just egg him on?

But it wasn't just Ben doing my head in. For starters, there was the unholy and fucking unlikely alliance of Jinty and Adie to soak up all my angry spores for one night. No one else got a look-in. She really disappointed me there, being absolutely honest about it. She came in with her new pal Petra, but I felt sorry for the girl. As soon as Adrian started up his shit with her, that was Petra dumped. She's all right and all. I had a laugh with her. But Jinty – I thought she'd see right through a twat like Adie. Far from it – she was all over him. It was like she'd been given an unhoped-for oppor-tunity to socialise with one of her own. The way the two of them were hooraying on about cars – fucking *cars*, for fuck's sake – and all these mad places they've been. I hate all these knobs who go on and on and on about their fucking gap years and how chilled it is in Kaoh Tang and how shite Koh

Samui's gone now it's completely overrun by tits like them! I can't believe them, some of the abject crap they come out with! Jinty, man – she really surprised me, coming on like that. I just didn't twig to that side of her. She must've had me nailed as quite an OK lad, but limited, because the slightest mention of Tuscany by fucking Top Gun and she was off. She was in rhapsodies, man. Tuscany this, Tuscany that, the light, the silences, the special, special oh-so-impossibly-perfect sunsets . . . well, she's shown her true colours, anyway. I'm quite saddened by her, really I am.

But this isn't even about her. It isn't about Adrian Dangerous. (Oh yes! Not only is that the name by which he'd like to be known, but he bestowed it on himself! Loudly. What a tit!) But no, I'm not laid low here now because of her, or them.

I roll on to my back, stare at a lone and tiny web on the ceiling and try everything in my power to suppress the thought. I can't stop myself. I can't hide myself from the truth that last night a girl came on to me, blatantly, and I shat myself. Nobody but me knows the truth. This is one of the things I've been dreading about coming away to Sheffield. It's true, it is – it's sick but it's fucking true – and it's this: I've been dreading all the sexual opportunity. Laugh out loud, but that's what it is. It's a no-win for me. If I'm social, like I can be, if I'm funny, like I can't help being, then people are going to like me, going to want me in the gang. But if I'm in the gang, out drinking, being me, then girls are going to like me. They're going to come on to me. And sooner or later someone – some sly twat like Ben or Adie – is going to pick up on it. They're going to notice. The only alternative, the only way I can keep a lid on this is by keeping myself to myself. I can't do that. I can't just stay in my room. I'd top myself. If there's any saving grace at all about the girl last night, it's that I doubt that she knows for sure what went on. She probably went away thinking that she hadn't made herself clear enough, or I just didn't fancy her. Wrong, on both counts.

I'd gone up to the bar, glad to escape Ben's voice. I glance over and he's holding court, spread across the little table in that lurid 'Jamaica – Land O' Mi Birth' T-shirt and he's got them all eating out of his hand.

'You might've read about that lad that accepted a lift in a lorry and ended up held hostage for forty-five days before they executed him and sent his head back to the British Embassy? Well, that should've been me.'

Too fucking right, I think, and turn round slap bang into her. She's heart-stoppingly pretty. Just as I don't believe I look like a student, neither, in my opinion, does she. She's immaculate. From top to bottom, she is something else. She's wearing jeans, skintight over her bottom and slim thighs, fraying out into small flares that only half cover her tan Camper shoes. I *love* those semi-flares, incidentally. Many of the guys and gals in here favour huge, massive, stupendous baggeroonies, jeans so voluminous you could hide a keg of ale down either leg – but this girl knows how to wear jeans. No Snoopy sweatshirts for this one, either. She's got a plain white T-shirt on underneath a round-neck, jade-coloured cardigan – the sort of cardy that's usually one part of a twinset. But her face – my God, her face is mesmerically pretty. Pretty is just exactly what she is, this girl. She's got a fantastic body, great tits, great little arse, beautiful, long, shiny hair – but she's not *gorgeous* in a sexy, sirenly way. She's not a *babe*. She's pretty. I know all about this. I've done little else for the past six years other than watch. I've read a ridiculous number of books, picked up a ridiculously large vocabulary and looked and looked at girls. I am the great observer. Pretty well the whole of my adolescence has been devoted to the distant but intensive scrutiny of females. From *Heat* to *Hollyoaks* I've soaked it all up, all the nuances of hips and lips and eyes. I really do know the difference. There's a candour about this girl's face, an openness, an innocence. She's *pretty*. I look into her eyes, she stares back and smiles. I'm dumbstruck. The thing that jags through me, slices me up from top to bottom is her smile. It's a smile that's beyond beautiful – it's powerful. She has these very flat canines that give her smile a radiance and an innocence that gets me right away, right in the heart. What a smile! What a face! I look away. I concentrate on getting served, unable to get her off my mind. Fuck, but she's lovely!

Innocent is the one thing she is not, though. It was her, it must have been her pushing up against me at the bar. I was as sure as can be that someone was pressing into me on purpose, pushing into my back maybe more than the crush to get served necessitated. I liked it, but I was too paralysed by nervy indecision to turn around or make anything of it. I just let it go, pretended I hadn't noticed. That didn't stop her. When I finally got served, I felt this jabbing in my side. I ignored it the first time, thought it could easily have been an accident, but it came back again, one short, hard jab to the ribs. I turned round sharply. It was her, just as I hoped it would be.

'Aren't you going to offer me a drink, then?'

I can only surmise now that I must have reacted like a blowfish with toxic shock. She looked at my face a little more closely than I'm used to, then winked at me, beautifully.

'I'll pay for it, like! Just that you're served now, innit?'

Another Midlands accent, but different from Ben's. She's not girly, but I don't know – I just like her voice. So often girls have girly voices. (Do their voices go through that humiliating adolescent thing where they *break*, I wonder?) I like her voice. I like her. She nods at three geeky-looking girls sat uncomfortably over at the furthest corner table.

'Don't think they've quite grasped the concept of rounds yet.'

She tries to slot a fiver into my hand. I jump to attention and try to make amends. I grin at her and turn away as I'm talking.

'Don't be daft. What d'you want?'

She wants an Aftershock. I buy it, turn around, hand it to her – then I totally do not know what to do next. Thinking on it now I could have asked her to join our lot – she's with three girls she'd be happy to escape from, she would've jumped at it. Or I could have taken the drinks over to our table then come back and chatted with her. I could have done something, but instead I did nothing. I shit myself. There was a long, horribly silent pause where she swayed on the spot, her pretty head cocked to one side as she gave me a look that was saying: 'I really like you. You won't have to try *that* hard to get me into bed, you know.'

It was a cool and inviting look that any man with a bit of charm and ease about him would have taken up gladly. Me? I bottled it. I put on a pathetic, embarrassed shrug and said: 'Well. Better get back to my crew.'

And to show her I was in charge of the situation I lifted one finger and went: 'Steady on the Aftershocks.'

I am a gutless wretch. I'm a wanker – literally, I'm a wanker for saying that to her. I said, 'Steady on the Aftershocks,' and I turned my back on her, a failure, walking away. I didn't have it in me to see it through with her. I walked away, just in case. I walked back over to our table, where people I don't really know and don't really like were telling stories and lies to impress one another. I walked across the pub floor and I despised myself absolutely with every step – but still I hoped that That Girl had noticed my arse is as pert as hers. I drank silently, empty with despair, numb with self-recognition. I'm a coward, a wanker, a just-in-case man. Fuck, but I hate that! And fuck, but I'm powerless against it. I'm feeble. I sat there and drank and I tried to fight the fear inside me, looked deep, deep within myself and reasoned it out. What, but what could go so badly wrong? And if it *did* go so badly wrong again, who was going to know anyway? Who would she tell? I told myself it was worse, far worse, to just let her slip away without even trying.

I swilled hard on my pint and forced myself to my feet, ready to take this on, head on – but she'd gone. She'd already gone. Their table was occupied by some hearty mountaineers or, if not mountaineers, lads with beards, anyway. She, That Girl, is probably waking up with someone now – someone with a bit more about them than me.

When we finally got kicked out of the pub last night it was belting down outside. It wasn't just raining, it was a deluge – you could actually feel the weight of the rain as it slammed into your face and your back. We cowered in various shop doorways until Jinty ran out into the middle of the road, screaming: 'Come on! Let's have it!'

Everybody followed, squealing and yodelling as we sprinted maniacally through the downpour. To all but myself, that'll form a wondrous memory, one day. That wild and carefree charge through the rain – they'll have loved that. Not me. All I'll remember is what I was thinking as I ran along too, pretending to be part of it all. What I was thinking was: you wanker. You fucking coward.

Loads got as far as the cop shop and gave up, or sneaked off to Balti King, but six of us ended up in Jinty's room, passing a litre of Jack Daniel's this way and a big fat doob the other. We slumped and talked and talked and talked, talked rubbish mainly, but I loved it. That was just what I needed, that meandering, bullshitty, stoned-drunk talk. I remember Jinty lifting her lovely head and fixing those fucked-up blue eyes on me and going: 'Kit. What the fuck were we talking about? Just then?'

And I was in bits, laughing and laughing. It was exactly what I needed right then, right after the cop-out with That Girl. The thought of her sends me sick with despair again. I bury my head in the pillow. I'm not hacking this. I'm just not making it. I want to go home. What's so fucking bad about that? I'm admitting it – I want to go home.

I drag myself out of bed and click on the mouse, desperate

for some kind of hit from outside. I hate it, hate myself for needing it so, but I rely on these messages, no matter how bland. I have to have emails to get me through. I'll reply to anyone just now. It's like tending the garden. You send the emails out and you'll get one back. You'll be in touch. I watch the inbox download and I'm pathetically pleased to find a reply from little Emma. I've missed her. She asks nothing of me, Emma. She thinks I'm just great. I write back straight away, trying to sound chatty and confidential.

Hiya there Em, how's it going? Glad you're
remembering to feed Guzzle. He's depending on you
for his daily fix of fishydust. It's good here. I'm
meeting lots of new friends from all over the country.
I think you'd like my girlfriends Jinty and Petra. I
mean, I'm not two-timing or anything, I have two
good friends what is both girls, seen? Jinty is a giant.
Really. She's about eight foot tall. When you come to
stay, you can stand on her shoulders and see France.
We all went out last night, got a bit tiddled and went
back to Jinty's room to talk rubbish. I can't remember
much about it. Don't tell Mum – she thinks I'm
spending my time acquainting myself with the library
and taking tea with my professors!

Well, little Pie, you be good for Mum and Dad. I
hope the house doesn't feel too big and boring and
empty for too long. You'll soon get used to having all
that space (and the telly!) to yourself and you won't
want me back at all.

Take care baby,

Kit xxx

I hit Send and throw myself back into bed, crushed at the thought of her, missing me like that, but battered more by the deceit. I mean, yeah, she's only a kid, Emma, and she doesn't want her heroic big brother piling all his woes on her. But I've gone completely the other way there. I've given her the full jaunty student bullshit number. *Got a bit tiddled.* Yeah. You got spannered, mate, so that you didn't have to think about how badly you fucked up with that gorgeous, gorgeous girl. *I can't remember much about it.* Not true, actually. I can remember pretty well everything. For example:

1) Jinty is twenty-four. Gosh! Who'd have thought it? Depending on whether you accept the 12.23 a.m. version of her story or the 2.56 a.m., she has recently dumped or, it seems likely, been dumped by a man of some forty-five years of age. Someone as old as my dad, indeed, has eradicated dear Jinty from his life, having previously, one presumes, been taking his fill of this lovable if unorthodox-sized lass on a fairly regular basis. How very odd life is, to be sure.

2) For reasons I can't begin to fathom, she seems to be attracted to the awful Adrian Dangerous, and he to she. Partly out of pique at this, I have taken to calling her Miss Jones. She's seems not to mind – indeed, she seems actively to like it. She laughs a lot every time I say it, anyway. The downside, of course, is that she calls me Rigsby.

3) Ben is a psycho. He plainly cannot, will not, ever tell the truth. That, or he has given up a remarkable life of travel and adventure to study English and philosophy at Sheffield University. From now on he shall be Benny Bullshit to me. Miss Jones, Adrian Dangerous and Benny Bull.

4) Surprisingly, and officially, Sheffield is the Safest City in England. I never knew that.

5) Simon is a top fella. Admittedly, he likes Moby and,

although he later qualified the remark and even later again fundamentally denied he'd ever said it, he also ventured an opinion that Faithless are 'wicked'. But he's a nice lad. He's into bands – Coldplay, the Delgados, the Libertines – all of that dirgy, introspective carry-on. Even though I've told them, untruthfully, that Autechre are numero uno for me, myself and I, and even though Autechre offer up the most unsettling, unnerving, unrelaxing soundscapes known to God's lost wretches, he's got it into his odd-shaped bonce I'm into 'chilled' music. Chillout, for fuck's sake! Perish the thought! Perish the fucking *word*! *Chillout!* But he's just trying to make a connection, isn't he? Probably only likes Moby for that cheesy, synthetic guitar riff in 'We Are All Made of Stars'. Can't rip him for trying to be friendly, can I? Like I say, he's a nice lad in that quiet, inner-confidence sort of way. He's quite sussed – you wouldn't think he was from the badlands of Baslow, exactly fifteen miles south-west of this very room. But he talks *dead* fucking slow – an affectation, I think. Has to be. It's weird that he lives so close, yet he's here, in halls, just like anyone else. That shit is wacky – I can't make him out. I like him.

6) I really like Petra, too. Petra is from their block. She comes from Stirling, I think she said. Or Strathclyde – somewhere with a university. Her dad's Indian but she says her mum's *Indian* Indian. She's dead funny, Petra. She knows loads about football, films, fashion and music – fuck it, she knows loads about everything. She can deconstruct Bollywood in a socio-economic sense, but still be interesting with it. I wish I fancied her. When she asked me what sort of music I like and when she wouldn't let me get away with 'all sorts, you know?' and I gave her a few names to appease her, she said: 'Well, you've come to the right place, haven't you? All those Warp loonies.' I mean, it's another of those, isn't it? She's trying to be friendly.

44

I know she was mainly just trying to let me know that she knows her stuff, but I found it a bit forced. I'm a bastard for finding it a bit forced, I know I am. It'd be different if she was a honey. I'm just being honest. It's the way of the world. When Petra leans forward to tip her ash into the can, you can see two things on her lower back. A tattoo of an eye. And hair. You can see hair. I know that if you couldn't see hair on her back, I wouldn't be so ready to notice that she's trying to impress me. If I fancied her, I'd be more than ready to talk about Warp tracks with her. I wouldn't find it a bit forced at all. But the fact is you can buy Aphex Twin tunes as easily in Stirling as you can in Sheffield. You don't specifically have to come to Sheffield to locate and purchase the wares of Warp. But I like Petra. I like her a lot. She's funny.

7)   Petra thinks the World Bank will collapse before we complete our degrees.

I sigh hard and stare at the ceiling and listen to the rain. It hasn't let up all night. I was conscious of it in my sleep, felt its presence, but it never quite tore me back from my slumber. I slept deep last night, but as soon as I woke I knew it intrinsically. I've tried to bat it down, but it's hopeless. I had to let it up. I had to let it out. I had to let myself, had to *make* myself go over all that so I can start all over again. I'll see her again. I'll see That Girl and I'll do better, this time.

I turn over and face the wall, as though the act of doing so will leave the niggling memories and the crippling truth behind my back. I won't get back to sleep, but I can't get up, either. I'm disabled. A dreary tristesse is yawning through me, laying me low. I lie there, existing through varying layers of consciousness, though never fully asleep.

Half-hearted knocking at my door. I ignore it. More knocking, a voice, then the scratch of paper as it's pushed under the

45

door. Forty-four hours ago I would have yelped for joy at the very possibility of being so wanted. Now I want them all to go away and leave me alone again. What day is this? Friday. Just the weekend to navigate, then I can lose myself in coursework. Oh fuck, but life is shit!

I doze, I come back round, I need water. I cannot, *can* not move myself from this warm and lonely bed, this hide of mine. I think of her again. I think of her breasts and her bum, her lively breasts pointing from that white, perfect white T-shirt. I stiffen as she comes to life for me and, with heavy heart and grim inevitability, I reach for myself. Yet again, yet more seed is wasted on the sheet.

The sky is dark even now, dark and low and heavy. The air is bitter. It's stagnant and damp and it smothers me. Weighed down, sullen with this not-wanting, not-feeling drag, I trudge, head down, along Shore Lane. I slip as I turn into Fulwood Road, and the shock of it, the sudden chain reaction, jolts me from my torpor. Sodden leaves are everywhere. The mulch and the mould squelches underfoot as I deign to walk off my dolours. The stink of a dying year decomposes in my lungs, my reluctant feet skid and slide through the rotten fall. Everywhere, everywhere piles and slats of slick, copper leaves. I hate it. This, that I'm walking through now, I hate it – but I carry on. I don't want to be here – but I carry on. I carry on because it takes me forward at least, and leaves all that behind.

I pull out the scrap of paper again, straighten it out. '*No wussing out! See yez in Bar Two at 1! Cy.*'

It'd taken me a while, that one. Firstly, the implication that I'd made some arrangement last night that I might, on second thoughts, not want to keep. Secondly, that I was in communication with a person called 'Cy'. Momentarily, I was mystified. I was reading it in my mind's ear as Kye, then Kee, then C-Y and it took me by storm when the penny finally dropped.

My new buddy Simon was taking barbarous liberties with his name spell – the fool. It was too true, though – we'd made an arrangement. Last thing, last night, when Simon and I were actively bickering about music (Coldplay, tortured genius ensemble or a tedious gang of drips?), we said we'd check out the university's allegedly avant-garde fortnightly scene the Gecko Club. We'd do it together.

But that, in itself, might be no straightforward matter. We'd have to join first, a process which, as Simon timorously informed me, would certainly involve some degree of humili-ation. The extent of that humiliation would depend, more or less, upon ourselves. He told me he'd been trying to pluck up the nerve to approach the Gecko Club's politburo for three days running now. I'd seen their stall in the Societies Bazaar yesterday, without properly twigging what it was they were punting. They were all set up in the Foundry, right there between the Fly-Fishing Soc. and the Gooners Soc. (This turned out to be a drinking and shouting club for Sheffield-based Arsenal supporters and not, as I had hoped, an appreci-ation society for the late Spike Milligan and company.) But whereas Fly-Fishing tried to woo potential members by means of a fat guy shouting, 'Relax. Catch fish. Eat them,' the Gecko Club's recruitment programme was manned by two wizened anorexics who killed the day gossiping while ignoring the desperate attempts of newcomers to catch their eye. Simon reckoned he'd loitered hopefully by their display three or four times, receiving nil encouragement. I hate that. I hate people who think they've got something going on.

I shove Simon's note and my hands way down into my parka's deep pockets, and try to put a move on. An antlike trail of students descends Whitham Road, huddled and yet certain, somehow. Their flushed faces are alive with antici-pation. I feel nothing. I stomp on down that dull hill, resent-ing all those other shuffling figures their easy-come beatitude. What's to be so fucking *excited* about? It's dank, it's horrible, it's a shit, shit day in an awful life. Passing the park I witness besotted newly-shags staring maddeningly into each other's eyes. That's all they're doing. They've met last night, they've talked revolting, naive cack all night, they've fumbled a lame shag together and now it's today and they're stupefied by first love and they're sitting on some wet bench by the art gallery holding hands and fucking staring at each individual spot on each other's gormless dials. It tires me out just looking at them as I pass. Simon better be there. The mood I'm in, I feel like just snapping my fingers at these Gecko Club poseurs, whoever they are, and shouting: 'Service!' That'll get them moving.

Simon is there, is delighted beyond all acceptable norms to see me and, in spite of his thin wedge head which appals me all over again, I'm quite pleased to see him, too. I decide not to bring up this 'Cy' business for the time being. He scurries off to get me a pint, fuel he seems to think necessary for the trials ahead. We settle into our drinks, picking up where we left off last night.

'Fischerspooner? No *way*, man! I *hate* electro-clash!'

'But you listen to Royksopp?'

'Yeah, yeah, fair dos. There's a time and a place for Royksopp – the acceptable face of ambient lounge.'

'So where's the difference? Why all the labels, man? It's just prog rock, isn't it?'

'Blimey, Simes – where's the *difference*? The difference is in the sensibility, not the fucking label. Trance, techno, ambient, whatever – it has to have intelligence, right? It's got to move you in some way, it has to have some . . . *edge* to it, yeah? Like, I can be moved by something totally fucking alienating –'

'Twiddly-twiddly bollocks!'

'No, mate – it's not –'

'That's what it is! Call it what you want, mate, but all that bleep-bleep crap you listen to is just one short hop from prog rock –'

'Don't talk shite, man.'

He's insistent. 'Seriously . . .' He's got one of those unfortunate sibilants on his esses that's common to dullards who want to sound more interesting. '. . . that last Sigur Rós album . . .'

'Utter, flawless beauty . . .'

'. . . pretentious crap. Twenty-minute fucking "sonic landscapes", man. I mean, one of the tracks has a *drum solo*, for fuck's sake! How's that not Yes, Kit? How's that not . . . Van der Graaf fucking Generator?'

'Which track? Sigur Rós do *not* have drum solos! Which track has a drum solo?'

His eyes pop in a hateful way I hadn't noticed before now. Behind his specs his eyes gleam and bulge. He's puffing up with righteousness.

'Well, exactly – my whole point about them, *exactly*. I mean, how do we *know* which track? They're *so* fucking up themselves they don't put *any* fucking info on the CD, do they? CD doesn't even have a fucking *title*! It's a symbol, man – a fucking shitty symbol! I mean, how crap is that, nicking an idea off fucking *Prince*? Only fucking words on the thing are Sigur-Rós.com!'

He opens his eyes wide, inviting me to come back at him – if I dare. He thinks he's won. His axehead skull is red and pulsing. It's only now I realise he's completely wankered. Dear Simon, *Cymon*, my daft-looking pal from the Baslow badlands is absolutely hog-whimpering drunk. I can't help loving him for this – and can't help needing to goad him on, too.

'Look, Si – I'm sorry I said mean things about Coldplay. I don't think they're that bad at all – if you like monotonous sixth-form first-love poetry dressed up as introspection. But Sigur Rós cannot teach Coldplay a *thing* about artifice. Coldplay are *the* most pretentious, self-indulgent, *boring* bunch of twats –'

'*Boring*? Well, if you're bored by heartache, bored by –'

'Bored of listening to him drone on about that bird he fucked off –'

'*A Rush of Blood to the Head* is *the* most searingly honest, insightful . . .'

I drown him out singing in the dullest, most banal and atonal whine I can squeeze from my spleen. I clamp my nose as I sing.

'"*Questions of sci-ence, science and pro-gress* . . ." fuck! That's a good lyric, isn't it? See what you mean, mate! Wish I was the bird he dedicated *that* to . . .'

I'm eyeing him dangerously, now. He's in my sights and it's in for the kill. Affecting to laugh at the lyrics I've just hit him with, I think once, think twice, think fuck it, why not?

'And talking of pretentious . . .' I pull out the note he slipped under my door this morning. '. . . I take it I'm talking to a Grand Master of all things false? Or should that be *faux*?'

He blinks at me. He isn't sure what's coming, but he senses it is not good. I point at various words.

'*Wussing* we'll let pass. *Yez* we'll leave for another day.'

I turn and face him directly. I can feel the sparkle of my eyes, playing with him, letting him know this is just fun. It's just a bit of fun – so long as I win.

'Sir Simon of Baslow, I put it to you that you have thus far lived a drab and unexceptional life . . .'

He nods, smiling, trying to be in on the joke to lessen its sting.

'. . . I further put it to you that you elected, upon leaving the teeming mean streets of Baslow, the Peak District, Derbyshire, to radically reinvent yourself . . .'

He smiles and affects to hold his head in his hands – which might hurt, if he caught himself on the angle.

'. . . you would indulge, Simon – *you would indulge* in complexities of facial hair as a matter of urgency and you would investigate the acquisition of a tattoo as soon as possible.'

I stop and wait for him to look up. He peers at me gamely from behind his hands.

'Come on. Let's have it!'

I give it my best barrister's face, full of disdain at the mire in which I daily have to tread in search of truth and justice. I brandish his note at him, looking away as I point wildly at the evidence. He grins and hangs his head.

'I put it to you, Simon of Baslow, that you have know-ingly and cynically fucked with the composition of a good and honest, an *honest* and *innocent*, name.'

He howls and hides his face.

'Simon says Simon is a bit of a crap name, doesn't Simon?' I lift his chin with my finger. I speak quietly, and with regret. 'Simple Simon's never been good enough, has it? Simple Simon is a bit of a fucking embarrassment, truth be known . . .'

'Spike Jonze does it!'

'Spike Jonze has, and always had, enough dough in the bank to play whatever pranks he wants on the world. And make shit films.'

Simon's looking perplexed now. 'Anyone can reinvent themselves. That's the whole point, isn't it?'

'Yes. Unless you're from Baslow. Not even Laurence Llewelyn Bowen can give you a makeover that gets you free of Baslow, man . . .'

He looks like this has suddenly gone beyond a joke for him. I decide to quit while we're still friends.

'To your new friends and associates, you may well be *Cymon*, Simon . . .' I hang my head theatrically enough for him to be sure I'm just having a laugh. '. . . but for me you will be for ever simply Simon. Good day.'

He smiles, relieved. But he's not leaving it there.

'What about you, then?'

'What?'

'Fucking Kit!'

'What about Kit?'

'What's wrong with Chris? Or Christopher?'

'Nothing . . .' I need to rein myself in here. I know how smug and twitchy I can get over this. I'll just keep to the bare facts and we can all move on. '. . . it's just that neither is the name I was given. That's my name. Kit.'

He eyes me warily.

'Shoo-ah it is!'

'It is. That's all there is to it, I'm afraid.'

He sits back and slugs his beer. He laughs to himself.

'What?'

'Nothing.'

'Go on.'

He looks at me, and I can see he means what he's saying. 'I've never met anyone like you.'

I drop my head, aware of my own false modesty but sure enough that he hasn't picked up on it.

'Good or bad?'

He grins full on. 'Oh, good, good. You're a one-off, man. Yeah. Definitely good.'

He finishes his pint. 'One more for courage?'

Petra is already there at the Gecko Club stall, being grilled by the two wire-thin atrocities running the show. One of them, the more emaciated of the two, has bleached white hair in a messy spike cut so mussed up you can see his pink scalp. He's wearing black – tight, tailored, silken shirt over tight Lycra trews – and stands with a mannered hand on his hip. The other specimen – who is completely bald but no less pink of scalp – wears a cropped Manchester United shirt. A *cropped* football top, no less, exposing three or four inches of hard white tummy – and when he turns round to change a record he has, no word of a lie, the word *Posh* and a number 7 emblazoned on the back. Stifling hysterics, I approach, amazed at my companions' bashfulness. How can they, how could *anyone* be intimidated by this pair of whoppers? Petra's doing her best to impress them.

'Loads of stuff, really . . . mainly guitar bands but I'm into all sorts. Beefheart, Pere Ubu, Royksopp, Badly Drawn Boy . . .'

They seize on this.

'*Pre* Mercurial Prize, *naturellement* . . .'

'And we won't even *go* down *About a Boystrasse!*'

'Strictly Beggars tip, *oui*?'

Their camp bitchery is tired and lame, as outré as Graham Norton, as threatening as a plastic *Scream* mask. Why Petra should grovel to them, only she knows. What I know is that there's no way I'm joining their shitty music club, no way I'll willingly spend another minute in their company. I can't resist asking just one thing, though.

'Gecko? Is that to do with Banco de Gaia?'

They look at each other. The one in black takes his hand off his hip, nibbles his longest nail without taking his eyes off me and goes: 'Not necessarily . . .'

'Not exclusively . . .' says the other one.

They look at each other.

'He interests me.'

'Yes. He's not entirely without va va voom, *n'est ce pas*?'

'You interest us.'

'What do you *know*, anyway?'

'Yes. Elucidate. What d'you actually *know*?'

I look at them for a moment, look at the floor, shrug and say: 'Fuck all.'

And with that I'm gone.

Week 0: Day 5
Weather: Bleak – Unremittingly Bleak
Soundtrack: Górecki – *Symphony No. 3*

I knew it. I knew my first Sunday would be the biggest downer of all, but I seriously was not prepared for anything like this.

Everything that could stack up to make today unbearable has come down to haunt me. There's a feeble but unrelenting whirr in my head, like the bustling click of playing cards flicked at speed. Tomorrow, Day One, is a staggering twenty-three hours away. I've got to get out of here. I've got to walk this off.

I'm ravenous but I'm not going anywhere near breakfast. I can't face anybody, not even Jinty. Least of all Jinty. I'm praying, I'm begging that it wasn't her. For an hour, half an hour, an eternity, however long it was, I lay morose in my room listening to Dangerous pleasure some girl. Was it Miss Jones? Fuck knows. All I know is that she loved whatever he was doing to her.

'Bastard! Oh fuck, yes, you bastard!'

That was what she was coming out with.

'Bastard! Horny fucking horny bastard!'

And all I could see was Adie. There was no wall between us, no divide. I could reach across and touch his head, touch the muscles that stood out in his shoulders as he propped himself up on the flats of his hands and pummelled his girl. That's what he was doing – he was hammering the girl, bucking and thrusting for all he was worth, while she lay and took it and groaned with satisfaction. I lay there too, lay there and saw all this. The mystery girl on her back, face buried in Adrian's chest as he fucked her and fucked her, looking at me, eyes glinting and taunting me. And I liked it. I reached down and stroked myself slowly, listening and liking it and getting hard at the sound of him fucking a girl next door. When I pictured the girl, the girl getting rammed by Adie, it wasn't Jinty. It was Colette. I listened and got hard and wanked myself off while I thought of Colette getting fucked. Another suicide committed in my lonely bed.

We'd all been down to Juice, those of us still here. Yesterday morning heralded a stampede home after the last of the real freshers' week activities ended with a West Street pub crawl and an Ibiza Foam Party at Sorby Hall on Friday night. A madly excitable throng of new boys and fresh girls got out-rageously drunk and set about passing water-filled balloons among themselves using only their chins, breasts and ale guts. The climax of the shenanigans appeared to arrive when a buffoon, frankly, calling himself DJ John de Blow, caused foam to gush from four immense tubes and urged his revellers to wallow in same. It was all harmless if faintly absurd, memor-able only for Willie Wilson's attempts to communicate and my utter inability to comprehend a single fucking word he was saying. I've never seen a human being so wholly intoxi-cated as my former Culcheth High contemporary as he wobbled around the Sorby bar, grabbing girls and double-bluffing the lads who tried to defend them. If only his doughty ma could see him. If only mine could, too.

Over breakfast yesterday morning, Simon — sorry, *Cy*mon — announced he was heading back to Baslow for a mate's eighteenth birthday that night. Quietly, insincerely, he added that anyone who wanted to come along was welcome so long as there weren't more than three. His car would only take three, maximum. Ben, to his utter shame, jumped his bones to be included.

'Don't worry about your class As,' he winked. 'Sorted.'

I felt abandoned, betrayed. There's no justifying that, but I felt like Simon had led me on, only to leave me high and dry. I mean it — I'm not one for throwing myself headlong into friendships, me. There's Erk, and even he's let me down. But Simon, well — I thought I could make a proper friend of him. It's come as a timely warning that people can let you down badly, just like that, if you let them. Like, I could've gone with them, gone to Baslow and enjoyed the notoriety of the new kid in town. It might have been all right. But it's just running away, all that. It may well have been a laugh, but it's only postponing the inevitable. We're here. It's our own choice. We have to make the best of it. At the end of the day, I didn't want to run away so soon after making myself come out here. I wanted to tough it out, see it through. They went right down in my esteem, going back, going *home* so soon after making their move.

That left an odd-fit gaggle of me, Jinty, Petra and Adrian fucking Dangerous to take on the horrors of Saturday night down the Union together. *Every* twat was going on about it, Juice this, Juice that, are you going to Juice? By the time I'd had my shower I was shaking, literally. I was in bits about my first big Saturday night but, being quite honest, it wasn't so bad at first. It was all right. Our original plan was to hit all the Broomhill pubs on the way down to the Union, but that took a nosedive right from the off. A boisterous pack of second and third years had taken over O'Neill's main room, loudly going on about Fresh Fanny. Adrian was all for panning them, Petra wanted to humiliate them, but ultimately we did neither. We sloped out to the Fox and Duck. The Fox and Duck, for all that Mum's nonsense should have scarred me for life, is a bloody brilliant pub. It's normal, even on a Saturday. There's loads of students in there, but there's loads of old men too. There's middle-aged local couples in for a swifty, and dodgy revolutionary types on the pull. There's the odd professor or doctor or other sundry admirers of the tweed jacket. There are nurses and shopkeepers dropping in for one on the way home, and the overall effect is harmony. It's cosy in there, you can hear yourself talk but it feels alive, too. I'm starting to buzz a bit by the time we move on.

We line our tumtums at Fat Jack's, dive into the Place for Vodka Reef chasers then stumble on down to the Notty House for more beer. It's *packed* in there, but the atmosphere's crackling. I can't help myself, I really can't – I feel great. I'm almost giddy with good cheer. We have a little spat over whose round it is – not over the money, but because the queue for the bar is bedlam.

'Ah, come on, Big Bird! It's a doddle for you, isn't it?'

'Hang on, hang on – I'm only just getting used to Miss Jones. It's fucking Big Bird now, is it?'

Petra interjects. 'Frankly though, Ms Jones, it'd be inverse sizeism of the worst sort for us to simply ignore your *length*. That, in and of itself, is a more invidious form of sizeism than the blatant but frankly predictable and thus harmless catcalling of our diminutive friend here. As a person of race I feel perfectly well qualified to comment.'

Once she's stopped her caw-caw guffawing, Big Bird gets the drinks in.

In spite of my pleas for circumstantial – the queues'll be twenty-deep, the ale's served in plastic glasses and we're having such a great time already – we drink up and head down to the Union. The snap of the cold night air blasts both thrill and foreboding through me. My soul aches with a lusty anticipation, a deep and joyous hope for big things – things going right, things working out. But that thing, the very thought of it, the knowledge that it's all out there, down there, mine for the having and the holding flings me deep into an anxious funk. I want to go to Juice. I don't want to.

But I'm fine once we get settled down at the Foundry. We get a cosy little outside table near the doors, with one of those big parasol-style outdoor heaters giving a lovely glow to the night. It's fine. Petra is funny as fuck. I think she and Miss Big Bird are going to be big-time pals. Even Adie's all right. He's a snob – or he'd like to be – but there's something about him, something vulnerable lurking not so far below the surface show. And he can't help his fucking stupid posh voice, can he? I'm still not sure whether it's for real. He sounds like Prince Charles. It's worse, really – he sounds like Alistair McGowan taking off Prince Charles. He's an awful, stuffy parody of himself and there's something about that that makes it hard to completely dislike him. He even says 'one'. I don't know – I've just never heard that. Hyacinth Bucket on TV, perhaps some of the older royals, but I really didn't think 'one' was in common usage any more. Adie says it. He *says* it.

'I mean, it's quite a comedown for the family to be sending one to a provincial redbrick. Quite the black sheep, actually. Both the brothers are Oxbridge, Diana's at the Sorbonne . . . I'm telling you − if I don't get a *bloody* good degree I'm done for. I mean it. Fuck up here and I'm totally up shit creek without a paddle. There's no way the parents are going to lend a hand if I don't pull down a first, actually.'

I honestly do not know what to say in reply to him. I find myself staring at today's badge − 'I'm With Stupid' − and it makes me feel very weird. It's like he's trying to acquire a persona. He's saying, 'I'm a little bit mad, me,' and it's heartbreaking, really. In one sense, it helps me warm to him, but the truth is he's a hard guy to make out. With his shrill and overconfident braying, Adie can come across as a wall of opinion. Even on subjects of which he *has* no opinion, Adie has something to say and he says it with certainty.

'I'm not so well up on the new stuff, personally. Actually, there *is* one guy I *really* love. David Gray. I *love* that mother!'

That he's investing bland crooner David Gray with some sort of edge and danger goes right over my head. I'm just stuck on Adie's face. I hadn't seen it up until then, but his face freezes when he's expressing excitement. It seems to sort of overload and, well, *stop*. That's what it is − his entire face just stops at the moment you'd most expect it to lose control. He seems to have muscles all over his face, muscles that twitch and flex when he speaks, when he frowns and when he gives off his cold smile. I've become quite used to the little pops and dints of his face in motion. But it does − it short circuits when he's happy! While I'm sat here working him out, naughty Petra is working him over. She's rolling her eyes and her 'r's in a show of bliss that's real only to Adie.

'*Deeevid Grrrreeee!* Ah *love* that bastard!'

'Really? Me too. *Love* the motherfucker! Though I don't think the last album's quite . . .'

She can't quite keep the pretence up to the extent of a

full-blown debate over the relative merits of *White Ladder* and *A New Day at Midnight* though, so she pulls her chair closer, eyes wide with fascination. It's a bit too much, I think. Bit cruel. He's just another soul trying to make his mark, isn't he?

'And what's your degree again, Adrian?'

'The Law.'

Sorry, but that's just fucking blown it. All and any sympathy is shot to bits by what he just said. I really, really hate him for that – for the use of 'The' before 'Law'. What a pompous, muscle-bound div he is! Petra makes her big brown eyes even bigger.

'The *Law*? Gosh!'

The irony is lost on Dangerous. He just nods and tries to affect modesty.

'Yah. Tough rap. Should be worth it.'

It's like he's thinking out loud, trying to convince himself. Petra smiles over at me with her eyes. She holds my gaze just a tad too long, before swooping back to Adie. She's needle-sharp – I'd hate to get on the wrong side of her.

'God, yah, I mean . . . who ever heard of a skint lawyer, hey?'

Jinty joins in.

'You gonna be a lawyer, then?'

Adie doesn't suss it. His forehead creases up, a young man taxed by his options. He studies his pint closely.

'Don't know. Might specialise.'

I catch her and Petra winking at one another.

'Oh – so might you be a surgeon instead, or something?'

He looks up, anxious now, nervous that he hasn't explained himself properly.

'No, no, no – The Law. Definitely. No question of fucking medicine! No *question*!'

Medsin. It's my turn to get them in. I get up and pad back into the bar, pondering how it can be that Adie should hate another academic discipline. That's how he comes across. He *hates* medicine, hates medics, feels a terrible rivalry between The Law and the great and good vocation of making folk better. I push my way through the crowds, buzzing with a semi-nervy beer charge, suddenly feeling good about everything. It's great here. I like it. It's good.

The music has barely started and the dance floor is still sparse. I am resigning myself to a good twenty minutes queuing at the bar when there she is, there I am, right in her face again. That Girl. I feel safe enough here though, ten-deep in the bar queue. It'll be fine. We can make small talk as we wait, I can find out a bit more about her and, bit by bit, we can work towards maybe seeing each other in the new year, something like that. I've got to say it – she seems really pleased to see me. Her face is one big smile. Little dints appear just below her eye sockets as she shows her little baby teeth and I have to say this, too: she's divine. She's just plain lovable. She's got a face and a smile that you can't help losing your heart to.

'Well now – I think I owe you something, don't I?'

She's doing that half sort of swaying on the spot motion she was doing the other night.

'Who's counting?' I say.

She leans closer.

'Who says I'm talking about drinks?' she whispers.

Two things happen. My dick quivers – and I panic. I feel ensnared by her. But this time I'm going to fight it through. I'm going to take my *medsin* and look this thing, this fear, in the fucking eye and I'm going to see it through. No way am I letting this girl go, this time. I draw down all my reserves of calm. I physically, knowingly, steady myself and force myself to go easy, but I just can't think of anything good to say.

'Better tell us your name then, hadn't you?'

'Colette.'

'Kit. Enchanted, I'm sure.'

That was better! She titters as I mock-bow and kiss her

hand, and I'm good at it. I'm getting away with it. I'm good at talking to girls! I nod in the vague direction of over there.

'I've got to get that lot a bev. Aftershock, is it?'

'Twist my arm, then.'

Love that throaty Brummie accent of hers. *Love* it. She pulls me close again. Her lips touch the nape of my neck as she whispers: 'But you've got to let me repay the compliment.'

I'm tingling with the dual forces of heightened sexual antici-pation and abject terror. I manage to attract a server and get the order in. I take the others their drinks, tell them I'll be back in a mo and hurry back inside to talk to Colette (not a name I love, incidentally, but we can't have it all, can we?). We get along brilliantly in spite of having virtually nothing at all in common. It's just one of those instant-click things that sometimes happens. We're plugged right into each other straight away. We're engaged, we're drawn right in and I just can't get enough of her. I'm interested in her, interested in the minutiae of her brother and sisters, her awful mother, her philandering father, the Salvation Army, the whole caboodle. She tells me about Tapton, about the Married Couples who mope around all day waiting for each other to get back from lectures. I tell her about Adrian Dangerous, DJ John le Blow, Club Gecko and Benny Bull, and suddenly it all seems tame and cartoonish. None of it, none of them seems such a threat any more.

I spy Jinty and the gang heading on to the dance floor. The opening strains of 'Dancing Queen' are clearly too much to resist – Jinty and Petra are already giving it loads before they've even hit the floor running. I can half accept that sort of kitsch admiration of Abba's inimitable shiteness – but these two seem to genuinely love them. They cannot wait to get on that dance floor. Dangerous tags along, massively self-conscious. I wave fervently, eager for them to see me with Colette, but the room is rocking. Hands, legs, arms and hair flail rampantly. I can snatch the occasional glimpse of Jinty's yellow tank top or Adie's Harlequins shirt, then they're lost again in the tumult.

I signal to Colette to follow, and mole my way through the crowd. She has me giggling like a boy when, having failed magnificently to get me on the dance floor, she stands facing me, taking off Adie's clueless, arrhythmic thrashing. He looks like he's throwing a rugby ball from side to side and Colette manages to dance alongside him, imitating him without him knowing. When she comes back to join me, I throw my arms around her and plant a chaste kiss in the middle of her forehead. She looks into my eyes, ready for the next bit, but I feel something or someone looking at us. I look up and there's Jinty staring over intently. It's not jealousy, it's not hurt – she just looks worried. She looks ever so fearful.

I'm quite drunk and quite confident. I pinch Colette on the arse as I shuffle away to the bogs, tell her I'll be two ticks. She gives me that adorable smile again.

'You'd better had be. I'm starting to get a little bit . . .'

She finishes the sentence with another of her smiles. Direct. Unflinching. Unambiguous. Devastating. In every way, she has laid waste to me with that smile. I lock myself in a cubicle and I can't piss for the fucking terror of it, can't think straight. Fuck! Shit! How do I get out of *this* one with my name intact? How did I get *into* it? I *knew* how it'd end up. I *knew* I'd end up bottling out again, yet I walked straight on, straight into it, each step making it more and more impossible for me to back out. Fuck! I can't go through with it. I can't do it. I know I can't.

I come on out and throw cold water on my face. I stare at myself in the mirror. A voice I don't know, a vaguely Scouse voice goes: 'Still as fucking ugly as you were last time, mate,' and, although there's no malice at all in his tone, I want to smudge him, just blot him out, for ever. His dull and harmless comment has only got me looking at myself again, thinking about myself, about me. I take a deep breath and take the plunge. But instead of the plunge taking me out of there and into her arms and, perhaps after minor negotiations, into her Tapton bed, I walk straight up the stairs and out of there and down past the West End. I cross over the road and it's still early enough for me to catch the 60 bus back to Ranmoor. I know what I'm going to say. When next I see Colette (or Big Bird, or Petra, or whoever confronts me first with their disbelieving 'What happened to *you*?'), I'll tell her I blacked out. I'll allude to some mystical ailment that's fine so long as it's closely watched. I'll say I sparked right out in the men's bogs and the next thing I knew I was being woken up by security. That's what I'm telling her. That won't make her disdain me, it won't let her see through me – but it'll put her off. She'll go after someone else, in future.

I'm walking on, but I can't walk it off. I want to. It's all I want, just now. I want just to walk and walk, leave all that, last night, behind me but it's smothering me like some leaden pall. I tramp down Riverdale Road, turn right into Oakbrook, head hung low, Walkman on full, hands in pockets as I trudge on towards Hanging Water trying to blot it all out of my mind. It's not as though there's some twisted mystery to be leavened out, either – I know exactly what's going on here. I know what it's all about and, right now, I don't need to think about it. I just want to walk away from it.

I get down by the glugging stream and follow it back through the moist and musty woods, past the silent water-wheel back up the slopes and muddy banks of the hill. I'm having to work my head full time here. If I let it lie still for a microsecond it's back, he's back – him and her, Dangerous and fucking Jinty. So I'm thinking hard, casting plans and scenarios in my mind. I'm working towards the next step already, the next step of my life, the step that comes after this one. I'm not unaccustomed to this. I'm quite used to it, talking myself through bad things, bad times. I take Scanner out and hope Boards of Canada will help me through.

Knowing myself so well, so very, very well has not always

been a boon. I'm seldom taken by surprise, but I don't always like what I know. From an early age, I've been an onlooker. I can say this in the coldest and the most factual way. I say it without romance, without either self-aggrandisement or self-pity and without seeking sympathy. Partly because I'm small, people have often not noticed me. In particular, I have seemed invisible, or not significant enough to bother about, to adults. I've sat unseen and watched their habits, their deception, their ticks and nuances. I've been the silent watcher as sexual affairs have simmered between strangers in Corsican hotels, seen them flare up, seen the flames, the burns and the fallout. I've seen liars at work, masters of deception giving themselves away with their flickering ticks and their jerky legs. I've caught a glance between two seeming strangers and read it off, read the whole thing there and then – read it right. I know people, intimately, immediately. I can suss people out. And of all people, it's myself I've got pegged best. I wish there was more to know. I can at least hope that there will be.

The walk is good, the woods and the stream and the sky just too fresh, too beautiful. What it does though, all this nature, is remind me that I'm on my own. I'm locked inside of me, and I can't get out. Places like this, places of calm and space, are for idling with the ones you love. There's a family chasing a tiny, yapping puppy, laughing as it chases and chases its tail. There's two kids, teenagers, sitting on a tree trunk, quiet after an argument, mute but intimate. It seems queer to me that even ones as young as these should be so advanced in their relationship as to row. I'm so far behind them in life already. I stop at the flat swell of the lagoon and watch the water lap at my feet. It's a place for lovers this, not one for drifters. I'll come back sometime. It comes to me as real and true that I'll be back here with someone of my own one day, sometime when I've worked this out. For now I need company. It's with a rueful thrill that I think of Jinty.

*   *   *

The first mistake I make is that I go back to my room. I've come out without money and I half recall tucking the contents of my pockets inside my shoe before dropping disconsolate into bed last night. My second mistake is that I let the door slam behind me. That does my head in at the best of times – can't be doing with big, heavy doors slamming behind me, would rather take a second to stun its swing with my palms – but this time I've got double the trouble. As though the swoosh and clunk of the door is the hunt call he's been waiting for, Adie comes diving into my room, eyes ablaze with fun – *his* fun. He takes me by the wrist and drags me out the room.

'Wait until you see this, matey! This you *have* to see!'

He pulls me into his room, where an unmade bed and an unreal stink confront me. Fuck, but you'd think he'd open the window – it's sour, chokingly stale and sour in here. On his desktop there's a portable TV and a GameCube and the floor is littered with *GTA*-style fuck-'em-up games. He leads me right to the bedside and gives a flourish with his hand.

'And here, gents and gentlemen – what do we have? What do we see? Hmmm.' He points to his bedsheets. 'On first inspection we see a not atypical student pit. Bed bedraggled after only two nights' use, telltale pint glasses and tissues on the floor – nothing out the ordinary, yes?'

He opens his eyes wide and gives me the most chilling, the most inhumane smile I've ever been exposed to. I feel privy to an unspeakable act whose real nature is about to be disclosed.

'But no. No. Far from it, my friend. For what has taken place in this pit of passion, this lounge of lust, is far, far, *far* from the ordinary. No ordinary man could drive a woman to the heights of abandon that were witnessed within these . . .' he takes time out to point to each of the walls, '. . . four walls in the small, small of hours of this very morn. Come. Observe. Celebrate.'

He tugs me down on to the mattress. For one eternal

second I think this is it, this is where the public-school twat shows his true colours and bottom-rapes me. But almost as soon as the thought is thunk, he's brandishing a short sprig of wire at me. Copper wire.

'Exhibit One, Your Lordship – that rare and wondrous thing we know as . . . the Ginger Pube!'

Oh God, please God, no! Not Jinty. Please, please don't let it be Jinty! He wiggles his index finger at me, beckoning me closer. He points to a patch of browny red, the size and shape of an oak leaf. My face must be a picture.

'OK there, old boy? Looking a tad *blanche*.'

'What, me? No, no, no – I'm sound. Smashing.'

'Good-good. Didn't have you down as a wet.'

He makes a big thing of stroking the red patch, rotates his hand slowly around its perimeter then lowers his head to it, sniffing theatrically.

'Aaaaah! Can still smell it!' He jerks his head back round to me. 'Don't you just love it, Kit?'

'Yeah.'

'Virgin blood! Isn't it just the best?'

The penny drops. Thank fuck. It wasn't her, then. It wasn't Jinty.

'Too right, mate.'

That's good enough to keep him going. He laughs to himself, big, self-conscious heaving of his brute shoulders as he recalls the tender moment. He points to another patch, bigger, yellowish, like he's pissed his bed. Except that there is no way, no way remotely that Adrian Hewitt would ever wet his bed.

'Look at this! You know what this is, don't you . . . ?'

My stunned and blinking face would tell an ass the truth, but Adie isn't looking or listening. He doesn't want to know – he wants to show. He laughs madly, now.

'Oh fuck, my friend! My God! You should have seen it . . .'

He breaks off, helpless at the recollection, buries his head in his pillow for a moment and re-emerges, breathless, laughing silently.

'What a gusher! Boy, was she a gusher, mate! The virgin bride turned out to be a gusher, a moaner and a slasher!'

He pulls his rugby shirt up and shows me a network of livid scratches. I am poleaxed by the sight. Truly, I am disabled. This is a world, a world of broken-in virgins and lacerated backs, to which I can't aspire. It's beyond me. It's way, way above me, out of reach, out of my ken. He is — he's in a league of his own.

'Sadly not a swallower though.' He makes a mean, rodent-like face and starts to dribble and spit. He drools back his own spittle and laughs out loud. 'Did she go, though! God, for a virgin — she went like a rabbit at Catford!' He's shaking his square head again, seemingly dumbstruck at the wonder of yet another girl stupid enough to let him fuck her. 'God, but she made a fucking racket!'

I know. I heard her. It got me hard, Adie. He snaps back round to me all of a sudden.

'Didn't hear too much noise from the pump room, old boy . . .'

I look him in the eye.

'The girls reckon you legged it with some little choirgirl bint. Reckoned butter wouldn't melt . . .'

I've been here before. I know exactly how to play it. I wink at him. He beams back at me, jumps up off the bed and claps me on the shoulder.

'So you *did*! You old dog! I bloody *knew* it, you know! I said to myself, actually he's one of those guys that just, you know — does it! He doesn't make a song and dance about it, he *just bloody does it*!'

He eyes me with so much admiration I feel faint. He won't look away. He's looking right into me, his stupid dark eyes scanning all over my face.

'I didn't say that.'

'You don't have to!'

'Nothing happened.'

'Come off it, you hound! It's written all over you!'

This is my art. I've been doing it since Year 9. I'm a maestro. The more I deny sexual adventures, the more people will leap to their own conclusions – almost always in my favour. There's no need to lie. The truth does the job perfectly. Adie is all over me now. His face is just radiant with new esteem.

'Come on, then!'

'What?'

'Details! Details! Details! What *happened*?'

I give him my best 'I'm saying nothing' face.

'Oh, *I* get it. I get it all too well now. Seeing the little slut again, are we? Keeping the fifty-seven in the can . . .'

Two things: he's an absolute meathead, no doubt about it. But thing two, and remarkably – I actually almost quite like him. I mean, he's an acquired taste, for sure – but there's something weirdly direct and childlike about the bastard. I think he's just like anyone else. He wants to be loved.

'Or, no – hang on! It's worse, isn't it? Some black, black art has come to pass in Room 101, yes? Am I close? Am I! Are we talking bottom sex? We are, aren't we? The despicable crime of buggery has come to pass in that very room!' He knocks on my dull wall. 'Oh, *excellent*! Well *done*, old boy! I knew you wouldn't let me down! I'll tell you what, old fellow, Jinty may be the one doing the shrinkology, but she hasn't got a clue when it comes to my old mate Hannah!'

'Oh? And what does Jinty reckon, then?'

He claps me really hard on the back, this time.

'No, no, no – she doesn't think you're queer! Just thinks you're . . .'

I'm all of a bristle, and the more I try to effect nonchalance the more eager and desperate I must seem. Adie's face, half Tom Cruise, half Will Carling, is not helping one bit.

'You know – a *nice boy*.'

This cracks him up. He's down on the bed again, slapping his mattress for mercy, laughing and laughing and laughing. He raises his head for one last look at the nice boy from next door.

'Know when you were with that bloody arse-shag addict last night?'

I nod, trying to look grave. That's my girlfriend he's insulting, there. Well, it could be.

'She was watching you like a hawk. Bit bloody jealous at first, actually! But then she said . . .' He puts on a silly, girly voice. '". . . Aaaah, sweet! Little Kitty. He'll walk her all the way home and that'll be it. Won't even expect a kiss for his troubles."'

I'm stung. I wouldn't have thought it of her. Big Bird, a snitch and a gossip. She's one of those who'll talk about whoever's not there. And I can see it now, I can see it all. She'll do it in a *dead* low-key way, like as though she's concerned or sympathetic. I feel sick. Jinty has taken this thick jock into her confidence, and the subject has been me. He holds his head really still and fixes his eyes on me, like he's got me sussed. I really don't know whether he's going to laugh or cry, hug me or hit me. He looks at me like that for fucking ages, and then he winks.

'But we know better, don't we?'

And that's it. He's off again. I'm desperate to get the fuck away from here, from him. Before he has a chance to come back up again I've legged it.

It took me four pints of Stella to spit it out that I knew what she'd said about me. She was mortified. She didn't even try to deny it. For a moment she just looked at me, looked at me long and true, like she was trying to make her mind up about something. Usually I'd have made her, or whoever, tell me what was on their mind. I hate people letting me know they're harbouring something, but then refusing to let it out.

But whatever it was that Jinty was harbouring, I didn't want to know. Not this time.

It was great being there in the pub, just me and her. She calls it the 'pob'. That's one of the things I love about her, the way she talks. She makes everything sound better than it really is. That *is* a fucking nice 'pob', though, the Ranmoor Inn. It'd be good if we could just keep it as our place, somewhere me and Jinty go to get away from it all.

I know it's Sunday, but the pub doesn't have the feel of a student gaff at all. I don't think many people know about it. It's mad. You cut through the Ranmoor gardens and turn left on Fulwood Road and you're there, smack bang in the middle of studentville. Seriously – Ranmoor, Sorby, Earnshaw, Stevenson – all the halls, all the student flats and houses, Fulwood Road's the artery linking us with the world, and for most students the world is Broomhill. I almost sort of love Broomhill – it *is* a madly cute, insular, warm and welcoming student ghetto. I know it's the easiest thing to just hate the place because it's Student Central. It's safe. But the thing is, it is very quickly going to do my little head in if I have to rely on the Broomhill scene whenever I need to get away from Ranmoor. Turn *right* on Fulwood Road, though – well, it's mad. It's weird, almost rustic suburbia. Big, big houses, quiet, leafy streets – and the Ranmoor Inn. The pob. Hardly another student in there, just me and Jinty. Instantly, I loved the place.

I got directly into gabbling mode, just talking and talking, giving out my opinions and prejudices like I do when I'm happy. I've got on to a pet hate of mine: self-regarding drinkers. Broomhill is full of them, students – presumably from places like Baslow where not much has happened in their lives to date – who are actively *enthralled* by the simple ritual of going to the pub. They think themselves rakish, daring, slightly on the edge because *yet again* they are crossing the road and going to the pub. No need to ask where they're going or where they've been. They're going to get wankered.

'Know how they give themselves away?'

'Who?'

'The twats who think there's something mad and fucking wild about going for a drink.'

'Go on.'

She's smiling, amused, quite taken with her spiky little mate.

'They do this . . .' I put on a dim-witted face that's supposed to exude upper-class thickheadedness. I wiggle my eyebrows dangerously as I announce: 'Just nipping out for a few beers!'

She's in stitches, Jinty. This really slays her.

'Oh, God, Kit darling. I swear – you're fucking horrible! You really are a very fucked-up, very nasty boy!' She goes silent and looks me in the eye. 'Come here.'

For one split second I think she's going to kiss me, but she doesn't. She holds me close, and strokes my head. It feels heavenly. I don't want her to stop, but I jerk away and pull a goofy face.

'Few more beers?'

I love Jinty. I feel utterly, completely safe with her. I trust her. I've had a couple of false starts here, put my faith in people who've already let me down, but Jinty's six years older. She's a woman, for fuck's sake. She has no sexual interest in me – in actual fact we could scarcely be less sexually compatible, her being a giant, me being a pixie. Me and Jinty – we're friends. We said so tonight. She said it first.

'We need to stick together, you and me. We need to look out for each other.'

Like I say, I know people. I know that somewhere in what she was saying she was conning me a little bit. Not in any bad way, but in the way that older people always think they can pull the wool over the young ones' eyes. It's nothing sinister – just, they underestimate you sometimes. She was saying some things she maybe didn't really mean, and her eyes were saying something different to her words. *I* know what she meant, though. I know what she means.

I'm lying here listening to Górecki through my headphones. Don't want any sound, anything to let Dangerous know I'm back, so I'm listening to Górecki through the cans. The thought of sharing this music with a vulgarian like Adie hurts me, anyway. I'd *hate* to see his muscled head pop round the door, those stupid brown eyes toughing it out against the world – 'What's this? Quite nice, actually' – I'd *hate* to be responsible for turning Adrian Dangerous on to Górecki's Third. Nothing quite comes close to the daunting emotional sweep of this piece. I have never listened to it and not felt drained. I'm flat out here, bruised and raw from all that's gone on in these first faltering days, yet I'm serene, now. Serene and ready. That's the other thing about this majestic piece – it kills you, but it becalms you, too. I'm strong and prepared, and I feel good things are going to happen. Come what may, I'm ready for tomorrow.

Week 1: Day 1
Weather: That Slanting Rain That Spears
  Your Cheeks Like Javelins
Soundtrack: DJ Shadow – 'You Can't Go Home Again'

I don't think I'll be able to keep this up. That was just . . . *awful*. Why am I doing this module, anyway? Why am I doing this *course*? I may well mock at Adie (who I saw striding past the Notty House this morning, wearing a mad, full-on City gent's overcoat with a badge on the lapel saying 'Sex Starved'). The thing is, he's doing law and guess what? He's going to be a lawyer. Medical students end up being doctors and surgeons and the like. Architecture, engineering, business studies – they all have a natural outlet. So what of English with American studies, then? Where does that get you? I'm wasting my fucking time.

All last week I've been running the clock down, waiting

to get started. I've said to myself that, regardless of all the other shite, I really want to immerse myself in this stuff. I want to know *so* much, and this is just the jumping-off point. If I end up making loads of mates and being a normal student and maybe having a girlfriend or something, then great – but it's a bonus. What I'm here for, I've told myself, is the work. I want to work. But, I don't know – that was just so fucking *depressing*. I've sat there and I've listened intently and it's suddenly come crashing in on me: what is the fucking *point* of this? Why are you giving three years of your fuck-ing *life* to this? It's not a vocation, it's a whim. It's not your life's passion – it's the thing in your education to date that's bored you the least. And all those kids in there! Are they like me in some way? Am I supposed to have something in common with them? What's it *for*? What'll I do with the fucking degree, if I get it? I just feel flattened by the whole thing before I've even got going. I think I might be better quitting and starting all over – but what would Mum have to say about that?

I find myself by the tram stop and I just get on and ride and, without my being conscious of even passing anywhere or moving any great distance, there's loads of people getting off and I'm down by the train station. It's blindingly simple. I get on the train and I go home. I come clean. I tell them the truth. I. Do. Not. Want. To. Go. To. University. I'm sorry. I know it's not what they want for me. I know they want to be proud of me. But I'm making myself miserable here. I'm making myself sick. So yes – I'm dropping out. Yes – I'm running away. What's so bad about that?

What's so bad about that is not how they'll react – with silent and stoic support – but how *I'll* feel. I'll feel like a worm. I'll feel like a failure. I fucking hate it here, but I'm not throwing the towel in yet. I stare up at the grim grey egg-box warren of Hyde Park Flats and I start into a jog. I pick up speed and I run, and run, and run.

Week 1: Day 4
Weather: Startling Sunshine
Soundtrack: Underworld – 'Rez'

That was mad. By any standards, that was a mad, mad episode.

1) There are only five of us in the tutorial group.
2) Two of the five are fucking ancient. I know I've no right but I feel cheated, having them in the same group. I'm just being honest. They are called Mature Students, but personally I'd want to call that into question. I'm considerably more mature than either of them and I'm not quite eighteen yet. Yep. I'm one of those bright sparks that got in everywhere a year early. Grounds for being hated, I admit.
3) One of the Maturos insists on calling himself Jock. 'Just call me Jock,' he goes, when I asked him his name. I felt a bit weird about that. I really did not want to just call him Jock. I ventured an opinion that that was maybe a little demeaning and he just gave me a look. He never spoke to me again. Fuck him.
4) There was worse. The other Maturo seemed to take a liking to me. Sitting here on this lavatory, ten whole minutes after making my excuses and legging it, I can now see that her admiration for me stems from my use of the word 'demeaning'. It's a word she likes. Alex is from Memphis, Tennessee. She is, with all the best will in the world, carrying a bit of heft. She is absolutely barking fucking mad and she's on my case badly. I've had to flee in here to get shot of her.
5) Of the remaining two in the group, one of the girls is a friend of Colette's. Actually, *not* a friend, thankfully. The good news is that, yes, they're both in Tapton, but they haven't really seen that much of each other since freshers' week. The bad news is that this girl, Andrea,

thinks Colette is a bit 'odd'. That can mean anything of course, especially if you're a beady-eyed frump who writes down *every fucking thing* your tutor says. But knowing my luck, what Andrea's telling me is that Colette is bang at it and half the hall has been through her already. I mean fair dos, it's not as though I've got any opinion on the matter. It's not as though I've got any kind of relationship with Colette or anything that would vaguely *allow* me to be hurt. But I know exactly what this Andrea stick means when she says she's 'odd' and it severs my arteries to hear it.

It's like a summer's day, today. We're well into October and the sun is blazing. Everyone's dressed in jeans, T-shirts, denim jackets, one or two girls in skirts. I, of course, am wearing my Spiewak and I closely resemble Kenny from *South Park*. If only an errant missile or a distressed tree-feller would put me out of my misery, too.

Yet I'm not miserable – far from it. I'm unusually and abundantly high, right now. In spite of, though possibly, just possibly, *because* of my bizarre lunch with Alex, I'm just *tingling* with joy. It's rootless. There's nothing to explain it. I just feel glad that I'm me.

She pounced on me – as much as a twenty-stone woman can be said to pounce on anything – as soon as the tutorial broke up.

'Y'all got plans for lunch?' she said. I thought it was a group invitation and looked around at my fellow learners for some sense of quorum. The others just kept their heads down and shuffled out. Alex was, already, not an easy woman to love. Throughout the tutorial she was constantly interrupting with questions, almost all with a clear but, I thought, futile political agenda. Questions like: 'Can we assume that this text assumes a superiority of male over female?' 'Can we look at this text actually as an exercise in sex-race propaganda?'

The text we were looking at is *Walden*. All that happens is a man builds a shack by a pond. Alex was seeing it differently. Alex sees a lot of things differently. Unable to come up with a good enough excuse quickly enough – and not really wanting to hurt the woman's feelings – I said I'd love to have lunch with her. That's me all over. I don't know why the fuck I do it. A simple 'yes' or 'OK' would've done, but I had to put on this big mad smile and tell her I'd *love* to.

We wandered over to the Interval, me minutely self-conscious about walking alongside such a spectacle – and in the nicest possible sense, Alex is a spectacle. She has unruly red hair, huge, startled brown eyes, and skin so white it's almost transparent. But although she's wider than a Mini Cooper too, it's not so much her physical look that's eye-catching. It's her clothes. On four successive days this week, I've seen her in four quite contrasting and utterly radical outfits. First day of lectures she was in combat fatigues. Next day she was in a sari – she also had rings on every finger and a splendid red tear painted on her forehead. Day three she was in the dirtiest, smelliest Afghan coat I've ever seen. Even when that shepherd-coat/sheepskin thing was in fashion and girls wanted theirs to be slightly battered and worn, I never saw a coat that had bacteria. Alex has such a coat. And today, to celebrate the sunshine, she was Carmen Miranda – complete with plastic pears and bananas in her hair.

People double-checked as we made our way into the Union. Alex talked; I nodded and pondered my escape plans. To my delight, I spotted Petra reading her *What's On* – and there was no one with her. Fantastic! She could share the wonders of the Alex Experience with me. Even better, the two of them seemed to hit it off. You never can tell with old Petra, though. She's dead friendly, she really is one of those girls who's just easy to talk to. But she's a piss-taking little mare, too. You've got to watch her. Couple of times I've found myself getting sucked into over-elaborate explanations of dead simple things and she's just goading me on.

'But hang on – if a stanza's just another name for a verse, what's iambic pentameter?'

And you'll tell her and she's all wide eyes and open face, nodding her head going: 'Fascinating, fascinating.' Then she'll just crack up and go: 'You really are a sad case, Mr Hannah. You want to get a life.'

I might have felt shite about it, if she hadn't said that. People who say 'get a life' need to get a life, I tend to think.

But her and Alex seemed bang into each other. I found myself more and more marginalised as their conversation veered from Naomi Wolff to genetically modified food. I felt like I was on pretty safe ground there though, given that, like the pair of them, I'm no lover of heated flesh. It's been one of Mum's prize theories since I gave up meat at the age of ten that that's why I'm not six foot. It's not because she's a half-Taiwanese dwarf. It's because I don't eat meat. I leant over to offer up my tuppence worth.

'Stick to carrots, broccoli and a good range of beans and pulses and you won't go far wrong.'

There – that'll get me in their good books, I thought. Uh-uh. No way Jose. Whatever it was that I said, I said it wrong. OK – it was a bit of a bland selection, admittedly, and not a strictly accurate representation of where I'm at myself, diet-wise – but it didn't merit the tirade that followed from Alex.

'Really depends what y'all mean by carrot and broccoli.'

I looked at Petra. She seemed to know what was coming and looked away, leaving me high and dry.

'Y'eat *feeling* carrot and, sure, you're doing pretty good.'

She challenges me with those big, mad, staring eyes. She's got this infuriating thing, Alex, where she looks at you like she's peering inside your soul. Like she knows what sort of person you are. I hate all that. My mistake was to answer her back.

'What you on about? *Feeling* carrot?'

That was all the encouragement she needed. Fuck, was she ready for that!

'You wanna know about feelings? Let me fuckin' tell you then!'

(This, incidentally, two seconds into her rant, saw my favourite black lambswool pullover festooned with spittle and, if I'm not terribly mistaken, couscous.)

For the next five minutes she jabbed her plastic fork at me approximately every twenty seconds as she made point after point after point, drenching me in spit as she eyeballed me ferociously.

'How *dare* you assume that carrots have no feelings . . .'

I could have and I should have stood up and walked out there and then – but I was trapped. I was mesmerised. I sat there while she hectored me about crops and chemicals and wheat and cover-ups; vegetables that wilt and shrivel as a result of depression; broccoli that is so choked with colouring that you can hear it cry; baby corn and petit pois strangled at birth to provide novelty food for the White Man. And what became swiftly and abundantly clear is that I was the White Man. I waited for her to draw breath and with a world-weary sigh, said the first thing to come into my head.

'Wonder how long it takes for it all to turn into shit, though?'

Truly, she was speechless. Her chubby hamster cheeks froze, her wild eyes glassed over for a moment and she turned to Petra to check this was for real. I saw that as a good opportunity to make myself scarce.

'Speaking of which, I've got a good one fermenting here. Time to let it lovingly into the world, hey?'

I'm sure that was love on Petra's face as I scampered off.

It's great the amount of freedom we've got between lectures and that, but it's hard to motivate yourself to work. I've always been quite conscientious but just at the moment I find it *really* hard to concentrate. I just can't stick at it. I'm finding it all too easy to put it all off till tomorrow. I never thought I'd say it, but I'm starting to quite like the life up here. I'm finding I don't mind the whole thing of making my own decisions, doing what I want pretty well when I want to do it. I've never had that. I'm sat here in Vittles waiting for a second pot of tea, and life is OK, on the whole. Everything's all right.

They serve the tea in these ace little pewter pots. Well, it may not actually be pewter but the pots are quite heavy and, crucially, you don't spill half your tea all over the table when you pour. Most cafés serve the tea in those flimsy stainless-steel pots whose lids leak as you're pouring. I can't be doing with that, I really can't. It's a major, major plus to find a gaff like this. The tea, and the Welsh rarebit in particular, is just bang on. I come in here a lot. I sat here yesterday afternoon and wrote Erk a letter. We sort of had this pact whereby we wouldn't email or text each other. We decided that the art of the handwritten letter had to survive, and we were just the chaps to keep it going. I made it sound like I was having a brilliant time and hinted that I'd made loads of mates and copped off with Jinty and Colette, without actually saying so. I still felt a bit crap that I'd been first to write, though. It's sort of an admission that you haven't got anything better to do, for starters – and you're also half saying that you miss your mate. You're thinking of him.

I'm browsing the newspapers, but it's mainly a front as I listen to some crusty Peter Hook lookalike selling revolution to an eager young girl who, I note, is wearing suede Spezial trainers. Very cute. The line the Hooky fella is feeding her is *so* fucking stale. It's all that semi-harangue patter where he just tries to make you feel safe and privileged and green, just for being who you are.

'And did you know that just four miles away from here in

Darnall there's the thirty-third highest infant-mortality rate in the UK? You probably hadn't thought much about that, had you?'

He's got an accent, Kiwi I think, and he cannot keep his hands still when he's talking.

'Wow! That's so awful . . .'

'But it doesn't have to be "so awful" . . .'

The twat actually does those inverted commas with his fingers to ridicule her and, in making her despise herself, brings her warm flesh a step closer to his mouldy bed. I'm about to ask him where he got his Day-Glo orange fleece from when I spy Colette over the road. Shit! She's standing outside Blackwell's, seemingly counting money in her hand. I want to watch her, my God, do I want to just sit here and drink her in, but it feels as though my ogling is sending a message across the road to her, alerting her to my presence. I couldn't cope with her just at the moment. I'm just starting to make a bit of headway here, make a little bit of sense of it all. Just *seeing* Colette drags me back down again, makes me confront the things I want buried. I duck behind the *Guardian* until my second pot of char arrives. When I look up again, there's no Colette, and Hooky has left with his wide-eyed victim.

Traipsing back to Ranmoor, I'm uncommonly chuffed to see Simon hop off the 60 just ahead of me. I run to catch up with him.

'Greetings, bro. How it go?'

'Cool, cool. Good, yeah.'

'What you up to?'

He checks around us as though we're under surveillance.

'Listen, Kit, man . . .'

I flap at the backs of my ears.

'You're pretty well up for anything, yeah?'

Fuck, but he talks slowly! Did he always talk this slow, drawling and agonising like he's giving each word cunnilingus?

'Bit of a statement, Baslow.'

He gives an impatient little glance past me. This is no time for joking, he's telling me.

'What's up, then? Spit it out.'

'It's just . . .' He glances round again. 'I've heard . . .' He swallows hard. 'Don't go telling fucking everyone, right, but when I was back home last weekend this fella at the party was telling me there's this place, right, this stately home with acres and acres of lawns, right, and the people still live there so it's like *really* dangerous?'

'What is?'

He grins and slaps his forehead. 'Duh! Good point, Einstein.'

He gets out a ciggy, lights it, holds it with what must be unutterable discomfort between the last two fingers of his right hand and puffs effetely on it once, then twice. He pulls the sleeve of his non-smoking arm down over his fingers and shudders his shoulders against a wind that isn't there. It's nearly three and there's still heat in the orange fireball sun. He checks around himself again before leaning close and spilling the fucking beans.

'Mushrooms. I know a place where we can definitely get mushrooms.'

He fixes his specs on me. I can't see his eyes for the sun's reflection.

'You want in?'

Although I'm conscious of Simon's faintly ludicrous subterfuge over such an innocent sortie, I let it go.

'Sure. When?'

He glances up at the sun. 'Could go now, if you want? Still plenty of daylight.'

'Is it far, like?'

'Nah. Out in the country, like. But it's just past the last stop, innit?'

'I'm asking *you*, mate.'

'We can only try, hey? There'll be another bus along any minute – what've we got to lose?'

I shrug and grin at him. 'I'm in.'

'Cool.'

'I don't *have* to hear them. I just know they're crap.'

'Very broad-minded of you, Hannah . . .'

'No. *No.* That's just the thing. People are *too* broad-minded, if you want my opinion! If a band can't come up with a better fucking name than The fucking Music then they better pack up and go home now. *The Music*! Jesus! I thought Stereophonics was bad enough. Or The Burn . . .'

'Oh, and I suppose fucking Yes is a great name for a band?'

'I've told you Baslow, man. I fucking *hate* Yes . . .'

'Can, then. Faust. Low.'

'Erm, 'scuse me amigo. You can diss your Krautrock as much as you want. Minnesota lo-fi, though – be careful. Be very careful where you point your gun.'

He gives me a real huffy glare that only tells me I know more, way more about music than he does, and stalks off to his own corner of the grounds. I leave him to his imaginary conversations with Chris Martin and skulk around in the slick, mossy grass by the main path. There's nothing here. There's nothing at all, other than a constant feeling we're being watched. I scuff at the ground with my toe ends as I trudge back towards Si.

'Bum steer, man.'

'Keep looking. We've hardly been here half an hour.'

'Half an hour's well more than enough. If there was anything here, we'd have found them by now.'

For the second time today I find myself being yelled at. I didn't know Simon could *get* so cross.

'Bollocks, man! That's fucking bollocks!' He rounds on me. His little piggy myopic eyes are glinting madly. 'This guy, right – he's *not* a bullshitter!'

I hold my hands out for peace. 'No problem, man. We'll carry on looking for a bit. I'm just saying, like . . .'

'Well, *don't.* It's hard enough as it is . . .'

'OK.' I eye him warily. 'I think Ryan Adams is quite good.'
This, at last, brings a flicker of a smile to his smouldering
face.

'I mean it, Kit. It's just one field. It's absolutely *stuffed* with
mushrooms. You won't believe it when you see it.'

I bite my lip. Heads bent to the task, we plough on.

Week 2: Day 3
Weather: Gentle Autumn Mist
Soundtrack: Freq Nasty – 'Voices in My Head'

I'm starting to handle the lowies a little bit better now, partly
as result of coming to understand that I'm not alone here.
Everyone but everyone is complaining of feeling a bit down,
to the extent that I'm a bit depressed by it. I don't really want
every Tom, Dick and Harry feeling depressed.

The other thing I do, though, whenever I'm starting to
feel a bluey coming to get me, is I go on the run. I grab my
Walkman and I do a runner. I get on the bus. I fucking love
it. I don't care what bus it is, or where it's going – Walkley,
Crookes, Killamarsh, Woodhouse, I'll go wherever the bus is
going. There's even a place called Intake. When I first saw it
on the front of the bus, I thought it meant you could get on
but not off. I swore to myself I had to ride that bus right to
the end of the line, and that's just what I've done and I feel
brilliant for it. I don't feel brilliant in myself, so to speak. I
don't feel *good*. But, I don't know – I've just been driven right
through the heartland of a world I've never known, a world
I'll never know. I've just been through all these places, all these
lives, and I've looked out of the window and I've watched
the world go by – *their* world go by – and I just feel, in the
truest sense of it, enlightened. My load is lighter, somehow. I
have learnt nothing, have had no sudden flash of insight or

truth. But what *has* happened is I've got a better sense of the world. I've been out on a bus on a Wednesday afternoon. I've ridden all the way out, all the way through these places, and I've had a small sense of what goes on in those places. I haven't thought on it *too* hard, but one thing keeps coming back to me. I haven't been sat on that bus with eight laden carrier bags and a kid who fucking depends on me. I've been sat there because I wanted to. If I want it, it's still there for me. It's all out there, waiting for me.

Week 3: Day 3
Weather: Getting Cold
Soundtrack: Scanner – *Locked Up*

Got a very sweet text from little Emma.

> Miss u. When r u cmng home? PS Hope u r snggng lds of ft brds xxx

I sent her a reply straight away.

> If you mean fat birds then yes, I specialise. I miss you too – especially your adorable habit of scratching while you watch Futurama. By the way – DO shorten whichever words you want, but NEVER call a loved one u. Got that, Pie? I'll be home for my birfdee. Love you, Kit xxx

I think that last bit's true. Mum, in between her nervy and ill-concealed enquiries about my sex life, has been trying to make plans for my eighteenth. I really don't want any fuss. I don't see my relatives from one funeral to another. I just think it's unfair and unnatural to stick us all in a room together and try to pretend we like each other and we're having fun, just because we're blood relatives. If she insists on having a party, I suppose I'll have to go. Can't see Maddy coming back from Miami somehow. I wish she would. One thing that's happening lately – and it must just be all the time I spend on my own here, walking, thinking, thinking – is that I can let her back into my mind. I don't mind. I'm ready to see Madeleine again. Still, whatever, it'll just be nice to see lil' Emmakins, the sprite. To be honest, it'll be good to see Mum and Dad. I sort of miss them, in a weird way.

I carry on up the hill, increasingly and quite pathetically excited at the prospect of Welsh rarebit and a piping-hot cuppa at Vittles. After that I'm finally going to brave Scott's for my first barnet trim since I got here. The relationship between a barber, his client and his client's skull is a fraught one and one that depends as much on sheer good fortune as shearing skill. If you're lucky, your local barber's a good 'un – it's as simple as that. The alternative is too dire to contemplate. But it's got to happen sometime, and that time is this afternoon. We've let fucking Dangerous talk us into the Students and Nurses night down at Flares, and if I'm going at all then I'm going looking my best. I don't know – I just feel tonight's going to be all right.

Week 3: Day 4
Weather: Breath Visible on Broomhill Air
Soundtrack: Cabaret Voltaire: 'Nag, Nag, Nag'

Oh. No. Oh. No. Oh. No.

My head is thumping like an industrial tar flattener and my mouth is acrid, stale and stinking. And it's not just a headache head ache. Without even lifting my fingers to touch it, I know I've done damage up there. Even through the throb of the hangover, I can sense out the bruising. I've whacked my head on something and I've got a lump up there the size of a mango.

I feel like shit. I'm not someone who gets hangovers, but then I'm not someone who drinks twenty alcopops and makes a complete and utter prick of himself in front of large and appreciative crowds – appreciative because it's not them that everyone's pointing at, asking, 'Who's the knobhead in the grey hoody?'

There's no escaping it. No matter how many times I bury my head in the pillow, this will not go away. The thing that will not go away is the deep and morbid truth that I am a wretched, wretched, wretched human being. I am a coward and a fraud and if it should happen that nobody wants to talk to me today and tomorrow and the day after that then that's absolutely what I deserve. Last night, I was a twat.

It started out like one of those nights that you half hoped student life would be all about. Even if you pretend to be above it all, above all that self-consciously hearty business of getting trolleyed, deep down that's what you want. You want to go out with a big gang of mates and get twatted. That's exactly what we did – and exactly what did for me.

We did what we'd promised we'd do for a while. We did West Street. Every fucking pub, by the way, starting at the Harley and working our way down, crossing the road so we didn't miss out any of them. The Swim Inn, O'Neill's, Lounge, the Varsity, Muse, the Hallamshire, even the Saddle – we did them all. Bar V, 80s, the fucking Cavendish – we imbibed in every one of them, by Jiminy. We drank with gusto, and we drank to get drunk. In this, we succeeded spectacularly.

I looked fucking good, as well. Scott's did a cracking job on the Hannah crop, giving my pretty little face a slightly less pretty aspect. Not that I look hard when I've had my hair cut, far from it – but I don't look . . . I'm just not so fucking *pretty*, OK? Last night, I looked good. That was half the trouble.

The last good thing to happen was finding the money again. Somewhere between the Hallamshire and the Saddle I'd dropped a twenty-pound note. I knew I'd had it in the Hallamshire because I was on my way to the bar, money ready, when the girls decided they didn't like it in there. It was too smoky, too much of an old-time saloon bar in a street of gaudy fun palaces for them to want to stay any longer than the obligatory drink – and they didn't sell Aftershocks. Soon as we got inside the Saddle I went straight up to get the round in and it was gone. I'd lost the twenty-spot. Obviously, I was in with a chance. I knew I must have dropped it outside, but West Street carries two dozen tipsy students from bar to bar every thirty seconds. That chance, such as it was, was minimal.

I ran outside and, nose glued to the pavement and giving every impression of succumbing to the early symptoms of yuppie flu, I retraced my steps, diving on scraps of paper and shouting 'Shit!' when they turned out to be trampled club flyers. But then I saw it. It wasn't trampled at all. It was just . . . lying there. It was waiting for me, waiting for me to realise I'd left without it and come back for it. That is exactly how it looked and how it felt to me. The strange sight of a perfect twenty-pound note sitting unmolested on a busy city-centre pavement moved me beyond all reasonable explanation. I bent gently, picked it up and burst into tears.

'That's it!' I gushed to them. 'By all rights I shouldn't even have this little twentaroonie now. I'm getting the drinks in!'

'It's your round anyway . . .'

'Oh yeah . . .'

'Do we *have* to stay here?'

'Too fucking real for you, is it?'

'It's not that, it's just . . .'

'It's too *shit* for us.'

'Yeah. Let's go to Sola. Cheap drinks on a Wednesday.'

'*Homework* night though, isn't it? Isn't that school uniform?'

'Don't *have* to wear school uniform.'

'Hang on though! Sola – don't they put an apostrophe on their flyers?'

'What you on about, Kit?'

'They *do*! It says "Sheffield's legendary cocktail bar drops *it's* prices for one night a week!"'

'Kit? You're getting sadder by the day.'

'All I'm saying is we should stick to the plan. Some people are going to like some of the bars more than others. Come on, hey? Every pub in West Street!'

'Let's just go to Walkabout. This was a crap idea.'

'Just the one, then?'

'Not even one, Kit.'

Walkabout was the last stop before Flares, and the nearer we got to Flares, the more stupendously nervous I got. It was like the whole procession down West Street was just a suspension of reality. The real business – the business of finding someone who was willing to take their clothing off and press their body up against yours in a very small bed – was about to start. This was the hard bit, avoiding the attentions of sexually avaricious girls. It was going to be hard to put it off, in there. Loads of nurses, loads of girls, all there for just one thing. It was, to put it mildly, not a place for a shy boy.

The real problems started when I discovered that a) WKD is 2 for 1 on a Wednesday night, and b) Colette was at the bar. She hadn't seen me. I ran the options through my head. By far the most tempting plan was just to get the fuck out of there. It was packed to a point where nobody would have had a clue who was in there and who had left. I could tell them anything. Yet I'd had enough of running. I felt I should try and see this through somehow.

My next option was to buy myself two of said WKD alcopop concoctions, neck them fast at the bar, neck another two, then take the exquisite Colette on the run. If I could just go up to her and start kissing her, really go for it, with any luck at all she'd smack me in the face, tell me to fuck off and that'd be that. At least everyone'd see I had it in me. Then again though, Colette would most probably never talk to me again and what would be the point of that?

The only other plan was to stick with the drink-WKD-as-quick-as-possible scenario and simply lose myself on the dance floor. That would necessitate dancing to Abba and Donna Summer for an unfeasibly lengthy stint, but at least my compadres would see that I'm someone who's a little bit mad, someone who knows how to have a good time. Just as this course of action was starting to appeal, my mind was made up for me. Not for a long, long time have I felt so utterly crumpled as I did at that moment. Relieved that Colette had been up to the bar, got served and was halfway back to her friends without even coming close to spotting me, I turned right round to watch her go. Being honest, I wanted to clock her little bum. I wish I hadn't. A large and, I'm pretty certain, hairy hand clamped itself across her right buttock and halfway across her left. Far from deterring the groper with a slap or a warning finger, she leant up on her tiptoes and kissed him, long and hard, only breaking to look into his stupid, hairy-eyebrow face. She was staring at some simian bodybuilder type, and she was giving him the look of love. I hurled myself on to the dance floor.

That was my next mistake. Seconds later my Abba-loving chums Jinty and Petra were by my side, giving it everything. Both of them were gurning, both trying to shout in my ear. I couldn't hear them, but they were smiling a lot. I don't know why, but I didn't want to dance with them. No – I *do* know why. I was dancing out of anger. I was dancing out of madness. I wanted to dance alone and dance the pain away – it was an exercise in purgation. I turned my back on them and turned directly into a group of girls who were dancing in a circle and all had blonde hair and looked identical and the next thing I was kissing one of them. I was aware that, in the background, her friends had made a circle around us and they were all cheering and wolf-whistling, but I didn't give a fuck. The pair of us were out of it, sucked into our own little cocoon, sucking each other's faces off. I didn't want it to stop.

There was a small scuffle when Jinty came running in and dragged me away.

'Who's this? Who the fuck's she!'

'This your lass?'

'She your lass, you two-timing twat?!'

The gang of girls all had accents. They weren't sure who to kick off on – me or Jinty. Bit by bit, they started to side with Jinty. The girl I'd been snogging booted me up the arse and shoved me back towards the bar.

'Go on! Fuck off!'

I just stood there, gaping at Jinty. I really could not fathom what was occurring, just that I was at the epicentre of it, whatever the furore was about.

'What's going on?'

She jerked her head behind her. Petra was sitting on the floor, head hung low like she'd broken her neck.

'Can't you work it out?'

'What?'

'Jesus fuck, Kit! Are you *completely* dumb?'

'What. Are. You. On about?'

She stubbed a finger into her temple and gave me a hateful look.

'You prick!'

She looked back at Petra like she'd come off the worse in a car I'd just crashed. She shook her head sadly.

'Fuck, Kit? What's the matter with you? Don't you get it? She's fucking stone bonkers about you, isn't she?'

This is the bad bit. This why I'm having to stick my head

under the pillow again, just bringing the moment back to life through very reluctant recall. I'm having to sing a tuneless tune in my head so that the words and pictures from last night are fuzzy and distant. La-la-la-la! It didn't happen! It. Did. Not. Happen.

It did, though. I followed Jinty's eyeline over to Petra. What I did next was bad. I laughed. I laughed out loud at the thought that *Petra* had a crush on me. This was made worse by the fact she looked up at that moment, saw me looking over at her and, seemingly, laughing at her. She got up and dashed for the exit. Why I said what I said next, I do not know. I can't work it out. I'm not a nasty person. I'd have to lie down with a shrink, really, to come anywhere close to finding out why I watched her go, turned back to Jinty and said: 'See what I mean? It's ludicrous to even *think* it!'

'What is, Kit?'

'Me and Petra!'

She gave me a really serious, I-am-rapidly-losing-patience-with-you sort of look. 'Tell me then, hey? Why don't you tell me?'

I gave it one more nervous little laugh, then I told her. 'Well, look at her! I mean . . . her *legs*, for starters. Those aren't legs. They're just . . . *thighs*!'

When I looked back to check Jinty was with me on this assessment, her face was slightly thunderous but, more than anything, she looked troubled or confused – so I went further. The way I saw it I was just being factual. I was just supplying the raw info that was eluding her.

'I mean . . . there's no def*inition*, is there? Her thighs sort of start under her arse and they just keep on going – all the way down her shoes.'

With that, Jinty cracked me, hard, on the side of my face and went out to find her chum. I couldn't for the life of me work out what I'd done wrong, so I necked two more Irn

Bru-flavour WKD and went to find Adie. If anyone was going to empathise, it'd be Adrian fucking Dangerous.

I didn't find Adie, but I found the bog. I had not been so gone, so totally fucked on drink for a long, long time. I was staggering drunk, bumping into people drunk, head all over the place drunk. I was, in short, wankered. I was elated to find a free cubicle. I suddenly relished the idea of the peace and solitude of a poo cubicle and slumped on to the bog. My head lolled forward so that it was touching the door. Everything happened in slow motion. The floor came up to meet me and the next thing, I was lying crouched and cramped on the floor, kecks still round my knees, totally fucked. I couldn't lift my head. I didn't know where I was. All I knew was, I had to get out of there. I *had* to get back to my feet.

I could feel the bilious vaulting in my guts well before the retching started. I got down on my knees again and, knowing then that this was something I'd just have to give in to, I let my sad, sapped head fall into the bog basin and I retched and heaved and threw my heart up – except that nothing came. From the next cubicle, from outside, from somewhere else, delighted fellows made exaggerated puking sounds, but not even that helped start the avalanche. The acute agony of dry retching in spasm, in endless, uncontrollable volleys of the most intense pain and misery, was enough to make me sober or, if not truly sober, then well enough to get to my feet, tuck myself in and get moving again. My eyeballs felt like I'd been whacked so hard from behind that they'd almost shot out of their sockets. Acidic tears stung my face. I took one, two, three, four, five deep breaths, unbolted the door and stepped out – to cheers of ribald appreciation from a now sizeable crowd.

'Fancy a drink, mate?' chirped one naughty Southerner. It was as much as I could do just to get out of there.

The first person I saw as I emerged was Jinty. She was wearing that same patient/impatient face and she was leaning on the wall outside the men's, awaiting my return. She levered herself off the wall with her shoulder blade and she was straight at me.

'Right, you, you bastard – I hope you really suffered in there.'

I was trying to sound as wan and as needing of sympathy as possible. 'I did.'

'Good. Now you'll be pleased to know that not only have I protected your sainted reputation from the rest of us who hold you so dear, I've engineered a way ahead for you.'

I couldn't even be bothered asking what the fuck she was going on about by then. A way out was being offered. A way out.

'OK.'

'Good lad. *Good lad!* You're *learning*!'

I nodded dumbly.

'Now, what I've told young Petra is that you're having a particularly hard time because your girlfriend back home has just binned you. I'm the only person you've told, and nobody's supposed to mention her unless you do. This is why you've been behaving so very strangely this evening.'

'And?'

She widened her eyes. 'Well, *I* don't know, do I? All I do know is that I've straightened things out for you, nobody thinks you're a dick, you are free to join us at Nirmal's.'

I joined them at Nirmal's where, mindful of how it would give her completely the wrong notion but no longer knowing the difference between wrong and right, I sat next to Petra and made her giggle. The more her eyes sparkled with love and amusement, the lower I slumped inside. I was witty and engaging, told her mad and quite funny things, told her stories, remembered the first lines of a dozen crap number ones. I was the best-loved kid on the table until I threw up.

They got me into a taxi. It was weird. I could clearly hear

them talking about me, could absolutely take in what was happening, but it was like I wasn't there.

'Might have an allergic reaction, you know . . .'

'What to?'

'Dunno. Nuts. Wheat. Anything. Might just be a good precaution to get him down the Hallamshire . . .'

'Pump his stomach? Like it!'

'No, Adie, no. Just check him out.'

Next thing I was on my bed, fully clothed, shivering like fuck. I know Jinty smacked me last night. I know I fell down and cracked my head on the bog floor. But this is the one that got me. This is what's giving me the headache. I got to my feet and went to get undressed, little understanding I was still paralytic. Standing in the middle of this Ranmoor cell, I lifted my foot to remove a shoe. The shoe stayed tantalisingly out of reach, no matter how far forward I leaned. Standing on one leg, very drunk, I leaned so far forward that I over-balanced and went crashing, head first, into the wall. I have not even a sense of how I got into bed after that − but I'm still wearing one shoe and my head hurts when I blink.

I hate this. I hate myself. Lying here, head under pillow, skull split into a thousand splintering pain cells and my eyes throbbing, throbbing with such a deep and impenetrable sickness, all I want is to go back to the moment where I found my twenty-pound note.

Week 4: Day 1

Weather: Low Sky, Damp Air

Soundtrack: Two Lone Swordsmen − 'Kicking in and Out'

To my sudden horror, I realise it's Adie sitting in the park. The weekend was bad enough as it is, without having to start a new week with Adie's shite. The weekend was a horror that's been waiting to happen. It happened on Saturday night at the Datsuns gig. It happened before that really, when Si announced he was off home to spend the weekend with his girlfriend. That crushed me. Not so much the idea that he'd had a girlfriend all along, but, I don't know – I was knocked sideways a bit by the idea that someone had so much free will and so much choice. *I* don't have that choice. I don't even have a girlfriend. But I know that if I go home for just one day, never mind a weekend, I will never come back. It's that simple.

The rest of us went to see the Datsuns. I think they were amazing but the memory is already obliterated by horror-association. Dangerous and Ben – *Ben* forfucksakes! – copped off and will probably now spend all their time with their new girlfriends doing couple things like going for long, romantic walks and shopping for battered Penguin Classics and just occasionally, when they feel like company, making up cute foursomes with each other and only when they feel really, really tight, inviting their sad gooseberry of a mate along to patronise him and reassure him that he's lovely and it's only a matter of time before Ms Right reveals herself. Adie's girl was a honey, too. She looked really *nice* and happy and clever and lively. Dead pretty she was, dead happy with life. Why'd she choose Adie in his crap, newly purchased combat jacket? What was fucking Adie *doing* at a Datsuns concert? He should be hanging on the credit-card line for Bon Jovi tickets. I've given him *so* much already and all he does is use it to get himself the best girls. Downer. Fucking downer. And what about fucking Simon? And *Ben*, for crying out loud! If Benny Bull can have a girlfriend, then why can't I?

The system is, if I'm feeling OK I'll take the right at O'Neill's and trundle down the quick route – not that it's *that* much quicker. If I'm into a lowie though, I tend to take the long way in, dawdle past the park and what have you, take a little moment to look at life another way. I often see girls heading doggedly towards the Goodwin, gym bags in hand, already conning themselves they're into some fucking 'regime' by walking briskly and breathing in these deep mad gasps. I look at them and I feel like shouting: 'Too late!'

But they're entitled to go to the gym if they think it's going to make some difference. I like to take a moment or two just to sit in the park and try and picture how bland it'll look in spring and summer, when the trees have leaves and life and colour. I love it how it is now, empty in every sense. It's still and stripped and cold, utterly bleak and monochrome. I couldn't love a place more than the bench where I sit under the naked beech tree, my cold and damp and only bench. Where Adie, if I am not very much mistaken, is sitting right now. It's too late to turn back. Any kind of noise or movement will make him look up, and if he looks up he'll see me trying to get away from him. He looks up.

'Yo! Adriano! Aulroon to you!'

'Aulroodidoodi!'

He's the only one who's been in any hurry to adopt my occasional Erkisms, Adie. He's a lad who needs to belong. His voice is flat though, and he's hardly got the word out and he's back into his sledge. I sit next to him.

'What's up, man?'

'Ah, you know . . .'

I leave it a moment.

'Tell us if you want. If not, not.'

He kicks at a twig. 'It's nothing.'

I pat him gently on the arm. 'No worries, mucker.'

I get up. Adie cranes his head after me, anxious. I stop, but remain standing.

'Finding it pretty bloody hard, actually. Torts is an absolute fucking bugger.'

My first instinct is a slight disappointment that it's something academic. I was hoping it was to do with that lovely girl he pulled at the gig – some sexual or emotional disaster that might help close the distance between us. He leans down, picks up the twig and flings it, underarm. He stands up, all meek. This is not the Adie we know and most often detest. He hangs his head.

'I don't think I'm up to it.'

The temptation is to say, 'Don't be mad, don't stress, we've only been here a fucking month,' but I say nothing. The thing is, he's probably right. Like, I've no doubt Adie can swot and memorise and give his all, but he's no brainbox. He smiles. It's a real smile too, this one. It's a happy, feeling-all-right sort of smile and his face doesn't freeze.

'Thanks, mate.'

I give him a confused shrug. A 'what for?' sort of shrug.

'Thanks for listening. Best get myself over there.'

And he's off, sprinting hard across the park. I feel an absolute despicable wretch for ever hating that boy – but then I remember his 'Top Shag' badge and things aren't so gruesome after all.

Week 5: Day 4
Weather: Drizzle
Soundtrack: Boards of Canada – 'Pete Standing Alone'

I don't like cocaine. One reason I don't like it is that it is very expensive. Another is that it makes people who talk shit talk even more shit, even more loudly. The worst thing of all is that it gives me diarrhoea. Still, I think it saved me last night.

Ben, of course, was the source of the gak, but he couldn't just *get* it, could he? Not Benny Bull. There was this Irish guy with 'connections' who he'd met through his 'contacts'. Seeing a reliable and ruthless operator in the slack-jawed Midlander, Mr Big immediately put him to work. Ben is unable to reveal the details, of course, but take it as read that there's some *very* naughty people involved. It's more than his life's worth to say anything more. Just sit back and enjoy that rare and wondrous thing – free drugs.

We did just that. We were a strange fit, the four of us, perched on the bed and squatted on the floor of Ben's room. Apart from Benny Bull himself, there was Simon, me and the rather frightening presence of Adrian Dangerous. Adrian, at least, does not tell lies. He's admitted right from the start that he's never taken 'shit' and that, indeed, shit scares the shit out of him. But he's always wanted to do cocaine. The prospect of this ordinarily aggressive young man getting supercharged on ching was not one I was relishing. To make matters worse, he's been trifling with his facial hair. In a curious and genuinely disturbing tribute to Si's mad strimmer cartography, Dangerous has let his sidies grow long. His sculptured sideburns now occupy most of his jawline, getting narrower and more pointy the longer they get. There's a slightly perverse mismatch between the safe and sensible hairstyle and the somewhat leftish 'burns. There's only one thing you can say about him. He looks mad.

He swoops for his line and makes a proper fucking pig's ear of it, spluttering the grainy powder all over Ben's desk. I'm not wise in the ways of such things, but I'd have thought that gear laid on by the Man Himself would be slightly less gritty than this bleachy crud. Adie has another go, and this time he's hit the spot. His eyes bulge and shine and he sits back, momentarily silenced.

Ben, endearingly, becomes gregarious and expansive on beak. Loudly so, but it's no bad thing to have someone sit there and just snow you with compliments. I've made the mistake of telling them I'm eighteen in December, and I don't want any fuss at all. Certainly not a party – no way in hell. Ben's having none of it.

'No, man, you lie, you lie! You do not mean that! There

are people in this room who *love* you, man, there are those of us who *revere* you! Ain't that right?'

Mute nodding. Simon leans forward.

'Mind if I . . .?'

Ben passes him the wrap, chunky with bad cocaine, hardly pausing for breath.

'No, no, no! A party shall you have, man! It's one of them – one of *the* great passing-out rituals of adolescence. You must drink and snort and screw and make merry – and I shall be the man to make sure it happens!'

I'm starting to feel a little hemmed in, tiny bit paranoid. Ben rants on. He's holding my hands, now.

'When I had mine, right . . .'

Here we fucking go, I think. A barge laden with crystal meth and champagne glided up the Shropshire Union while the Gallagher brothers and Atomic Kitten danced to Benny Bull's Mobile Disco. But he's stuck. Conflicting fibs seem to have short-circuited his system and he's momentarily lost for words. He flaps his hand in mid-air.

'Anyway, it's not about me, man – this is all about you. My mate, right, he owns Atlantis, yeah? Best fucking club in Wolvo, man! I'll bell him now, sort out the full VIP for all of us. Stay at ours, yeah? I mean, it'll be cosy if you know what I mean, but if you're the kind of guys I think you are and you don't mind roughing it for one night on the baddest council estate in fucking Willenhall –'

'Is that where you're from?' Simon is wide-eyed behind his glasses.

'Yep.' Ben looks down, fiddles with the toggles of his hoody. 'Had it pretty rough, like, but that's the challenge, isn't it? We're born into one skin, born under the same sky. Got to make the best of it, haven't you?'

'Shit! That's *so* cool!'

I want to ask why, but Si is on fire.

'Wow, man! Are you, like, really from a council estate?'

'Yep.'

'Lol! Awesome . . .'

He's shaking his head in dumb wonder. He turns to me.

'What about you, Kit? You must be from somewhere really cool?'

'Me? Fuck no! I come from a very plain little place outside of Warrington. I don't even live *in* Warrington . . .'

'Yeah but, like, that's right by Manchester, isn't it? You can go to all the clubs and that . . .'

'Well . . .'

'See what I mean? You guys have all had such cool upbringings . . .'

'Well, hang on a minute! I mean, I'd love to just sit back and accept your bouquets, but, well . . . it just isn't *true*. I've got a dead nice mum and dad, they still live together, give every indication of being wholly devoted to one another and seeing the whole thing out. I've got a clever big sister who's in Florida being a marine biologist and an adorable little sister who knows more about music than anyone I've met. *She's* cool, little Emma. I've done fuck all, actually! I'm *ordinary*!'

Si stares at me with ill-disguised disappointment. He turns back to Ben.

'Are there, like . . .'

Ben laughs. 'What?'

'I mean . . .' Simon gulps hard. '. . . are there many blacks where you live?'

'Blacks?'

'Black boys. Like, gang members and that . . .'

I can feel a chuckling attack coming when Ben interjects.

'Oh ah, Jammoes? *Loads* of Jammoes round Willenhall and Wolvo.'

'*Wow! Cool!*'

Ben tries to look modest. 'Quite a lot of me best mates have been involved in gangs, like. Know the Burger Bar Boys and that?'

Simon nods, clearly not having the foggiest.

'Yeah, they were all me mates. Lot of them been clipped now. Need to keep me head down a bit. That's why I come here, really. Get out the crossfire.'

'Awesome. I mean – were there many, like, white guys –'

Ben cuts him short, shaking his head devoutly.

'No, mate. I'm a bit like Jimmy? In *8 Mile*? Like, I *know* these guys, seen? I grow up with dem bwoys – and some of they, they badass brothers, you know what I'm saying to you?'

He is now addressing Simon in a queer combination of Black Country with a Yardie twang.

'But I *down* with they. I dah Pussyman.'

He says *Pussyman* with a mad lisp. Simon sits up straight.

'You had a gang name?'

'Oh aye – Pussyman. Speaks for itself. Since the longest time, man, the fanny been all over me. You'll see it for yourself when you all come down, yeah? Your man Benjy is quite the ladies' man.'

He gives himself a self-regarding grin and takes another long draft of ching. Simon does that crazy finger-clicking thing, grinning his daft head off.

'Irie!'

Adie's come back to life.

'This is sounding more and more excellent by the minute! What's the flange like down there, anyway? Do they drop 'em?'

Ben winks at him. 'They will do if you're with me, mate. Know what I'm saying to you?'

'Fuck! Yeeeeessss!' Adie has screwed his fists together like he's just scored the winning try against the All Blacks. Even though he's sitting with his back to the wall, he's stamping his feet excitedly on the floor. 'On the razz in Woolveroon! I cannot bloody wait! When do we go? How are we getting there?'

If I had any say at all in the matter of my birthday non-celebrations, the window of opportunity has absolutely passed. Adie, coked up to the eyeballs, is on fire. His jugular stands out madly as he rants on.

'Had this one last night, yeah?'

He slaps me really hard on the thigh. It hurts.

'Probably kept poor Kit here awake all night, hey?'

I give him the nod he's been banking on. In all truth, I heard them start and fell asleep with my headphones on, wanking.

'Fuck! I tell you! What a *screamer*!' He eyeballs us all, making sure we're all in on it. 'Jesus! Never had one like it! You know when they look like butter wouldn't melt in their mouth but there's just that little something, that little look that lets you know there's kind of more to them than meets the eye?'

Enthusiastic nodding and murmurs of agreement and encouragement from the others. I reach for the charlie.

'Well, this one last night – man, what a moaner. Only went down to the Gale for last orders, just see if there was anything doing. Played the whole thing spot on, actually. Pretty cold, but I just wore this Blue Harbour T-shirt, yeah? I *love* those clothes, boys – real quality, says a lot about the guy that's wearing it.'

I finish up the half-inch I've missed.

'So, I can see her looking at me straight away. I have this little trick that I'm going to share with you guys, OK? All it is, is – you have to pretend you don't know they're looking at you. You hold your pint like this . . .' He crocks his arm at a savagely uncomfortable angle, making his ludicrous biceps bulge. '. . . so all they're seeing is this, right?'

To my amazement, Simon is nodding and smiling. If there is one man in this building less physically imposing than me, it's Simon. He's what you could faithfully describe as a wimp. Dangerous has his full and unflinching attention.

'So she kind of just sidles up to me and that's the moment. It's nothing she's said, nothing she's done other than that coy little half-look from the side. She's saying: "Fuck me!" What's she saying?'

'FUCK ME!'

Jesus! Was that me? It was, too. It's the coke. I don't know what came over me other than that coke-fuelled rush, but I'm laughing and clapping my hands.

'Been there, man! Been there!'

I am confident and complicit and Adie loves me for it. He tells his story, tells all about the girl tearing at his back and screaming the house down, and his entire focus of attention is on me. I don't let him down. For all intents and purposes, I am a young man revelling in the giddy ritual of a common experience, mutually relished. I laugh, and finish off sentences for him and give every impression of being a Dark Horse. I imply and insinuate and give just enough of myself for them to be convinced: Little Kit Hannah is a right one. Keeps it all to himself, but fuck has he had some birds! Simon goes very quiet and is the first to make his excuses and leave.

I feel sick, now. The only good news, blurted out after Si had gone, is that those nice, happy Indie Girls they copped at the weekend robbed their pockets while they were asleep. Nice one – we're all back in the same boat, loveless, listless, girlfriend-less. But I can't help feeling sick about it all. I'm sick at myself for selling my soul so cheaply, sick at the ravenous disparity between what they think and what I am but sick most of all from the mauling kill of the cocaine crash. To add insult to injury I have the wildshites now, too. This is not going to be a good day.

I've been looking forward to lunch with Jinty, but that is not now going to be an option. Oh, Lordy! I dare not fart for fear of following through. I make my way out through the main entrance, passing Ratboy who's lingering by the notice-board. As ever, he looks like death warmed up. I, of all people, should be more tolerant of a lad like this. I've lived through years of 'titch' and 'shrimp' and 'maggot-dick'. Even when schoolmates started liking me, I was still Nipper or Mighty – there was always some reference to my size. I've been on the receiving end, for ever, of appearance-based barbs, so I should not be party to all the cruelty that goes on behind Ratboy's back. The truth is though, I can't stand him. I mean, I'll qualify that. I don't know him so of course I can't revile him. I've never even grunted a hello at him. But I can't find it within myself to feel remotely kindly towards a lad who never combs his hair, deliberately wears clothes that even Help the Aged would reject and whose dental regime seems to involve a file instead of a toothbrush. And he definitely knows he's weird, too – he seems to *want* to exclude himself. He carries his work around in this big, stupid, old-fashioned brief-case, *huge*, it is, like a doctor's medicine bag. He carries that bag so that people will hate him – I know he does. Nobody but nobody in Ranmoor speaks to him. Nobody knows anything about him. You see him every now and then at meal-times, but only if you're really, really late. He always seems to leave it until there's no one else there.

I head off along Fulwood Road, head down, hands thrust deep into my side pockets, only vaguely aware of the trickle of students on either side of the road. A growing sense of numb inevitability is cracked sharply by a vision outside Somerfield's which is, truly, lunatic. It's Satanic Matt from the Ranmoor Christian Alliance, and he is *preaching*. I rack my brains for some clue as to today's special religious signifi-cance, but he beats me to it. He's holding up a dirty big placard with the word SIN on it, and he's babbling on about Hallowe'en.

'All Hallows' Eve, ladies and gentlemen. The night before All Saints' Day. All right? Ladies and gentlemen . . .'

The rock 'n' roll evangelist screws his face into a compound of distilled compassion. He makes a big thing of searching, humbly, for the right way to express himself. He's all self-conscious humility and reasonable pleading.

'. . . let's face it, OK.'

Again, his face agonises at what he's having to say here. I edge nearer. I'm unaccountably excited by the sight of Satanic Matt making a public display of himself. It's too fantastic – he's just standing there, the tit, shouting out loud at passers-by. He's holding up a placard and doggedly telling people things they don't really want to hear. It's madness. It's lunacy. I'm gripped by the same terrible compulsion that sometimes used to make me shout out in class, to amuse my pals. This time, this is for me.

'Christmas lost its true meaning some time ago.'

'When?'

The four people who've stopped to give the nutter the time of day turn to see who's heckling. Matt ignores me and soldiers on.

'But with Hallowe'en, yeah, we still have a chance.'

He pauses, half expecting an interruption. I smile back.

'We still have a chance, right, because nobody really knows much about All Saints' Day anyway. Yeah? So we can't really mess it up too much, can we?'

'Oh yes we can!'

One of the crowd laughs. His wife shushes him. Even from here I can see the flash of anger singe Matt's cheekbones.

'We can import as much of this witchy-poo, trick-or-treat, here's-another-excuse-for-the-merchandisers-to-coin-it nonsense . . .'

The shushing wife nods her head vehemently. She's with him one hundred per cent on that one.

'But every *Scream* mask, right, is masking Our Lord's message on this special –'

'Killjoys!'

I grin gamely, catching Matt's eye. He's had enough.

'Sir?'

There's no doubt about it – his eyes are glinting as he addresses me. He's manic. I point at myself and mouth the word 'Me?'.

He nods. 'Spare us a moment, sir?'

I feel a wee bit exposed now. It was funny when I was at the back of the crowd, but he's gone all serious on me.

'Step up here for a minute? Yeah?'

I have little or no choice. I'm going to have to go up there. Aware that my radiant grin now looks a little wan, I stride up with as much purpose as I can muster. Matt runs his eyes all over my face. He composes himself, closes his eyes for a second. He is summoning God's wrath to chastise me. He places both hands together over the pole of his placard, finger-tips joined in a praying position.

'What does this word say?'

I put my face right up close to his placard and pull what's meant to be a dumb face.

'Sin.'

'Thank you.'

He closes his eyes again, waiting to receive Our Lord's message. The signal is exceptionally good today.

'What is the middle letter of "Sin"?'

I search the sullen sky for answers.

'I.'

'Thank you.'

He relaxes one hand and beckons for me to stand down. I grip the hand hard and shake, staring into his eyes.

'Thanks, man. God. I feel . . . *clean*. Thanks.'

His upper lip is slick with perspiration. His eyes betray real anger, but he manages a smile. He spreads his hands out to the flock.

'So, you see – we managed to turn a sinner . . .' He plays it out, plays his pun for all it's worth. 'Into a winner!'

Three of the congregation start to applaud, but weakly and only for a few seconds. The fourth, the old lady, turns to her husband and whispers loudly: 'It was a fix. It's obvious.'

The old boy jiggles his little finger in his ear and thinks on this. 'Summat to do though, eh?'

I'm a much happier Kit by the time I reach the library.

Jinty has started shrinking me. Seriously. She's about six weeks into a psychology course and she thinks she's fucking Freud. Every nibble of pasta is accompanied by: 'You're not enjoying that, are you? So why plough on with it?'

And everything little thing I say gets: 'What's *wrong* with you?' Or, 'What's the *matter* with you?'

All I did was tell her about Satanic Matt, but she reacted like she'd found me going through her underwear drawer. She talks to me like this all the time, lately.

'What's wrong with you?'

'Nothing!'

'Oh, come off it, Kit. That's hardly normal behaviour, is it?'

'What's normal?'

'Society can't function without commonly acceptable notions of normality.'

'Commonly *accepted*, surely?'

That's about as far as we'll get, usually. She'll get annoyed with me, I'll deliberately say something to irritate her – typically something that demonstrates my unusually keen intellect – and we'll both go off into sulky silences. This time she goes further though. This time she gets up and she's angry. She's properly vexed with me. She stabs her finger in my chest and glowers at me.

'That's just not funny, Kit.'

'Mmmm. It is.'

I nod my head as I say this. I can feel how my face must look – slightly uncomfortable at her refusal to share in the joke, slightly unsure that it was all that amusing after all, but still defiant. Twitchy, but defiant.

'Made *me* laugh.'

She gets up, flushed. She's really cross with me.

'You, young fella me lad, are going to end up with no friends at all. D'you hear me?'

With that she's gone, ludicrously tall and ungainly in her haste. Temper does not become her. But once she's gone, I'm down and out. It's like some murderous virus, the way the blackness takes me over. For a long time, I just can't move. I'm sat there, staring at my plate, experiencing nothing other than a loose and sickly understanding that I am there. People come and go. I think some people say some things to me – probably just questions like: 'Is anyone sitting there?' But I'm lost. I'm way down deep inside myself and I can't come back out.

After a time I lift my head. I'm feeling things, sensing the basic facts, but I'm not thinking, yet. The thing I sense is that I have done bad and am continuing to do bad. By sitting here, immovable, I am keeping myself from fruitful acts. I am doing nothing. I'm aware that at some point I will have to stand up and walk towards the remainder of my life, such as it is. It is out there, and it awaits me. But I cannot stand. I don't even know how safe I am sitting here – but I know I don't want to go out there. My dull mind swoons and thickens, and I sit here and wait.

Outside, it's dark. Something tells me to go and sit in the West End, have a drink or two. A few beers. Hah! I told her about that one, didn't I?

'*You really are a very fucked-up, very nasty little boy.*'

How many people has she dragged into the conspiracy? How many people has she made aware of how nasty I am? I'm not, though. I'm not nasty. I just – I *tire* of people. I'm tired.

Without recalling crossing the road, I find myself by the English building. I loiter outside, listless. My mind's still discon-nected, but I'm getting closer. I'm starting to sense more than one sluggish thing at a time, starting to absorb the facts. Something, something sooner or later, will trip the switch and engage me again. I sit on the cold step. I stare blankly out at a green-black Sheffield sky. In the far distance bangers rap and rockets scream and zip. Already my breath steams the cold night air. Nick Roland steps around me.

'OK there, Kit?'

'Oh. Fine, thanks. Yeah.'

'OK.' The genial tutor doesn't move. 'Sure you're OK there, buddy? Nothing getting you down?'

This does the trick. Whatever makes you fully digest a question, compute it, process it and formulate your answer, I don't know and don't want to know. But Nick's kindly enquiry jolts me back, makes me aware that I'm giving out an impression and it's an impression I prefer to counter. I'm dazed and sullen outside the faculty building and I'm giving one of my tutors cause for concern. The way I feel, this should be the least of my worries. Instead of hanging on by the thread I should just give in, go under. But it's weird – all I want to do is get myself off the hook. I want Nick to know I'm fine and I want him to know it's fine for him to leave me alone.

'I was just, erm – I've got a little touch of the flu, I think. Just felt a bit short of breath. No worries.'

'Absolutely sure?'

'Really.'

He grins that blond smile. Fellas who stay blond into their forties all have that smile. It's the Robert Redford smile. He's a lovely bloke, Nick. If I was a girl, I'd be one of those who waits behind to ask him pointless questions.

'Good-oh. I was going to ask if you fancy a pint, but maybe that's the last thing you want if you're coming down with the dread lurgy . . .'

'Yeah, thanks. I'm just going to pick up some stuff, then I think I'll consign myself to the bunk . . .'

Why am I *talking* like this? So jaunty, so careless. Why not take him up on the offer? What's the worst that can happen?

'You look after yourself then, Kit. Good paper, by the way. Really very good indeed.'

He taps a cigarette from his pack, sparks it and gives me the once-over.

'If you're still feeling bad tomorrow, don't drag yourself in, you know. You're doing well. I'm not going to hit you on attendance if you're not feeling well.'

'Thanks. We'll see.'

I feel like the grown-up out of the two of us. He thumbs-ups me, pulls up the collar on his greatcoat and steps out towards the street with relish. I watch him go. I'm watching a man who loves his life – a man who's made sense of it at least. And I'm watching a man who knows I'm fucked but can't help me unless I reach out to him. There's no way. I'd rather top myself. I will never, ever confide in anyone. I will not tell. Whatever it is, whatever it may be, I can face up to it by myself. Consultation, confession, a problem shared – that's for other people.

Week 6: Day 2
Weather: Uncommonly Mild for Time of Year
Soundtrack: Aphex Twin – 'Windowlicker'

'WASSUP!!'

It must be three whole years since that funny-twice ad was last on the TV, but Adrian Dangerous still finds it hilarious. Moreover, he finds it hilarious to burst into people's rooms while they slumber, bellyflop on top of them and, before they can even think about drawing a breath from the recesses of their winded carcass, stick his drunken head in their face and shriek: 'WASSUP!!'

He's picked on the wrong fella at the wrong time, this time.

'Adrian. Get the fuck off my bed. Get the fuck out of my room. And get the fuck down to Maintenance and get that fucking door fixed before you even *think* about going to bed. Savvy?'

He stands back, stung and unwilling to be censured.

'Ouch! Touchy . . .' He sits on the edge of the bed again. 'Just tell me, though . . .'

He leans close. He absolutely reeks of stale beer. He grins at the recollection he's about to share with me.

'Few of the men went down to Stevenson, yeah? Completely *wrecked* the fucking place! Bangers, rockets, stink bombs, the lot . . .'

'Want to watch yourself, Adie. You'll be getting the call-up. Your country needs reckless diehards like you . . .'

'Just *shut up*, will you! You'll be bloody fucking interested if you'd just fucking shut up for a second!'

I sit up and cup my ears. 'Go on.'

An evil smile spreads across his face. He eyes me intently.

'Met a chap who knows you. Knows you well.'

My heart plummets. I can see the whole picture. Willie Wilson. Drunk with the beer and high-jinks crowd. Meets Dangerous. Pair of them besotted, of course – peas in a pod, the oafish pair of jackanapes. So what happens? What is *bound* to happen when New Mates discover they share Existing Acquaintance? They slag him down, don't they? They rip him to shreds. It was only a matter of time of course, but old Willie Wilson has seized his opportunity – big time, by the sound of it, too.

'Oh aye?'

'Oh yes indeedy, Kittykins! A certain Mr Wilson . . .'

I knew it. Willie fucking Wilson. My spirits could not plunge lower than this.

'. . . and what he had to tell me was *very* interesting!'

I can feel myself burning up. Of course there were the usual jibes at Culcheth, but nobody escapes that. For myself, it was almost always to do with me being so tiny.

'That dick of yours actually *work*, Nipper? D'you need tweezers to have a wank? Can your bird actually feel it when you're inside her?'

But I didn't have a bird, of course. Occasionally, some of the real bastards would take pleasure in grilling me in front of the class.

'Think you'll ever find a hole small enough to accommodate that sorry little cock of yours, Mighty?'

Willie Wilson was never quite bold enough to be one of the tormentors – but he was always there in the background, smiling his malicious smile. I turn and face the wall, ready to take my bullets.

'Oh yes – I think there's one or two of our friends and neighbours who'd be *very* interested by what your Mr Wilson told me!'

'Why do I feel so pitifully underwhelmed by this?'

He moves closer.

'So you don't deny it, then?' His voice is getting closer. 'Is it the case, Mr Hannah, that you do not dispute Mr Wilson's version of events? Is it? Is it not the case that, far from disputing these allegations, you actually *revel* in them?'

I give the weariest, the most bored sigh I can manage.

'Wilson's a bore and a virgin, Adie. Virgins always have a goodly supply of speculative gossip to distract attention from their own miserable plight.'

'Eloquently put, Mr Hannah, and almost certainly reliable. Also, on this occasion, entirely irrelevant to the matter in hand . . .'

I turn and face him. He's puffing his chest out, thumbing his ribcage like a Dickensian barrister.

'You are familiar, are you not, with the Portobello Street area of the city?'

My relief is immense. I could leap up and hug Adie. Again, and with accuracy now, I can see what this is all about. I see it all in a second, before he needs to say another thing. The evening I nearly blacked out. Hallowe'en. Just after I'd seen Professor Roland. He tugged up the collars on his overcoat and walked off into the night, and he looked content. He looked complete, walking off like that with someplace to go. And that's what I wanted, too. I wanted a place to go. So I did, I walked – vaguely, at first, no real sense of where I would go – I just wanted to walk.

Then a notion suggested itself. I shuffled up to West Bank and stood huddled by the flyover, uncertain which way to turn, waiting for the traffic to clear. My eyes were drawn to an old fella over the road, doubled up and coughing hard. The air was cold and damp, yet sickly exciting with the rip of fireworks and the drift of bonfire smoke. Not so long ago I'd have been gripped by that smell – the woodsmoke and the lure of a winter's night. Not now. I watched the old man go, and there it was in front of me. Jessop's Hospital. All the leaflets, all the advice told us to steer clear of Down There – the area behind the hospital. Yes, they cried – Sheffield is a Safe City. Yes, the streets in question are fine and lit and you're really not going to suffer any mishap. But try and avoid Down There, if at all possible – and if you *have* to go after dark, make sure you don't venture down those mean streets alone.

So that's where I went. That's where I go. I walk past, whenever I can. I act like I'm passing through, but I'm drawn there, like a fascination. I know why the Union urges avoidance. There's another world down there, a world that's cold and hungry, a world that comes out after dark. Girls huddle in ones and twos, some smoking, some talking, all bored and dull and slack with resignation. There aren't many attractive ones. Some of them look very young. Now and then they shout out when you walk past.

'Just looking, gorgeous?'

'You can have it for nowt!'

'Inee tiny, him! Aaaaah, come 'ere, darlin!'

The first night, the night I was confused, I just walked and walked, away from their braying laughter. The image stayed in my head, though. That one girl, the one in boots. She was beautiful. I got to the junction and stopped to look back at her. They thought I'd gone, but I watched them for ages. After a time, there was shouting back there, and a clatter of feet running towards me. Willie Wilson was in the gang, laughing madly as two black lads chased them. He was deranged, Willie, laughing and coughing as he ran. He was really enjoying the chase. They all stopped at the corner of Rockingham Street, breathless, eyes shining, bent double with hands on knees. The tallest of them, an ugly big lad with terrible, *terrible* acne shouted back, loud and aggressive: 'Come on! Who fucking wants it! Slags!'

Another one ran back up Portobello and hurled a bottle. I heard it smash on the road.

'Scum!'

I didn't think they'd seen me. I turned and slid away.

When I got back to my room Jinty had left me a note.

Kit Darling – so sorry if I hurt you before. I came back but you were just sitting there and I didn't know what to say. Two things: I'm about to come on. No excuse, but you know what we're like when we're raggy! But in spite of that, honey, I AM worried about you. I'm your friend and I want to be there for you. I was going to take you to the Inn for a good old natter. Will you knock for me when you get in? Big Love, Big Bird xxx

I felt OK anyway, and I felt better still when I read that – but I didn't go and knock for her. All I wanted to do was get under my duvet and think about the girl in the boots.

I didn't even get a proper hard-on before I'd dribbled all over my hand. A miserable orgasm born out of shame, but blessed relief nonetheless. I slept without the headphones that night.

I smile knowingly at Adie.

'Look. Yes. I was down there. I mean —'

Adrian Dangerous flings himself on me again, smothering me with my pillow.

'You dog! You dirty fucking dog! Jesus!'

He sits back in admiration. What his face is telling me is that he admires me more than any living thing. To Adrian, I have a depth, a mystique, a dark side so grotesque that he withers in my presence. He shakes his head.

'Jesus, Kit. You really are something else.'

'No, man — it's not like that at all . . .'

And I'm not saying that just to make him think it's *exactly* like that this time, though I can't deny I'm relishing the sensation of being thought a rogue. I can see how they all get off on it so much. It's thoughtless and it's boorish but there's something great about being one of the boys. If only. He looks deep into my eyes as he shakes my hand.

'Get the door sorted right away. In awe of you, mate.'

He backs away, stands to attention, salutes and departs. My sleep is troubled by dreams of the awestruck Adrian Dangerous in thigh boots, diligently wanking me off with tweezers.

Week 6: Day 3
Weather: The Sky Was Green All Day, Never Quite
  Sure Whether It Was Dawn Or Dusk
Soundtrack: Plaid – 'Myopia'

We found the mushberters, me and Si. That wild fireball sun was just starting to burn itself out and me and him were just starting to hate each other's guts when I spotted one. And, once I was sure that this particular little pixie's hat was the real deal, I spotted hundreds of them. Thousands. I didn't shout to him straight away. I picked ten, twenty, thirty, forty, put them in my Somerfield bag and strolled over to him, smiling.

'Found any?'

He was morose, almost funereal.

'Nah.'

He kept his head down, piggy wee eyes searching the ground for any sign. I stood back and watched him, waiting for him to get angry with me. He didn't seem to notice that I'd given up the hunt, so I tapped him on the shoulder. He ignored me, carried on raking the grass systematically, grazing the dewy surface of the vast lawn with the tips of his fingers in the fading hope of turning up one, just one psycho-fungus. I prodded him again and wafted the bag in front of him. This time he stood up straight, ready to get mad again. I delved into the bag and produced for him one thin and bedraggled mushroom.

'This one?'

He ran his eye over it and, at the exact moment he was going to dismiss it, he went into this mad comedy lurch, snatched the root from me and held it as close to his sightless eyes as he could get it. He started beaming wildly and weirdly. It was truly a wonderful moment, enchanting yet uniquely sad to see close up the strange pleasures felt by strange boys. And at that precise moment last week that's all he was, Simon – a little boy, thrilled to bits with his find. I threw him the bag and he just lit up.

'There's more?'

I tried to sound blasé as I gestured behind me. 'Oh aye. There's loads of them – just over there.'

'Where!'

There was panic and mania and mad, mad excitement in

that one sharp word he barked at me. I led him over to the crop and the boy was in heaven. He dropped to his knees – seriously, it was as close as you'll get to a religious act – and he was picking, rooting, foraging frantically for the bountiful fungus. He plucked and grabbed and stuffed them in the bag as fast as he could go, like the mirage was suddenly going to disappear and he'd be left with nothing.

'Come on!' he grinned at me.

'We've got loads, though. Shouldn't we be heading back?'

'Fuck off! When are we gonna get a chance to come back here again?'

'Tomorrow? Day after?'

'Fuck off! They might not be here tomorrow!'

'We might not be, if we swallow this little lot. There's enough here to take the whole of Ranmoor down . . .'

'Just get picking, will you?'

I stood there, not picking. Simon craned his head round. 'Please?'

I could half understand his excitement as we dried them all out on his floor. There were 457 psilocybins arranged neatly on the middle-page spread of that day's *Guardian*, and I have to admit it, they looked beautiful all laid out like that. We shook hands on the deal. Nobody was even having a nibble until Bonnie Night.

Even now, sat here on the bog examining yesterday's fuel, I can't get a sense of whether last night was a nightmare or a necessary evil. I mean, I know I freaked out on mushies. I know I had a whitey like never before. But there's none of the typical self-downer that so often accompanies mornings-after like this. I feel all right. More than anything, I feel like I learnt something last night and, although I can't for the fuck of it redeem whatever it was I learnt, I have an innate certainty that it was good. Last night something good happened.

We'd agreed that we'd make tea. Out of the handful of hallucinogenic experiences I've had to date, mushroom tea is by far the most intense and long-lasting. I've done microdots, made omelettes and cakes, had a few good trips and a few living nightmares, but each time I've had tea it's been good. Our plan was that we'd all meet in Si's room at five – me, him, Ben, Liaison (as we've taken to calling Adie), Petra and Jinty. We'd all partake of the tea and ramble down to Endcliffe Park for the funfair, the hot dogs and the fireworks.

That was the plan – but Simon and I proceeded to fuck it up gloriously. With my Civil War tutorial over by three and Si having a blank afternoon, we thought we'd get back and get the preparations started. Not that there was a whole lot of preparation necessary – the mushrooms were good and dried and we were just eager to get the fun started. I brought a bumper pot of Maltesers round and we drank hot coffee through the chocolates, enjoying the sickly sensation of the sweet melting malt. As I sat there, I counted out fifty mushrooms and laid them to one side.

'Gonna need more than that, man. Well more.'

'I don't know, you know . . .'

'Yeah. Definitely. Want to make sure we get something off it . . .'

'Ah, we'll well get something off fifty . . .'

'Only just . . .'

'What about people like Adie and Jinty. It'll blow their little minds if they ain't done any before . . .'

'So we're going to sacrifice our own thing so that they can have a good time, yeah?'

I drop the mushrooms in frustration. Simon scoops them up, careful not to miss one.

He leans in close to me.

'I know! How's about thee and me have a little dabble *maintenant*, hey? We can get a little brew on the go, neck a few cups now and by the time the others come we'll be well away!'

Something about me and drugs: I mean, I've got to say I quite like the whole thing of getting out of it, if I'm honest. I'm not one of these habituals. I've never – well, hardly ever – gone out in search, gone out to score, let a whole evening revolve around the acquiring and ingesting of the drug. If it's there, all right – I'm in, more or less. But I can't get *that* excited about it. And I've never been one for getting completely twatted. I'll have a little go, but I'd rather it was other people who everyone was talking about next day.

This new plan of Simon's sounds dangerous. I'm feeling trapped. Once, years ago, at primary school we made a big human train and climbed to the top of the slope at the far end of the school field. I was the smallest, so I went on the end. On the count, we started to run down the slope. The sheer momentum of all those little boys running at once meant we picked up speed too quickly, and everyone had to run faster, just to stay upright and stop the chain from breaking. My little legs were going like demon pistons, driving and driving as fast as they could go. The train dragged me on and I could feel it, and me, lurching out of control. I could see what was going to happen. When we hit the level, the shock absorber of the flat field would act as a natural brake, and that immediate impact would buckle through the train and make it collapse on itself. I could see disaster about to happen. Everyone would go down, everyone would get crushed by the boy behind them. That feeling of terror, of powerlessness, has never quite deserted me, yet all I needed to do was let go. I was the only one in the chain who could have let go. It's like that now. Simon is up and filling the kettle, about to set a chain of events in motion. Unless I suddenly remember I've got a lecture and flee from this room at once, I'm going to find myself setting out on a ride I just can't stop. I won't be able to get off again until the ride comes to a halt.

'You fucking fiend!' I grin at him, convincingly.

He beams back. 'Lol!'

I sit back and wait to take my medicine.

By the time Adie knocks, I'm already half gone and it's one of those that could go either way. Liaison sits down and prescribes my fate instantly.

'D'you buy that one, hey? D'you think black guys make better lovers?'

In other circumstances I might not have answered him, but my sensitised mind is analysing everything from an exterior point of view, keen to let me see myself as others do. I, in turn, am extra keen to give nobody cause for offence. I'm almost meek in my response.

'I dunno, Adie. I mean, I think, in general, it's just not good to generalise.'

Simon's on it in a flash.

'And that's, like, not a generalisation?'

Adie's on one, though.

'I just think they've got a fucking cheek, expecting girls to fall for them without putting *any* fucking effort in! Do you know what I mean?'

'I know exactly what you mean!' the wild-eyed Simon gurns. 'What you're saying is that somebody's beaten you to some girl you've had your eye on and you don't like it one little bit!'

'Guy's fucking in love with himself. Rolls into lectures with these *ludicrous* fucking jeans on. Guy doesn't *walk*, he's a fuck-ing . . . *pimp!*'

'Fascist!'

Simon's winking at me, urging me to join in, but all I can focus on is Adrian's attire. Adrian Dangerous, terrifyingly, is wearing a black polo-neck jumper. I can't take my eyes off it. I am, sincerely, *glued* to Adrian's outrageous black polo. Actually, there's nothing remotely outrageous about the jumper at all — it just looks crazy on a jock like him. I'm going to have to hang on here or I'm in real danger of losing it, badly. I close my eyes. Shortwaves swoon across my eyeline like anaesthetic. Their voices come in and out, detached and disembodied.

'Guy thinks he's a fucking gangster. Christ knows what he thinks he's doing studying the Law!'

'Is there the mildest tad of race prejudice hiding behind your antipathy, Adie?'

'Race prejudice? Me? You cannot be serious! Jesus, mate . . .'

I open my eyes again. Adie is shaking his head solemnly. It seems like his head is shaking in ultra slow motion, giving him a mournful look that's totally out of whack with his smooth and blameless face.

'Ask Sammy Millar-Jaja about that, why don't you?'

'That's a made-up name!'

'Captain of the First Fifteen three years on the trot, mate. Bloody excellent man, Sammy. Superb.'

'You cunt!'

Simon has fallen to his knees. He's breathless with mirth, pointing at Adie and looking round at me for support.

'There is no such person as Samuel Milton-Umbongo, you cunt!'

Adie looks at me to check whether this is serious. I shrug. I have better things to occupy me – such as the large, smiling ladybird perched on Adrian's shoulder, kissing him on the cheek. He turns back to Simon.

'Fuck off and give me some of that mind-bending fucking tea you've been going on about all week, you soppy little tart!'

The ladybird winces at his language, pulls a face at me and strokes Adie's head besottedly. What is left of my self-determination persuades me to give in, lie down and succumb to the squiggles and squirls.

We've been in the park an hour when the fireworks start – in more ways than one. Petra has been monging out badly, but every time Ben offers to walk her back to Ranmoor she cowers away, eyes wild with terror, and starts hugging herself and whimpering. Jinty's not much better, although she, at least, has cause for paranoia. Whereas hallucinogens, bizarrely, make most people hallucinate, they serve only to make the priapic Adrian even more randy. He's been sidling up to Jinty, whispering profanities into her ear and standing back smiling, sincerely expecting her to take him up on his suggestions. She's freaking out, both her and Petra are – Ben and Adie are agents of Beelzebub and they want the pair of them out of sight.

Incandescent flashes and showers of light tear the blue-black sky apart. The air is pungent with the smell of cordite and bonfire smoke and onions frazzling, but it's all happening over there, away from me. I walk towards it, towards the light and the crowds and the crackling buzz of anticipation. I've forgotten about my friends. All that is on my mind is the spectacle over there. I keep on walking towards it all, but I seem to get no nearer. Somehow, what is happening on that side of the park is an illusion, a trick. The further I walk without getting anywhere, the more I begin to panic at this *trompe-l'oeil*, this trap set solely for me, to lure me away.

I turn and scan the crowds madly, desperate to spy someone, any one of my gang. I can see none of them. What I do see scares me to the marrow of my bones. Every single person is turning towards me, facing me, looking at me like they know what's going to happen next. They're doing everything very slowly and deliberately. Even their smiles take for ever to waft across their white and undead faces.

Two black guys walk towards me – except they're not really walking, they're sort of hovering, deep in conversation with one another. Just as they get parallel with me though, they turn and leer right into my face. They stop and tell me with their eyes that there's no place to run, nowhere to hide – I'm done for. I start to breathe quickly and sharply, in-out in-out, think, think, thinking what I can do to get out of this. I'm surprisingly calm. A superconsciousness seems to have over-ridden my subconscious self and it's fundamentally accepted I'm a goner. Anything else, therefore, is a bonus. This I under-stand, without having a notion what the fuck is going on here. I walk to the brook.

On the other side of the brook are the woods, and just through the woods lie Riverdale Flats, student accommo-dation a stone's throw from Sorby and Halifax – friendly terri-tory. Half the residents of Riverdale and Earnshaw and all the other halls must be out here, now, but there's not one face I know. I'm spooked yet serene, ready for whatever fate befalls me.

Suddenly I see Jinty – yet there's no way that it can be her. There is no way that that can be going on. She's just over there, on the other side of the little stream. She's naked and smiling, and fuck does she look good. There's a small encamp-ment there – a fire, shapeless people busying themselves in the background. In the foreground is a small black man with a hugely distended belly. He's dressed in tribal garb. Jinty is kneeling at his feet, licking his cock. She has a look of bliss on her face as she turns to me, beckons me on, then turns back to the chief and licks his thickening shaft again, licks him and sucks his cock with relish. She's running the tip of her tongue under his balls, opening her eyes wide at me, then closing them, in raptures as she sucks and licks him. I try to shout to her, but I can't make a sound. I just stand there and watch. I seem to blink in ultra slow motion and the scene shifts, but I can't work out how or where or why. I look again and Jinty's face has changed. Her eyes are wide with horror now. I squint hard, I try to focus fully and only on the encamp-ment and I can see now that her arms are bound behind her back. Her arms are tied and her legs are splayed and a line of men is waiting for sexual gratification. These men have bones through their noses. To their left, a large pot boils furiously on a roaring campfire.

I run towards her. From behind, two sets of hands grab me and haul me towards the woods. I can hardly think, let alone shout out. This is happening, this is happening now. I am being taken into the woods and I am going to be boiled alive in a pot. My feet are trailing along the ground as my assailants drag me towards the stream. If they get me to the other side, to the woods, then I'm dead. I look across at Jinty and I see from her evil smile that she was in on it from the start. She stands up, and her bonds fall away. She was never tied up in the first place, it was all an act to get me there, and somehow, from somewhere deep within me, I knew that, too. I summon up all the power, all the will I can mine from within me, and I throw everything into tearing myself free.

'Fucking heroic, man!'

We're in Jinty's room. She and I are being, if not force-fed then strongly encouraged to eat the chestnut roast they've purloined from the Riverdale Flats bonfire party. I'm OK, now. I'm fine. I'm even enjoying the story. From what Ben has told us – and he's told us at least three times so far – Adie and Simon were convinced I was about to pass out with fungal poisoning. They both supported me on their shoulders and were trying to rush me to the first-aid tent. Apparently I went crazy, knocked Liaison out with a haymaker then started trying to pull his jumper off him as he lay there, prone. Ben's eyes are on fire. He's loving it.

'It was unreal, man! You're just stood over him, going: "Polo neck! What's with the fucking polo neck"!'

He cracks up laughing again. I bury my head in my hands, loving it too as they tell me what happened next. I can just about remember this bit. What happened next was I turned on Simon and chased him all round the park, threatening to hack his filthy dick off and stuff it in his own mouth. Then I went over to Jinty and tried to persuade her to press charges.

'Oral rape, Jinty! Oral rape!'

I'm wincing, but Jinty throws her head back and laughs that throaty laugh. I offer a nervy chuckle myself. Petra pats me on the thigh, and leaves her hand there.

'There's more, sadly . . .'

Jinty takes over.

'I'm in a bad way myself and you're starting to spook me. Your eyes are just . . . *gone*, baby, you've got these *eyes* and you're as mad as anything, telling me I've got to go to the police, and I'm saying, like, *why*? Nothing's happened? And that's when you *really* lose it. You're saying to me: "You call *that* nothing?"'

She looks at the others and makes a coy face, swooning comically.

'I'm not so sure I'm able to continue from this point. I feel a little faint.'

I look round the room. I still haven't quite landed. Part of me's still out there somewhere, fervently resisting bogeymen. Petra strokes my leg as she speaks, like I'm her husband and I've been missing at sea for days, but heroically I've swam back to shore, too tired to tell of my miraculous escape.

'You know what they say about the best surprises coming in small packages?'

That cracks them up. I beg her not to go on, but she tells me. She tells me how I chased Jinty round and round the bonfire with my penis in my hand, shouting: 'Come on, then! It's *nothing*, is it? What about mine, then? What's wrong with this one, hey?'

I'm cringing. Ben pats me on the shoulder.

'Priceless, Kit man. Fucking heroic.'

So that's it, then. Those of my friends I have not hospitalised, I have exposed to the sight of my diminutive penis. I may as well pack up and leave now. Simon lowers some more nut roast towards my cakehole, opening his mouth reflexively as he goes to spoon-feed me. I nibble a bit, swallow it and hold my head in my hands.

'Was it that bad?' I ask him.

'Folklore, mate – Seriously. Fucking *epic*, man!'

I glance over at Jinty to make sure she's OK with it all. She's looking at me oddly. In my current state, I can't make out what's so different, but there's something. She's just sat there cocking her head, looking at me carefully, taking it all in.

I shift on the bog seat, arse uncomfortably numb. I give it one last squeeze, but there's nothing else to come out. There's no point in analysing it, allocating it, doubting it – I just feel good today. It's the sixth of November, I'm a tiny bit notorious and my ablutions are robust. The chestnut roast has done my excrement no harm at all. Sadly, I can't stare at my shit for ever. I have a lecture to attend.

Week 8: Day 4
Weather: Fucking Freezing
Soundtrack: Brothomstates – 'Qtio'

I've saved this – nay, *savoured* it, by gad – all day. His letters are a rare source of joy and comfort. In Erk, I know of one living miscreant whose life is more wretched than my own. Since his ejection from the student flats – on grounds of consistent bacon theft from the communal refrigerator on his floor – Erk has written regularly. He's moved out to a spirit-sapping room in an old widow's house in a place called Acock's Green. For the most part, his letters describe in detail the dreariness of his bedsit existence, his debilitating bouts of influenza (brought on, in no small part, by his addiction to niggardly hand-rolled cigarettes) and his failure to make one firm friend. He has not even been in a situation where he could meet a woman socially, let alone set in motion a chain of events that might lead to sexual intercourse. He's obsessed with sex, Erk. He gets none. He spends his life on the bus to and from Acock's Green. He makes me feel triumphant. He's truly pleased, I think, at the success I've made of life here in Sheffield. The slightly ambiguous and occasionally exaggerated tales I write of in my own letters to him have perhaps encouraged him to draw that conclusion, but I'm definitely having a better time than he is. It's got to a stage where each fresh instalment of his own weary plight makes me rejoice. I'll admit it. I'm revelling in my best friend's misery.

I had a feeling there'd be a letter this morning. I had to wait about half an hour – OK, three minutes – while this married girl searched and searched, refusing to accept there was nothing there for her. Her name's Marie and she's from Oldham. I had a sort of non-conversation with her once, in the queue for Sunday dinner. I wasn't chatting her up. I don't do that. I was just taken by how unspeakably unhappy she looked and I felt quite good and strong as a result of that and I thought I'd try and cheer her up. Story was that her fella had been up here staying with her since Friday and she'd hoped he'd stay a bit longer but he had to go back first thing to play football. She was missing him badly. He was on his gap year but, with her language course being four years, she'd started straight away – as all good people should. The good news though, the thing that lit her up when she told me about it was that Stuart (bad name, incidentally) would be coming to Sheffield next year. They already had their name down for rooms in the same block. It was Marie's intention to spend her entire time at Ranmoor so that she and Stuart could start saving up. Jesus. Only once she'd accepted that Stu hadn't written to her today could I snatch up the latest instalment of *Acock's Green*. Periodically throughout the morning

I've patted it in my pocket, quite tempted to open it up in lectures and get a little taste. But I've resisted. I've waited until now. I've bodyswerved Alex, made it down West Street without bumping into would-be lunch companions, and settled myself down in the Hallamshire. God but I love this pub! Virtually no students use the place. It's never that busy, just the usual old boys and alkies that gravitate to places like this. Until a few weeks ago I'd never drunk brown ale at all, but that's what I've been supping, in tribute to the great unfortunate one. That's what I'm doing right now. I'm settling down with a bottle of Mann's and living through Erk's hell with him. I take a sip of the sweet beer, sit back and let it roll.

Aulroodidoodi Old Bean – good to hear you sounding more desperate than me. Hookberters, hey? Now there's a thought. Not a very long thought, though. Even they'd knock me back. I'd have to pay double and even then they'd find some way of getting out of the actual rudities.

Needless to say the rudeometer is below zero. I've got no chance. I've well spent my loan, bladdered my overdraft, didn't realise I had to buy books out of this pittance, too. I can't even afford a bottle of brown down at the Guild, let alone any kind of proper night out. I'm up yon shitte creeke without nay paggle. Clearly there is nil chance whatsoever of my seeking employment – which is by way of introducing my latest tribulation.

My latest tribulation is that I have been caught shoplifting and shall appear before Birmingham Central Magistrates' Court on 4 December. This would not be a matter of such supreme humiliation were it not for the fact I've been nicked for snaffling fucking textbooks! The shame. I doubt that the

128

wigberters are going to jail me, but that might be preferable to the living hell I go through daily. Wake. Wank. Wait at bus stop. Watch bus sail past, full. The very act of finally getting out of this killing Birmingham cold and on board a fucking bus is comfortably the highlight of my day, these days.

Whatever there is of my free time I spend shivering in the library, trying to make eye contact with girls. Unanimously, they take me for a potential sex offender and move to a more populous part of the building. Guilty by proxy, I slope out into the rain, which I find suits me well. I walk for hours and hours in the chilling drizzle, making no attempt to keep my head dry. I fantasise about catching pneumonia and having to be rushed home, where Mother begs me to hang on, to fight, not to die. I consider this, recall that it is she who insisted I take the offer to study metallurgy at Aston and die dramatically in front of her very eyes. Many hundreds of female students attend my funeral, walking in sombre procession behind the extensive cortège. They place an enormous wreath on my grave. It says:

WE THOUGHT YOU WERE A WEIRDO –
BUT YOU WEREN'T

I guess that's about the size of it, except to mention in passing that I'm growing a beard. Oh yes indeedy, me old lambserooni! Also, and this is a very sincere and serious enquiry – will you jot down for me the location of a) cashpoint machines, and b) supermarkets within a walk of Sheffield mainline station? Please don't crucify me, please don't mock my moribund life – just tell me what I need to know, yes? Actually, wouldn't mind coming up to Sheffleburgh this weekend. Sounds a thousand times ginsher than fucking Aston – and you're bound to have dough. Piss notice, I know, but you can email me at the ac. address if there's any massive negberter. Whatever, send us the info on Sheffield shops and banks so's I can get on with my project.

May your sons have many sons,

Erk

Accompanying the letter are several pages of bizarre cartoons, captioned with words like 'MISERY' and 'REJEC-TION'. Boy, do I love him! The thought of him coming up, coming here fills me with a mad and giddy thrill. It lasts five seconds, swiftly replaced by a cloying funk, driven by a sordid vision of the reality of Erk in Ranmoor. For starters, my chums will like him more than they like me. He's urbane and funny and dry. Everyone always comments on how fuck-ing *dry* Erk is, whatever the fuck that's meant to mean. It's going to look like I've copied everything from him. They'll all see it in a stroke, see where I get some of my more agree-able idiosyncrasies. Like, he has this lunatic way of talking, everything's hyper and gushing and so, so arch. He'll go: 'Aulroodi', for hello, and he puts mad little things on the ends of words. He's a lot older than me, Erk. No way is he coming to Sheffield. They'll use his visit to find things out about me.

I sup up my brown, slip his letter back into the envelope and hasten out to send him an email.

Week 8: Day 7
Weather: Wild, Wild Wind
Soundtrack: Disadvantage/elephant – 'Sunday Service'

I'm not the only one who finds Sundays the killer. It's become the day that me and Jinty slope off to the Ranmoor Inn, but I feel a bit tight on Si. He really feels it bad on a Sunday. His folks live a half-hour drive away, he's got a car, he's got nothing really keeping him here but I've brainwashed him it's a cop-out if he gives in. He thinks he's wimping out, running home to Mummy for a big mad Sunday roast. Couple of times he's invited the brood along, couple of times I've really felt like saying, yeah, fucking right, that's *just* what I need, but, speaking strictly for myself, I know it's no good. You can't keep running away from it.

And to make the thumping dull crawl of another Sheffield Sunday even more unforgiving, every bastard has flu. That's all I can hear – people trying to hawk up mucus, people almost rabid with coughing spasms – the whole halls is rocking with coughter. I've got a bit of a tickly throat, bit of a runny nose, but I haven't quite gone under, yet. I'm sitting here trying to work out whether *Moby Dick* is one of the wonders of creation or a very long and rather boring book written in oldspeak, when he taps at the door.

'Kit? You in there, man?'

Before he even opens his mouth I know what it's going to be. His mum has some special herbal remedy concocted from the wild and notable berries of Baslow which will cure everyone's coughs and colds. But he'll have to nip over there to collect the hallowed phial and, well, we might as well *all* go and eat some decent tuck while we're there, too. Still, I'm more than happy to be distracted from *Dreary Dick*. I hop to the door. Simon *and* Petra. Well, well!

'Come on in,' I say, wondering how long he'll go round the houses before he gets to the point.

Today though, Si has come up with a winner. Decamped to Adie's sickroom, he tells us about this pub out on the moors, dead old coaching inn it is, and it's miles away from anywhere, remote, meant to be haunted and it does great food. Anyway, he reckons they have big open fires and on

Sunday evenings there's this sort of ramblers-type thing, the Hearthside Club, where people sit around and tell ghost stories. Today, Ranmoor is almost unbearably bleak. The wind is battering the skimpy trees outside, takeaway food cartons chase discarded newspapers in fast and furious tornadoes and outside my window all is grey. The sky is sullen, there is no light, no light at all. A spooky old pub on the moors sounds just perfect. I mean, I'm picturing folk with hair growing out their ears and thick socks protruding over stout walking boots, but I don't know – I just have a hunch it's going to be bang on. Ben thinks it sounds 'wank' and Adie stops coughing for long enough to stick his fingers down his throat – but for once I am madly fucking enthusiastic and I insist that, even if it's just the three of us, we go.

Petra, Jinty, me and Si squeeze into Kurt, his dodgy old Polo. I feel a bit iffy about taking a lift in a car that has a name, particularly a lad's car. For me there's Herbie, the Love Bug, and then there's other cars. I don't really think you need to be giving cars names. I can't be doing with all that, but old Kurt does the trick. It starts, it goes, it gets us there. After heading out towards the Snake Pass we take a right into the middle of nowhere. It's dark and windy, and there are only very occasional beacons of light in the very remote distance. These moors, only twenty minutes outside of the city, are desolate. What on earth must the Romans have been thinking, wanting to march through all this in skirts and armour – let alone wanting to *own* it? Brrrrrrr! We head off down a bumpy, potholed track and after a while you can just about make out the silhouettes of buildings. We pull up outside this pub called Strines and I have to say it looks well spooky and I can't wait to see what it's like inside.

Inside, I am unchuffed to spy the replete rear view of Alex, waiting at the bar. I know immediately and instinctively that it's her – she's wearing a donkey jacket and DMs – and she seems to sense me out, too. She turns, gives the four of us a big smile, then seems to check herself, realising belatedly that she only knows Petra and me. We're in there now and we're staying, so I stride on up to her and give her a big hello. Away from classes she seems a different person. She's less guarded, less crabby; more *friendly*, in a nutshell. Petra goes into that slightly embarrassing hysteria routine that girls sometimes do when they haven't seen each other for a while. She gives her a big hug and greets her loudly.

'*Hiya*, girlfriend! Whatcha doing out here!'

'Every Sunday, babe!'

Petra covers her mouth like she's been told she's won on *Blind Date*.

'No way!'

'Sure . . .'

Alex takes a step to one side, ready to indulge in her favourite pastime: lecturing people.

'You know – y'all got some of the most awesome fucking scenery I seen anywhere in the world round here. I don't get it with you guys. Y'all just sit around drinkin' and bellyachin' when you could be out here!'

Petra's quite happy to take the tongue-lashing. 'That what you like to do, then?'

'Hell, yes! Every Sunday I can, babe! I'm out at first light, walk the hills, walk the moors, drink it all in, you know?'

I have to allow, it sounds fucking perfect.

'And then, to wrap it all up, this is my little treat to myself. You ain't been before?'

We shake our heads.

'Y'all are going to *love* it! It's *amazing*!'

She scans around the room.

'Coupla guys I know from the footpaths . . .'

This is when I twig what the friendly front is all about.

'. . . usually good for a ride back into Sheffield. I don't see them here just yet.'

Out of nothing more than embarrassment, I can only imagine, Simon pipes up: 'Oh, God, don't worry about that! Stick with us lot. If your friends don't show up, we can drop you off.'

She looks at him like she's been to Gratitude School. I mean, she genuinely is pleased and thankful, but she's so *gracious* about it. I just don't know if you can be *that* grateful for a lift home.

After half an hour or so, a cherubic man in a wax jacket approaches our table and asks us who fancies going first. We look at one another, puzzled. Alex steps in.

'Oh – you guys don't know about this? Right, this is how it works, right? Like, one guy from each group gets up and takes the fireside, right, and tells a tale . . .'

I look around. There are only two other tables occupied in this side of the pub, and one of these is manned by a geriatric with a hearing aid. With the best will in the world, I can't see him standing up in front a roomful of strangers to spin tales of the macabre on the High Peak moors.

I am wrong, though. That's just what the old man does. In a slightly crackling, slightly quavering voice – a high-pitched voice, fundamentally – he weaves us the legend of the Barren Beauty. I'm spellbound. The yarn has all the usual elements – the beautiful virgin, the evil and lecherous landlord who owns her tiny cottage, the thunder and lightning of a week-long hurricane, the tall dark stranger – yet it's an unusual tale of the supernatural. This young beauty, Megan, is the pride of all the moorlands, admired though, interestingly, not desired by every man. There's a brave young conscript who turns up at the village inn one night, and who she marries on the eve of the Napoleonic War. Soon afterwards, a terrible thunderstorm descends on the little village, forcing everyone to hide behind battened doors. Nobody could leave their homestead for six wild nights.

At this point the wind is screaming under the pub's big

oak door and down the chimney breast. It's fantastic. It feels so safe, so warm and cosy as he tells us this biblical-sounding fable. Apart from the squall outside, the room is in absolute hush. The storyteller tells of the landlord breaking down Megan's door to bring her supplies. He finds her unconscious and almost on the point of expiry. A short time later, the beauty becomes pregnant. There are apparitions of God and the Devil, both giving conflicting advice. The Devil urges her to keep the child. God tells her she must obliterate the bad seed within her. Tormented, and slowly going mad, she sends word to her young soldier. She hears nothing back. She takes herself up to the crags and throws herself to her death. Some years later, the valiant young hero returns to the village inn, to discover his young wife has perished. He's heartbroken, but before he goes he asks why no other man asked for the hand of such a beauty. He's told that the girl had a freak accident when she was thirteen. A wild horse fell on her, crushing her and making her barren. The legend was that only the Devil could impregnate her. The young soldier looks at the barman with unadulterated evil in his eyes. 'So what became of my child?' he asks.

When the old boy's finished I'm first to my feet, applauding with, I hope, real feeling. He holds his hand up for me to stop. A couple of middle-aged fell-walker types half glare at me.

'The moral of the story, if there is one, is this: things aren't what they seem.'

He picks up his pint off the mantelpiece and takes a swig, letting us know that – now – it's over. I try to make eye contact with the old guy to let him know how much I've enjoyed his story, but he keeps his eyes on the stone-flagged floor as he makes his way back to his table. I'm about to go across and offer him a pint when everyone shifts in their seats and looks up. To my considerable surprise, Alex has got up.

'Erm, hi, everybody. Like, I'm Alex and I guess one or two

of you out there know me by now and you're thinking, like, *at last* – she makes a contribution!'

She pauses for the uncomfortable laughter that ensues. This seems to take away whatever small traces of nerves she had.

'Well, look y'all – I don't *have* a story, yeah? I truly appreciate the way you guys have taken me in these last weeks and I guess I just wanted to reach out to y'all and let you know how much this whole scene means to me, and . . .'

I'd swear she's filling up, here. She's stopped and she's rattled and, fuck – she's chewing her lip! She draws breath and strength. She laughs in a kind of false-modest, Miss World-accepting-her-prize way.

'That story moved me. Sincerely . . .' She looks over to the old man and mouths a 'thank you'. She sighs hard again. 'And, like . . .' She looks at the table as she speaks, now. '. . . well, I guess I wanted to share something with you guys, too.' She looks up. This is it. 'When I was a little girl I was abused, also.'

There are audible sighs of anguish from the small audience. Alex pauses and makes direct eye contact with as many drinkers as possible.

Petra's eyes are moist. She clenches her fist. 'You go, girl!'

The beer has loosened my mind as well as my tongue. I can't stop myself. 'Here we go . . .'

Jinty shushes me. Alex gives me a look, but carries on.

'Except I never really thought of it as abuse.'

I just can't help it. My mind is surging and stinging. Little pinpricks are niggling and digging at me. I can't stop myself. I *have* to say what's on my mind. Hand over my mouth I whisper to Jinty.

'Fashionably abused . . .'

She rounds on me, wide-eyed with rage. 'For fuck's sake, Kit!' she hisses.

I snap back at her: 'How come every girl you meet these days has to have been fucking messed with?'

Alex pauses and waits for my attention. She catches my eye and speaks quite calmly.

'This is, like, really hard for me? I'm sharing some issues here? I'd appreciate a little support?'

And just like the evil soldier in the story, I'm possessed.

'You're making it up!'

She bursts into tears. Simultaneously, Petra and Si shout things at me, meaning I can't hear what they're saying. Jinty storms out, shaking her head, but I really, truly do not care. I'm driven on. I know I'm right.

'Listen to the guy's story, anyway! That's the whole point! She doesn't *get abused*!'

Suddenly the old guy has got to his feet. Again, he's holding up his hand up for quiet.

'Excuse me. The young man is quite correct. Megan of the Moors is of course not a victim of rapine. She is seduced by the Devil in disguise. But please, I urge you. This is not a platform for such things. You must settle your differences around the table, not in public. Thank you.'

The remainder of the paltry crowd applauds. Alex nods to him in deference and sits back down. Petra and Simon both give her a little squeeze as she takes her seat again. Simon then cranes his head away towards the door, ensuring no interface with me, while Petra just sits there and glowers at me. I give Alex a sullen look.

'Sorry.'

'No problem.'

'No – I mean it. I was out of order.'

She observes me closely, but not unkindly.

'You were out of control.'

She's right. I was. And still, still it's there, snagging at me. I can't bat it back down. I can't kill it.

'I just . . .' I look down at the flagstones. What is this? Why do I *have* to make my fucking point? I can't stop. I just can't – I have to say this, let it out. 'It seems to me like an awful lot of girls have been abused. I admit it – I'm cynical. Either it's become like a fashion thing – it adds somehow to a girl's depth of character and experience if she's been through an ordeal like that – or there are suddenly an awful lot of really evil dads and uncles out there.'

'Interesting you assume the perpetrators to be male.'

'Well, aren't they?'

'In my case, no.'

She's solemn and dignified here. I feel bad.

'Look . . .'

'No, Kit. No need. You said what was on your mind.'

'I did. It doesn't mean I can't regret it though, hey? I was wrong. I often am. I'm sorry.'

Her face actually bursts with pleasure. She's smiling, and she looks nice. Only now does it hit me I've hardly seen Alex smile. She's always challenging, spiky, contrary.

'Really – not a problem. I'd far rather people were honest. It's a much better thing than hidden agendas.'

Petra's nodding stridently. 'Absolutely. Subterfuge is the mother of all evil.'

Jinty returns from wherever she stormed off to. I sense that attack might be the best form of defence with her.

'All right, Big Bird. Finished being a drama queen then, have we?'

She gives me a withering look. 'Got them all back on your side, have you?'

'Er – no? Don't think so?'

She's got me feeling really edgy and foolish. I feel dead self-conscious.

'I'm just trying to make amends. I just . . .'

Simon and her look at each other. The exchange confirms to me what I've long suspected – that Jinty talks about me to whoever will offer an opinion back. Simon, the yokel sneak – I might've known *he'd* be up for a bit of gossip. I don't care. Let them talk about me.

'I've apologised. OK?'

Jinty sits down. Her face softens. 'You can't *do* that, Kit! You can't just savage people then say you didn't mean it and expect everything to be all right.' She looks around the table, her eyes beseeching their support. 'I'll say this here and now, Kit. Some of us are a little bit worried about you. I mean it.'

Simon lowers his eyes to the floor. Petra leans over and takes my hand gently.

'It's like you're constantly angry . . .'

'Am not!'

'Or, like, you're playing to the crowd . . .'

'What?'

'Oh, come off it, Kit! Just look at some of the things you've done . . .'

'And you're *such* a cool guy . . .'

I try to make comedy eyes. 'Am . . . bloody . . . *double* am-not!'

They laugh, Simon louder than the rest.

'Look. Leave me alone. I don't know what happened, right. I shouted out. I shouldn't have. I've lost the plot a couple of times, lost it in public. OK. But it really is not, *I* am not worthy of your ongoing analysis.'

Petra looks to Jinty. Shit! *They've* been at it, too. Alex leans over.

'Give the kid a break, yeah? We all say shit we don't mean.'

The ride back is uncomfortable, not just for my making the jam in a sandwich of Alex and Petra.

I can't sleep. My mind is whizzing and popping with ideas and revelations and conspiracies. They've all been talking about me. My friends have sat in huddles and picked me apart. I'm aware that people do that. A good way to feel better about yourself is to find fault in others. But am I so bad that I'm a candidate for that kind of bitchery? Am I an easy, obvious target? I've never thought of myself that way. I'm hurt that they've half been encouraging the more outspoken side of my personality, then, first opportunity they get, they've pilloried me for it. I don't like them talking about me like that. I don't like it.

Not often does it seem to me that I have actively done wrong, but I feel rubbish about tearing into Alex like that. I go over and over it in my mind. It seems unreal, like that was some other person pointing the finger and mouthing that stuff. Most people have a vague belief that some subconscious will controls our inner selves – our *real* selves. I don't discount that, but I have an intrinsic certainty that there's something else besides, something way more potent when it comes to defining the things we choose to do.

I believe there are three factors. There's ourselves, the people we are – the walking, talking, wide-awake folk we present ourselves as, day after day. But while we're battling away trying to be Petra who's funny, Ben who's seen it all, Kit who's full of ennui, there is the subconscious that senses and smells, sends reliable messages to us about when we should be scared, when we should feel sexy and so on. I'll go along with that, too. There are definitely functions and factors I can't explain – instinctive things. But to my way of thinking there's a third animus again, a *super*conscious that overrides everything and that, more than any other impulse, makes us do the things we do. It doesn't necessarily make us choose – it makes us *do*. What is the thing that compels you to make that leap off the top board? What is it that urges you to get up on the dance floor? What makes Kit Hannah shout unkind things in public? It's your superconscious, and mine is particularly well honed. If I could have explained all this to them on the way back, they may not have bid me night-night, then dashed to each other's rooms to talk about me. On the other hand, it would probably have given them even more to talk about. He's mad, Kit. Proper mad. I lie on top of the bed, mind aching, knowing that I won't find rest until the birds start singing.

Week 9: Day 2
Weather: Winter Sunshine
Soundtrack: Rae & Christian – 'Swansong'

I've missed breakfast. Not, regrettably, for the reasons most of the other blessed inmates here miss their breakfasts. Not because I've been staring into the sleepy eyes of the girl I love, the girl I've spent the night loving and with whom I am now sharing intimate and eternal moments, moments of my youth, my life, before reality bites. I haven't missed breakfast because I'm hung-over, even, or because I've plain slept in. It's none of that, sadly. I've just been lying there, looking at the ceiling, wondering when the fuck my life will start. Out there, I hear voices full of cheer – excited voices, voices full of life. Where are they going? Where have they been? Those people are alive – it's all so easy for them. I think of Professor Roland. *He's* alive. I mean, he's old, he's done it, the best is already behind him – but the way he walks, the way he is . . . he just *loves* his life. I hate mine. But I know it isn't going to just change, just like that. I know it's up to me to make things happen. That's the depressing part. I know, I *know* absolutely that it's beyond me to take those steps and start myself up. I can't even get out of bed, so shite will be the hours that lie between now and whenever I place myself back in this cot. I just want to turn over and sleep it all away.

The consolation of missing breakfast is that I can trundle down to Vittles, take my time, let things drift. My tutorial is not until twelve. If I had a bit more vim about me I'd already be down the library, plotting out the things that make the difference between functional, effective academia and real brilliance. That thing is passion – the will for knowledge, the *need* and the curiosity to learn all about the things that intrigue you. I have days and moments when I am gripped with a thrilling awe for the possibilities of this course. Through the privilege of dedicated study, I can learn all about America. I *want* to know, too. There's a module I'm taking entitled 'The Idea of America' and I swear there are times I wake up almost palpitating with enthusiasm for it. There's so much I can discover, and it's well within my capabilities to absorb it all and give back something special. The days I feel fine, that's what I want. I don't want to just go through the motions, tick the boxes, fulfil my requirements. I want to do something great. I have a notion that I'm going to do a major analysis of the American Dream told by way of gangster tales. I know how I'll go about it. It's perfect – 'The Idea of America' through the looking glass of Noodles and Tony Montana – the ones who came and saw and took what everyone else had. I can get impossibly jizzed about this – yet I can also feel numb to it. Today is just another dull day when it seems pointless and unoriginal and hopelessly ill-conceived. I can't find any enthusiasm for it. I might mention it to Nick later on – but I'll probably just bin it.

I try to muster a smile for Mary, who's always pleased to see me.

'Usual is it, my lovely?'

I've got to admit it – however crap I'm feeling, it's great being called 'my lovely', and there's something oddly reassuring about being someone who has a 'usual'. I take a place in the window, flick at the *Guardian* and, with a great, gushing spasm of pleasure, I remember Erk's letter. I try to keep calm as I open it.

Aulroodidoodi, me old pippin – sorry for cock-up on Sheffroon jaunt. As it turned out, my masterplan wouldn't have allowed time for any fripperies, anyway. But thanks for fucking me off. It assists me in the general and weighty business of wallowing in self-pity to know that my one true friend is having such a fine time of it that he couldn't spare an hour for old mucker Erk.

My heart sinks. Fuck. I've upset enough people, lately – not dear Eric, too. This is shit. What could I have done about it? He gave me, like, *minus* notice that he was coming!

Nah, only messing with you. It was one of those spur-of-the-moment things. Would've looked pretty damn stupid if I'd have seen the whole ruse through and come tapping at your old digberters and you were out of town, what?

Relief. Big relief.

Hey, there's a thought. Next time you're legging it, YOU give ERK a bit of notice and I'll come and stay at old Sheffberter and have a stab at being you for a weekend. Ginsh, or what? I couldn't really do a worse job of being you than you manage to make of it yourself, hey?

I'm smiling. I'm fucking well smiling!

Anyway, Lord of Loon, you may well be having a fine and SUCCESSFUL time over there in doughty old Yorkshire (are the people REALLY dour and gruff – and are even the young people quite old?), but I, your good friend the Erk, have been involved in cunning and audacious skullduggery. Oh yes, my friend! I am a kwimi-nal! It woz The Law wot drove me to it, though. They fined me two fucking ton for the bookstore heist – I ask you! How's a poor student meant to pay THAT back? Here's how. I planned this fucka meticulously and I jolly well think I've got away with it. Hallelujah! My money problems could be over! So here, without no further ado – whatever 'ado' may be at the end of the day – is your ten-step guide to viable bank fraud.

My little pewter pot has been sat there, steaming beguilingly – but I'm gripped, here. The tea can wait.

1) Write to your kindly bank manager and tell him your chequebook and Switch card have been zapped. If necessary, follow this up with a confirmation phone call, even a visit, during which you will exude sincerity and a tiny element of embarrassment at allowing such a felony to be perpetrated against you.
2) Wait for your replacement goodies to arrive.
3) After consulting the great big train timetable that gives you ALL the times of trains to and from everywhere, find a service that places you in a new city in roughly ninety minutes to two hours. That's a good time. You will see why.
4) In my particular case, that place was Sheffield. I made sure to purchase a modest repast in the Aston Guild complex, paying with my brand new Switch card. This placed me in Birmingham at 22.07. There are no trains to Sheffield after nine pee-em on a Sunday.
5) At dawn, I hitchhiked my way to your fair city. Hitching is easy-peasy when you live in Brum.
6) At precisely 8.30 a.m., bundled up against the wind – and recognition – with scarf, Oxfam tweed trench coat and new beard, I blocked the cash machine of the Sheffield Pond Street branch of HSBC with chewing gum. Thanks for the detailed location info, incidentally.
7) At 9.01, pointing out to bleary Monday-morning staff

that the cash dispenser was buggered, I withdrew £200
in cash – using my old, reportedly stolen chequebook
and a signature sufficiently different for it not to be my
own, if scrutinised – but close enough to convince the
cashier this morning.

8) At 9.04, I hastened to Drome in Division Street, where
I purchased a very elegant leather overcoat by Massimo
Osti for a reasonable £650. I paid by Switch, using the
old card with the botched-up, quite good signature.

9) Next I sprinted to Tesco Metro where I purchased a small
meal of fillet steak and mustard mash from the very good
Tesco's Finest range. I accepted a sum of fifty of our
English pounds as Cashback.

10) Stopping at Sainsbury In The City for wine and vodka to
accompany my meal, I gathered another fifty pounds in
Cashback and jogged to Sheffield's quaint and rather chilly
train station. Using the cash method of payment, I boarded
the 9.29 to Birmingham. Having shaved and divested myself
of the 50p overcoat, I alighted at Birmingham at 11.02,
stowed my bags in Left Luggage and by 11.07 was conspicu-
ously withdrawing a niggardly £20 from the New Street
cash dispenser – using the new card and mugging up lustily
to the CCTV camera.

Genius, or what? This mind, this beautiful mind of
mine could be put to such better use. Nobody cares,
though. They see Erk and they think Nerd. Let's see
what the bank thinks, eh? Certain as they may be that
the Sheffield Steal was orchestrated by none other
than Grimes, E.P.P., are they REALLY going to try
and stand it up. It sounds preposterous, doesn't it?
What student would go to such lengths as to get up
at 5.30 a.m. for £350 and a big leather overcoat?
How can they prove it?

I shall toast you this evening with flint-dry Sancerre

and frozen Stoli, as I munch on prime beefsteak and think to better days. See you at Chrimbo then, old bean.

Over and out,
Erk

PS – What do I think of Coldplay? I think Chris and Gwynnie will make adorable babies. Here's praying he doesn't write songs about her, or them. Why d'you keep asking, incidentally?

PPS – The leather coat's going for two ton if you're interested.

Erk, the headcase! He's always been like that, plotting the minutiae of these mad little schemes. If I turned on the TV and saw him getting led away by Special Branch, it wouldn't surprise me one little bit. I know him well, well enough to know that nothing is beyond him – yet I know him not at all.

There've been posters and flyers about this World Debt protest all around the Union and the flyover, but I'm a trifle taken aback when Liaison asks if I'm going. If anything, you could see him on a Country Alliance march through town – so long as it didn't last too long, was followed a damn good piss-up and a roll in the hayloft with some busty landed lady. World Debt, though? What's the plight of the planet's millions and minions ever had to do with Adrian Dangerous? I'm so shocked at his approaching me in denim jacket, baggy-ish jeans and, yes I'm sure it's deliberate, *spiky hair* that I just nod agreement.

'So you'll be there?'
'Er . . . yeah, yeah. Sure thing.'
He carries on scrutinising me.

'Everything OK?'

'Sure.'

'You look like a ghost's just walked through you.'

I give him the once-over, once more.

'Adie?'

'Yap?'

'What's erm . . . what's with the clobber and that?'

Adie glances down as though examining himself for the first time ever.

'You like it?'

I clear my throat. 'Well, yeah, it's *new*, I mean . . .'

He beams back. 'Good, good. Didn't want to look too, you know . . .'

I smile encouragingly. He shrugs and grimaces back at me.

'Didn't want to be the only square there, you know?'

I nod. The hair suits him, strangely. It's one of those boy-band, gelled-up, studiously scruffy cuts, but with his clean looks it counterpoints his face well. I can't tell him that, of course.

'You look fine, Ade. They'll never have you sussed as under-cover . . .'

'Ha bloody ha,' he grins, but he looks wounded. I'd swear he has a badge that says Ha-Ha somewhere in his collection.

To my considerable chagrin, the rally is chaired by that motley ponytailed Peter Hook scruff from Vittles – not that you could call it a rally, truly. For me, a rally needs to involve loudhailers, should preferably take place outside and incur an unjustifiable level of heavy-handedness by the local constabulary. Hooky, again favouring the orange fleece, has attracted around sixty hardy souls to the Raynor Lounge in the Union. Petra's there with some woman in a burka. The eyes behind the burka give me a friendly wink, but Petra barely turns round. No doubt Big Bird has decided the time was right to enlighten her about the real Kit. It was just an observation, anyway. There *is* no definition in her legs. We don't all have to fall out over it.

Even though we're all singing from the same hymn sheet, Hooky launches into a diatribe about the evils of globalisation and, in so doing, implies that us miserable capitalist wretches gathered before him are the chief perpetuators of world debt. What somehow makes his tirade not just uninspiring but really quite irritating is that it's delivered in a wheedling Antipodean accent. He's no orator. He just shouts things.

'Kinsil the World Debt *now*!' he orders.

I can feel it coming. I really am having a hard time quelling it. I can hear my voice, hear how funny it'd sound if I just pipe up: 'Is it, like, a Direct Debit?'

The tragedy is, my confidence has gone. Right up until Strines, any time at all really, I would've just come out with it, just to amuse myself. And it would've been no more than this tit deserved, either. With his glaring, beady eyes raining hatred down upon us and his mouldy hair and clothes and his flagrant self-righteousness and his thorough lack of humility or humour, I would love to shoot the bastard down. Who is he to stand there in an orange fleece telling us how things should be? I'll tell him how things should be. In a perfect world there would be no ageing Trots shouting slogans at young people like us. We're not thick. There's just no need to shout at us. I really hate him, and I hate his hairy ears and his orange sweatshirt most of all. He clenches his fist and twists one last drip of bile from his rhetoric.

'No to the G14!'

At the front, a slender wrist is raised in support. It's the girl from Vittles with the ace training shoes, now a fully paid-up conscript – paid with flesh as well as fury, no doubt. Even now, at the height of her involvement and acceptance, she isn't one of them. Try as she might, she can't make a fist.

Nothing in her life to date has given her need for fists, and the closest she comes now is a kind of elegant royal goal celebration. Her allies hug her at the end of the meeting though, and they seem a nice enough bunch. They've got open, generous faces and they want the world to be a better place. I shouldn't be so harsh on them, but the Hookys of this world plain do my head in.

As the meeting starts to break up, Petra and her friend idle over. The woman in the burka gives me a gentle punch.

'What did y'all make of it?'

Alex. She truly is a case. I don't know what compels a big-hearted, big-boned Tennessee girl to go out in fancy dress every day, but I'm glad I don't have to find out. I concentrate on the eyes peering out at me, eager for an answer at least, an argument even better, and I try to remember what she's asked me.

'He's erm . . .' I look into her eyes and elect for the honesty route. 'He gets on my tits, that fella, quite frankly.'

She takes a step back. 'Oh?' The two eyes eye me yet more avidly. 'He does?'

I nod and flash a look up at Hooky, surrounded now by really good-looking girls, all eager for just one deferral, one moment of this passionate revolutionary's time.

'You hide it well. I kinda thought Nick had a soft spot for you.'

It takes an age to sink in.

'Nick?'

I look back at Hooky. Alex's voice exudes an amused, maternal patience.

'The tutorial, duh! I was just wondering what you made of all that . . .'

Next thing Alex, too, is making inverted commas with her fingers.

'*American English* subtext.'

I can feel myself getting cross. I wish I didn't get cross. I try to breathe deep, try not to let myself get so riled. The best I can do is to talk a little more slowly than usual.

'Well, like, no. I don't think there *was* a subtext . . .'

'Uh?'

'I think there was no attempt by Professor Roland to disguise his meaning and, in truth, there *is* no ambiguity. There's no question. American software concerns are at the forefront of an America-led undertaking to convert the world to American. American English is merely the bridging period.'

Her eyes sparkle with rage. Her hand flies up and drags the mask piece down.

'*What?* Are you *serious?*'

'Absolutely.'

'Jesus!'

She comes closer. It seems like she's going to hit me.

'There's just no fuckin' *give* in you, is there, Kit?'

'It's not really about me, it's a case of –'

'Fuck you! I have really *tried* to reach out and be a friend to you, Kit. I really have tried to understand and just . . . *be* there for you!'

'I'm not sick.'

'Know what? Fuck you! Fuck *you!*'

There's a stand-off. Petra just looks bored. I look Alex straight in the eye.

'Look. There isn't even a margin for debate. It is clearly and demonstrably an ongoing campaign by the US to erode the culture and significance of traditional English and replace it with their own cheap, flimsy version. That is not a matter of opinion. It's not *my* opinion. It's a fact. I'll *show* you.'

Her eyes are still firing sparks at me.

'Show me. Asshole.'

'OK. Erm, erm, erm . . . *traveller*. Spell traveller for me.'

She rolls her eyes.

'Please.'

Pause. Sigh. Deep, sulky sigh.

'T-R-A-V-E-L-E-R.'

'See?'

'See what?'

'You stole it! You stole the double el!'

She shrieks with laughter.

'Stole it! Jeez, man, you should be *thanking* us for that! That's just natural fucking wastage!'

'Why, though?'

'Why what?'

'Why waste it anyway? I mean, it's been around for years. Why change it?'

'I dunno. It's confusing. It's excessive. It's just, it's like . . . it's *wasteful*! It's surplus to requirements. We're doing you guys a *favour* getting rid of those damn fussy, damn *stupid* extra letters and stuff!'

'Spell that! Spell favour!'

She makes a face at me.

'Same thing, Kit. This is getting boring. If your so-called American-English conspiracy is a White House-backed cultural strategy then I gotta say, I'm with them. Know what? We're simplifying your stupid stuffy language for you. Like for ever, we're the ones making things better and we're the ones that have to take the flak for that!'

I eye her carefully, playing out the moment.

'Spell Mississippi.'

'Say what?'

'I said, spell Mississippi.'

'M-I-S-S . . .' It dawns on her. 'You really are a sick little fuck. You know that?'

'I don't think I am.'

'Oh, believe me, boy! Y'all are *sooo* fucked up!'

A ponytailed man in an orange sweatshirt approaches.

'Comrades! Thanks for giving of your time and, even more importantly, of your minds.' He holds out a tin. . . . 'If you could also spare of your funds . . .'

Reluctantly, Alex drags her face out of mine.

'Whatever you can spare, comrades.'

Alex goes into her bag, opens her small purse and picks out the only, much-folded note. She gives him the fiver.

'I thank you, sister!'

'No problem.'

We start to shuffle to the door. He's round us and in our faces again.

'There's a Grants Not Fees meeting in the Broomspring Community Centre Thursday evening. Hope to see you guys down there. And in the meantime . . .' He delves into a thread-bare khaki satchel. 'A bit of fairly basic literature for you to take a dekko at.' No one is yanking his hand off to take the pamphlets. He begins to accept he's lost us. 'Go easy, comrades. See you around.'

Am I a bastard to loathe that man? Am I wrong to want him just to fucking well go away and never come back? Doesn't seem so unreasonable, to me.

Week 9: Day 4

Weather: No Two Ways About It – It's Fucking Freezing
Soundtrack: Suicide – 'Diamonds, Fur Coat, Champagne'

Soon as the tutorial was over I legged it. Things are still frosty between Alex and me, and I just didn't want any awkward-ness as we were all packing our things up at the end. Through intermediaries, she has expressed her sadness and puzzlement at my ongoing negative attitude, but it's gone beyond redemption for me. I don't *want* to redeem things. I'm happy being her enemy. I think she's mad. As soon as I got out on to Shearwood Road I legged it. I ran down to the tram stop, hopped on, got off at Commercial Street and cut through the market over the bridge past the old station.

My plan was to spend the afternoon just rambling through the heartland of the old steel industry. They've started tarting up a lot of the old industrial buildings on the edge of the city centre. There's a warren of trendy streets full of industrial chic bars and design companies just off the Wicker, but I want to get way out, way past there. If I follow Mowbray Street and Neepsend Lane out alongside the river I'll hit Kelham Island and Philadelphia and Parkwood and, past there, the huge forbidden cities of the steelworks and forges. It makes me giddy that there's this whole hidden Sheffield that students will never, never know. How many students know there's a quarter called Philadelphia here, for fuck's sake? I shoved my hands down deep into my parka pockets and walked like I knew where I was going.

The wind down there was scintillating. It was vicious, slicing my face like razor wire as I hit the Hillfoot Weir. It was like *Metropolis* down there: to my right, the awesome and enormous Neepsend gasworks. Ahead of me, looming and morose, ranks and ranks and ranks of sullen and powerful foundries. Hardly a vehicle or a voice penetrated the winter silence, the starving bark of a stray dog the only sound.

Dark came early and I had a brief jerk of panic about losing my way. 'Keep the river to your right,' I muttered to myself. Head down and mobile phone clutched tight, I ploughed on into the cutting wind. Where the walk out was stunning for its silence and its isolation, the same streets now were starting to come to life. Just ahead, in the dim-lit area by the Industrial Museum, girls stood off, waiting – just waiting. I was past them before it hit me I knew one of them. The girl from Portobello Street. The girl in the boots.

I wanted to stop and turn back. My animus, my *me* – that's what I wanted to do. That's what came so plainly to me – that I could walk over and do this, now. That no one but no one would know. That I could I let this girl do sex to me. I wanted that, really wanted it. But I kept walking. Some other thing took over, took control, and made me walk away, keep on walking, miss the trick.

I wasn't too bad on the bus back up to Ranmoor, though. I mean, sure, I knew I'd missed out on a big, easy opportunity – a real chance to nail this thing and get on with the real business of just being normal – but I was also more than well aware that she'd be there again. My puss in boots could wait until a better day.

I'd missed supper and there was no sign of the others. I wasn't that arsed. I was happily resigned to staying in, maybe doing a bit of reading, when the tap came at the door. It was Jinty and Petra – in school uniform. My immediate and crippling thought was that they were going to push me down on to the bed and seduce me whether I liked it or not. I affected ease in the form of a Kenneth Williams voice.

'Whale hay-*low*! Pleeeeeaase! *Do* come in!'

'Nah, mate. You come out. We have plans for you. Come on!'

I persisted with Kenneth.

'*Plans* you say? Reeeeally! I wasn't expecting this!'

I ran an eye over them. Petra looked cute. Schoolgirl suits her. She's got really lovely big eyes and a round, pretty face and I've got to say it, her tits looked great in that tight cotton blouse. Still don't fancy her, though. Jinty, on the other hand . . . I mean, fuckinell! She looked horny as fuck! Her legs – which you never ever see because she's forever clad in faded Beth Orton jeans – are just amazing. She has the most unbelievably long, graceful, beautiful legs and she's wearing shiny black stockings with a garter and suspenders, and a microscopic pleated gymslip and fuck me but my cock was vaulting! I still can't believe it was Big Bird. That is the thing I came to understand as I drifted off to sleep in a sinsemilla fug: I have a hard-on for Miss Jones. Badly. I have a thing for her.

Reluctantly accepting that there was not a cat's chance in hell of my donning school uniform nor even the slightest nod to any kind of theme dressing, the girls took an arm each and nibbled my earlobes.

'Now then, Kittykins – you just relax. Tonight is your night. We're gonna spoil you!'

These sentiments, no matter how well meant, had the reverse effect to that intended. Far from relaxing, I panicked wholly at the creeping notion that these two had been plotting. Whichever way you looked at it, the pair of them had had a tête-à-tête and come to the conclusion that I was someone with depth and it was their duty to get to the bottom of me.

'Where are the others and that?'

They adopt businesslike personas, ticking off our missing persons on their fingers.

'Adriano? Lifting heavy weights up and down with similarly squat fellows at the Goodwin Leisure Centre . . .'

'. . . there to make his muscles larger and more robust.'

'Simone de Baslow? Hiding. Obsessively counting every two-pence piece he's hoarded . . .'

'. . . he's saving up for the Christmas *Goodgreef.*'

'Good grief! How long's he been into fucking trance?'

'*Electro*-trance, darling! And ever since I lent him my Joy Kitikonti bootlegs. He's a man possessed . . .'

'Man in search of a fucking identity, if you ask me . . .'

'Leave him alone! He's sweet . . .'

'He's cool, Si . . .'

I make a determined effort not to get into this.

'Benny Bull?'

They exchange wary glances.

'Benicio Del Toro . . .'

'Has gone home . . .'

'Gone back to Wolverhampton . . .'

I hold my hands up, trying to keep a good nature.

'Look. He can bribe as many club promoters as he wants. I am not going to fucking Wolverhampton this weekend. It's not happening. End of story.'

They flash each other covert looks again. Petra raises her eyebrows at Jinty.

'Well – whatever, honey. That's up to you . . .'

'Yeah – it's your birthday. If you don't feel like celebrating . . .'

'With your friends . . .'

'That's entirely up to you. It's your call . . .'

'But *tonight* . . .'

'Yes . . .'

'Tonight . . .'

They shrug.

'We just wanted to take you out. That's all.'

'That's about the size of it, Kit mate. We felt like . . . we just wanted real time with you, you know?'

'Quality time. Time with *you*.'

They stand there in schoolgirls' clothing, making a visible attempt to crank the mood up a notch.

'Yeah, baby! Tonight is all about you . . .'

'We're gonna take you out for something to eat . . .'

'How bourgeois.'

They stop and make big eyes at each other and hold their hands over their mouths.

'See!'

'Sister, I see!'

'He can't even be nice when we're being nice to him!'

'Poor boy!'

'Yes!'

'We must redouble our efforts!'

'Yes!'

'As friends, we must help poor Kit through these dark days and steer him towards the light . . .'

'Oh, fuck off!'

156

I grin as best I can. It's not their fault. I'm chuffed they've gone to the effort – really I am.

'Do I get to choose where we eat?'

We ate at Pizza Volante, during which time we quaffed not one, not two, but three carafes of the pungent house red. Petra became very drunk, very soon into the second. She leant in to me, her big eyes fighting to focus on me as she launched into the remnants of a pre-worked speech. I did my best to do her the honour of taking it all seriously.

'Kit. You're a lovely, lovely boy. Everybody says that.'

'Why, thank you –'

'Shut up!'

I shut up.

'Right? Shut up while I'm talking to you. Shhhh!' Her head sways as she shushes me. 'It's like . . . well . . .'

She looks up at Jinty for encouragement. Big Bird gives her the nod, sits back and takes a good long slug of red.

'Look. You've got to forget her.'

I'm about to say 'who?' when she reaches across and takes my hand.

'I know it hurts, honey. It hurts like fuck. But you've got to put all that behind you, yeah?'

I'm liking the sound of this: Kit Hannah – lovelorn wastrel. Yeah, I could get into that part quite nicely! I lower my head and take a deep breath. Petra gives my hand a squeeze.

'Yeah. Well . . .'

I make a big thing of staring forlornly at the table. Petra drops her head to make my eyeline.

'All you've got to remember is that you're not the only one, Kit . . .'

Jinty leans over now, too. She takes my other hand.

'She's right, Kit. Sorry to just hit you with all this, but . . . we care, yeah? We *give* a fuck!'

I make like I've just snapped out of a reverie, and that reality is worse than the daydream. I stare at them dumbly. Somehow, I make my eyes blink silent tears.

'Oh, baby. You've got to let go, yeah? You've got to let your friends reach out to you . . .'

'You've got to let us *reach* you . . .'

I nod meekly, by now fending off a genuine emotional collapse. This is fantastic! I'm a waif, a stray, a damaged, heart-broken romantic!

'Look, honey – all we're saying is . . . we're here for you.'

'We're here whenever you need us.'

'If you need a shoulder to cry on . . .'

Petra puts her two index fingers to her cheeks, forcing a smile.

'Or a smiling face . . .'

'Whatever, Kit, honey. Don't bottle it up. We've all been there . . .'

Petra gives Jinty a supportive hug and lays her head on her shoulder. I sigh out loud.

'You're right. You're right.' I look up at the pair of them and force a smile. 'It's futile bottling this stuff up . . .'

Two sets of hands scrabble across the table to me again. I carry on with the smiling lark and hold my hands up in surrender.

'OK, OK! You win!' I shoo their hands back across the table, laughing. 'But ladies, seriously . . .'

They give me a reverent silence.

'This *is* a toughie for little me . . .'

Vigorous nodding from them.

'I'm only small.'

They do that face where girls go 'Aaaah! *Sweet!*' I'm on a roll.

'It's . . . like. It's the first time this has happened to me. It could be that I won't just . . . *open up* about it, yeah? I don't know. Maybe not for a long time, anyway.'

More heartfelt nodding, plus the hands. The hands are all over me again, as are the wide, sincere eyes.

'Just . . . well – just bear with me, hey?'

'Course we will . . .'

'And I'll try – I'll *really* try not to be such a moody bastard.'

At Homework, emboldened by my brave new story as much as by the wine and the vodka shots, I get up on the karaoke stand and sing 'Tears of a Clown' and pretend not to see Jinty and Petra nudging each other and biting back tears of their own.

It's been bugging me all evening.

'He is not cool! Si's my mate and all that, but be serious! No way in the world is he *cool*!'

'He *is*, Kit. He's just . . . he's dead laid-back.'

'He's chilled.'

'Oh, fuck that! What the fuck does that mean? It means he talks in a . . .' I put on a really slow, druggy, hippie voice. The renaissance Kit Hannah of Homework karaoke fame is already a dim and distant memory. '. . . dead . . . slow . . . voice. But doesn't really say anything. Cos he hasn't really got anything to say . . .'

Petra takes a long toke on the spliff as we huddle against the cold. Walking back seemed like a great idea half an hour ago. Now, I'm frozen to my bones.

'You're not by any chance a tiny bit jealous of our laid-back friend, Mr Hannah?'

'Jealous! Of *him*? Why would I be?'

Petra shrugs. 'Cos he's cool.'

I stop dead outside Record Collector. 'He. Is. Not. Cool.'

Big Bird takes the joint, sucks, speaks as she blows. 'He's got a certain certain something about him – a certain sort of . . . *vulnerability*?'

'Maybe. But the last thing he is is cool. Right?'

'Why?'

'He can't be.'

'Why not?' She exhales hard. 'Tell you what. Instead of us

telling you why he is, why don't you tell us why Simon's so *not* cool?'

'It's obvious to anyone who knows the difference. He just *isn't*, right!'

'*I* think he is. He's got a great haircut, really cool clothes –'

'What? He wears fucking *Quiksilver* clobber!'

'Looks great on him.'

They walk on, leaving me dumbfounded. Quiksilver doesn't look good on *anyone*. I run to catch up, tug Jinty back.

'Look. Listen.'

I try to catch my breath. They exchange amused glances.

'Simon's from fucking *Baslow*! He *can't* be cool . . .'

Petra is spark out and, now we've stopped giggling, Jinty and I are scouring everywhere for grub. We've only smoked the two badboys, but fuck does that skunk do your head in! Petra's had a minor whitey on it. She cowered down in the corner of the room, staring at the two of us like she didn't know us and we were about to do something bad to her. We managed to calm her and get her to lie down on Jinty's bed and now, seconds later, she's snoring her head off. I never knew girls could snore like that. I'm in bits with her. I can't stop laughing, and that sets Big Bird off, too. She crawls to her cupboard.

'Where are those bickies?'

'Fucking starving!'

'Me too.'

'You got anything?'

'Nah. Thought I had a pack of digestives . . .'

'Ooh! Don't tease me, missus! Digestives, mmmm . . .'

'Could leg it into Broomhill . . .'

'Fuck that. There's got to be something . . .'

Then it hits me. I pull myself up.

'Back in a mo.'

She starts laughing and is still laughing when I return with a bumper box of Maltesers.

'These'll put hairs on your chest.'

I throw myself on the bed next to the comatose Petra and chuck Jinty the goodies. She starts to eat them, one at a time, very deliberately. Her long legs are stretched out on the floor below me, slim and lustrous in her sheer black stockings. She's slumped back against the wall popping Maltesers and her long legs are parted and I can see her white schoolgirl's knickers. She sees me looking up her skirt.

'Makes me horny, grass.'

I gulp. She eyes me.

'Does it make you horny?'

'I can't move.'

She pops another Malteser, eyes on me the whole time.

'You don't have to.'

She moistens a finger and lightly strokes her inner thigh. She closes her eyes.

'God . . .'

I'm poleaxed. I want to get out of there, badly want to run away, but I can't move. And I want to watch, too. I want to watch.

'D'you feel uncomfortable?'

'No.'

'Would you feel awkward if I . . .'

Her eyes are burning into me. I say nothing. She un-buttons her blouse and slips it back over her shoulders. She's so slim. I've never quite appreciated what a fantastic-looking girl she is. She's so extraordinarily *long* that you tend not to view her in those terms. But she is – she's stunning. Her shoulders, her slender arms, her beautiful neck – she's gorgeous. She's sitting down there in her bra and stockings, head leaning back against the wall and what I'm thinking is: 'You, Miss Jones, have a very lovely collarbone.' She puts her hand inside her knickers and closes her eyes.

'What's the horniest thing you two did together?'

Her voice is drowsy and faraway.

'Who?'

I realise my gaff and sit up to make good my slip-up, make something up. But it's OK. I open my mouth to speak and before any lie can tumble out I hear her gentle snoring. Jinty too has taken the knock. She's flat out. I leave the pair of them to sleep it off.

In spite of the sub-tundra chill of my room, I take off all my clothes and stand on the end of the bed so I can see my cock in the mirror. It's heavy and arched. I turn slightly and look at the dip of my hips and the sinewy pout of my buttocks. Jinty doesn't know what she's missing, here. I lick my finger-tip and stroke my dick till it's hard. My breath mists over on the air. I'm starting to shiver. I get into bed and the ice-shrill freeze of the sheets shocks me and thrills me right through. I ply my cock and think of Jinty's long legs and I come in wild spasms all over my frozen belly.

This morning there's a note pushed under my door.

Nightmare! Awoke with an awful compulsion that last night ended badly. Did I behave disgracefully? I hope not. That would be unforgivable at any time, but frightful in light of the headway we made earlier on. Tell me it's all a bad dream, Kit darling.
Love,
Jx

Headway? What does she mean by *headway*? Likelihood is she's saying that me and her and Petra made some big connection last night. That'd be the obvious reading of it. But you could, if you were a real desperado, interpret it that she's thought that me and her were on the verge of getting it on. Crikey! That's one to keep an eye on, but whatever, it won't be a problem. No one needs to know what's happened but me and her. I head down to lectures with a real spring in my step, and only I know why.

Week 9: Day 5
Weather: Still the Brass Monkeys They Sit on
    My Shoulder
Soundtrack: Black Dog – 'Carceres Ex Novum'

The reason I've been so chipper is this: wanking. To be absolutely blunt, the suicidal ecstasy of masturbation has been an area that's started to worry me lately. Me, I've been having to . . . well, the truth is, I have to *try*, I have to really concentrate just to get through a wank, these days. Since I've been at Ranmoor a lot of the joy's gone out of it. I mean, I wank relentlessly. I wank whenever I'm alone, whenever I get just half an opportunity. That impulse mechanism is still there. 'You-are-alone. You-must-pull-down-your-trousers-at-once.' The very *thought* of having a wank is one of the great moments of any given day. Just the thought of it – it gets me all excited, the knowledge that I'm about to yank my jeans down and make stuff up in my head that makes stuff churt out of my knob. More often than not though, just recently, the actual manipulation itself has been a bit of a chore, being honest about it. My knob goes to sleep halfway through. I mean, there's not much I can do about that. I can change images, change the storylines, think some very bad thoughts – but once my superconscious has grown tired of the toss, it's as good as over. An apologetic dribble over my wrist is about as much as I can expect once the inner lights have dimmed.

    To tire of tossing is to tire of life, I tend to think. Yet all too often since I've been here, the sorry truth is I really can't be arsed. How crap is that, when a man's having to admit he can't even find the vim to spank himself off? So this is truly a cause for celebration. I'm back! Oh yes indeedy – last night and today I've been fucking supercharged! I must have had five wanks in less than twenty-four hours. What a stud! And it's all down to Jinty, really – Jinty and the girl in boots. These are the sights that haunt me, even in my sleep. Jinty in stockings. Jinty in boots. The young prostitute dressed as a schoolgirl. I can't get them out of my mind – and I don't want to. No matter how smitten I was with Colette, she never gave me the horn like that. I must've been thinking of her as a Future Wife of Hannah or something. But Big Bird, fuckinell! If only she but knew it, she has become an object of delirious and erotic fantasy for her good friend Mr H.

So up is my outlook as I bounce across the Union forecourt that I almost dive on Petra and hug her to bits.

'Hiya, you!'

'Wow! Someone got out of bed the right side . . .'

I give her a big warm smile.

'Look. Last night. Thanks, you know . . .'

'Nah, shucks. It was nuthin' . . .' She's looking a bit bashful. She addresses the flyer-strewn floor as she speaks. 'Listen. I know you don't want to, but . . .' Now she looks up, those huge brown eyes melting into me for the kill. 'Ben's been on wanting to know what time we'll be down. He's gone to a *lot* of trouble, Kit . . .'

In all honesty, if she'd have asked me to kiss her long and hard, right there, in front of the world, I'd have done it. There's no explaining it and I don't want to explain it. I'm as high as a kite, I'm excited, I'm *excitable*. Of course I'll fucking well go to Ben's. I've persuaded Mum that I don't want any fuss – at least not until I'm back for Christmas, anyway – so why the fuck not? I'm eighteen tomorrow. I'm an adult. I have everything to live for.

'What about your mum and dad, Ben? I mean – where are they going to sleep?'

He turns his back and looks at the wall.

'They ain't here, man.'

Anyone can see that. The little house is a pigsty. Apart from one family photo on top of the TV and a, frankly, very poofy-looking portrait of Ben sat at a piano with big dimples and a genius hairdo, the house seems unloved, abandoned. Apart from the smell of dog's or cat's piss, it doesn't seem lived in. We soon find out why. Ben turns to face us.

'I don't want no one making a big deal out of this, right? I don't want no sympathy. Yeah?'

We all nod, totally fucked as to what's coming next. He lowers his voice, and his eyeline.

'They're gone.'

He turns back to the wall. He walks over to the telly and picks up the family photograph, giving us time to let it sink in. Ben's an orphan. Fuck.

'But . . .'

Jinty steps forward and throws her long arms around him. 'Ben, darling . . .'

Ben looks as crushed as I've ever seen him. With his tubby little pot belly making a perfect ball under his Italia hoody, he looks like a kid. He seems tiny.

'Why didn't you . . .'

Ben just holds his hand up and shakes his head. He takes a deep, deep breath and forces a smile.

'Come on, ah? This is just what I didn't want. We're here to have fun, ah? We're here to celebrate a certain little man's Big Birthday!'

'Less of the little, thank you kindly!'

'That's more like it! Come on, ah?' He turns and faces the lot of us, wet teeth drooling in a set smile. 'Let's get fuckin' wankered!'

As we troop on out of the tatty little council house, I can hear Simon up ahead.

'This is *such* a credible place to grow up! It's *so* cool you live here, man!'

I allow myself one glance back at the well-fed family in the photo and my heart aches for poor Ben. Both those proud parents gone and both his brothers, presumably, left home a long time ago. It explains a lot.

'Will we, like, meet some brothers tonight? Will we meet your homies?'

The club was absolutely fucking superb. It was a carnival. Ben, true to his word, had the six of us ushered right past the door queue. Inside, a volcano was brewing. House music never sounded so good to me. The whole thing, the atmosphere, the people – it was just *happy*. Christmas had started early in Wolvo and it was like every dressed-up kid in town had come out to play. For ages, Simon and I just sat back on a sofa watching Dangerous trying to pull Bunny Girls. Literally, these girls had rabbit-ear headbands, fishnets and little tufty white tails pinned to the back of their black tutus. They were clued-up and sexy, the sort of girls who like shaven-headed doormen and bad lads. Adie didn't have a prayer, but that didn't stop him.

Ben brought a bottle of champagne over and, just for that moment, I was impossibly touched. These five people – they were there for me. For *me*. They like me! Yet, for all my good cheer and all the good vibe of just sitting there with my pals, sipping bubbly, I couldn't hold back the demons for long. I've given up trying to fathom this – it'll happen at the exact moment it shouldn't. My mind just went into reverse. The hissing, the snapping, the wire jam inside my head started up again and all I could do was sit there and ask myself who all these people were and what they wanted from me. I was helpless against it, but I kept on smiling and sipping the champagne.

The nastiness started in the curry house. Simon, who was trolleyed and sloppy by now, far gone and madly in love with the world, was telling Ben all about some snowboarding centre down the road in Tamworth.

'It's *so* fucking cool, man! And it's so *easy*! Anyone can do it . . .'

I cracked a poppadom and scooped up some chutney and tried not to listen. I tuned into Jinty and Petra giving Adie stick over his failure to pull. Nobody noticed me trying to join in the piss-take and all I could think was that Adie wouldn't even *be* here if I hadn't taken pity on the square-faced bore that first night. Who was it that invited him out with us? People forget so easily.

'The rush you get when you're hurling it down the slope at fifty mile an hour . . .'

That's it. I can't hold back.

'You have to wear shit clothes though, don't you?'

'What?'

'It's in the rules, mate. It's a prerequisite of snowboarding that you have to wear really bad clobber.'

Miraculously, Jinty and Petra can hear me all of a sudden.

'Kit!'

'Come on, baby!'

'Hey! It's your birthday.' She checks her watch. 'Yep, siree! It is now officially your birthday!'

'So?'

They're not rising to it. They're determined to steamroller me, flatten any voices of dissent that might put a downer on the evening. I glower at Mister fucking Cool from Cowpat City, but I shut my mouth and try not to bring the evening down.

'Hey, Kit!'

Simon. *Cymon.* I swear, there's something going on behind those eyes. No way is he the chilled, laid-back hipster they've got him down for.

'You're a grown-up now. You're a man.'

He's goading me. I flash him a look and let it pass. His time will come.

Simon's time came exactly three minutes after he fell asleep. I only feel a tiny bit shitty about it – the twat was asking for it. All the way back in the cab it was me, me, me – Kiss FM snowboarder festivals in Austria; word-of-mouth Ladytron gigs in Liverpool; post-Goodgreef comedown barge clubs on the Manchester Ship Canal. He was into fucking Coldplay two months ago! All I could see was his stupid, spiky hair and his lunatic sidies and his slow, slow, voice – so exaggeratedly slow that I could see it as well as fucking hear it. By the time we got back to Ben's I was burning up with hatred.

We sat around in Ben's front room, smoking and making up lists.

'Best five crisp flavours?'

'Sour cream and chive . . .'

'Ain't that just cheese and onion?'

'Smoky bacon . . .'

'Ugh! Repeats like anything!'

'Like anything.'

'Like anything.'

'Yeah yeah, got it in one, thank you muchly.'

'Do Wotsits count?'

'Sure do. A unique and wondrous taste well worth its place on the list.'

'Salt and vinegar. Got to have good old S&V in there, somewhere.'

'Roast chicken . . .'

'How do we actually know it's *roast* chicken?'

'What about worst crisp names, though?'

'*Monster Munch!* A stupendously bad name . . .'

'I was thinking more flavours actually. Cheese 'n' Owen, par example.'

'*Salt 'n' Lineker.*'

'OK – howbout this: sexually attractive animated characters?'

'What? Like Disney characters?'

'Can keep it to Disney if you want – or we can widen it out to include such erotic icons as Betty Boop.'

'Jailbait, man!'

'Penelope Pitstop.'

'The Little Mermaid. Sultry redhead eh? Phwoooarr!'

'Does Marina count? Aqua Marina off *Thunderbirds*?'

'Lady Penelope!'

'What about Parker, then?'

'Pervert!'

'This list is very male hetero . . .'

'Very *white* male hetero . . .'

'Who let Alex in?'

'Seriously. Your tastes are *so* predictable!'

'So bloody *safe*!'

'Erm, excuse me.' Simon. No passion, no expression in his voice – he just *says* it. 'Like, I think you'll find I nominated a mute amphibian?'

There and then, I decided upon his fate.

He was the last to drop, too. So pleased was he with his own contribution to the night that he just went on and on and on. I checked and checked again that he'd finally crashed out, and made my way to the kitchen. There was very little in the way of cutlery and kitchen utensils. What there was, however, was something far, far better. Stifling the fits in my stomach, gripping back the convulsive tittering that was tickling to be let out, I picked up the pinking shears. He wants a mad hairdo, he's fucking well going to get one. I went to bed a happy man.

The arguing wakes me. I'm in the boxroom, alone in the little bed, half dressed. A vacant sleeping-bag lies on the floor beside me. I can hear the drone of snoring from down the stairs. They must all have slept where they fell. The voices are coming from outside. Ben's voice is pleading. I haul myself over to the window to see what's going on. The pavement is directly below me, as are Ben, a big, dirty bloke and his big, dirty dog.

'One night, you said!'

'Michael, I'm not disputing that! But these kids are students, like. They don't get up before midday on a Saturday!'

'Thee dow girrup before *what*?'

Ben's in agony down there. He's looking up and down the street, panic in his voice.

'Look, Michael, shhh, hey? You're gonna wake them!'

'Yow said one night! I need me fuckin' 'ouse back!'

Ben delves into his pocket. He pulls out at least three tenners, maybe more.

'Look, mate. Go and have a drink, yeah? Have a drink on me. Come back at one and the house'll be empty.'

Things are becoming clearer. Michael gives him a sullen and resentful eye.

'It better be!'

'It will be.'

'And it better be fooking *clean*, too! Spick and span, just like you found it!'

'It'll be *gleaming*, mate.'

I smile to myself and lie back down. I'm overwhelmed with love and pity and respect; I really feel for poor Benny Bull. To go to these lengths, to go to all this trouble, just to convince Simon he's some badass ghetto kid with a heart of gold – it's heartbreaking. No way am I blowing him up. I'm not even telling *him* I know. I love the daft twat for this. He makes me feel normal. Downstairs, I can hear him starting to wake up the dead.

'Adie? Simon? Listen, each – we gotta start making a move. Si? Fookinell, man – what the fuck's happened to your *hair*!'

The blowback of demented laughter hits me at the top of the stairs, where I crouch. I smother the smile and pad drowsily down to see what all the noise is about. Simon is sitting there trying to look like he's in on the joke, but the joke is exclusively on him. Exactly half his hair is missing from one side of his head. Odd tufts and clumps spring out, but he's a man with half a head. Worse still, he only has one eyebrow. I pat the disposable Bic in my pocket and resolve to dump it as soon as Simon's own search is over. He's grinning madly and he's sick to the spine.

'Come on then. Who did it?'

'Dunno, mate.'

'I was first to fall asleep.'

'You could've been pretending, though?'

'Yeah. Interesting how it was you who discovered him, Ben. A felon always likes to be there at the scene of the crime . . .'

'Look, no big deal, I'm *laughing*.'

'So am I, matey . . .'

At that point, I can no longer hold it in any more. My sides split and I fall about laughing and everyone joins in, Simon too, laughing and laughing and laughing. Two hours later and ten miles outside of Sheffield, the slightest hiccup or snigger brings on a great gale of guffawing from the four of us. It's true what they say about laughter. It's good for your soul. So is a good job well done with a blunt pair of pinking shears.

Week 9: Day 7
Weather: Pale Winter Sun
Soundtrack: Seefeel – 'Spangle'

I'm pretty downhearted about Adie. His new chin stud, his Hip List and his apparent ease in the face of a sexual calamity are all reasons to resent him – but the things he's told me, the stuff that's really going on with him? Well, it gets you thinking, that's all. The old boy from Strines is only right. Nothing is ever as it seems – that's the one thing I can say with certainty after this fucking fucked-up weekend.

I've got my headphones on and I'm back at Hyde Park Flats. There's something so bleak about the whole layout here – the concrete, the mean uniformity of the rows and blocks – that it fits my Sunday downer perfectly. Yet there's something about that view, too – the scale, the scope, the sheer infinity of possibility when you look right down from way on high – that gives me hope. More than that, it fills me up. It makes me know, somehow, that things are going to be just fine. I lean right out and I can see, in miniature, cars and buses and people busy-busy-busying themselves around the Park Square roundabout. Round and round they go – round and round.

I look at the card again. No cheesy message, no in-joke, nothing whatsoever alluding to a birthday at all, let alone an eighteenth. It's just a moody portrait of thunder cracking over the Florida Keys – pure Madeleine. The message is, too.

Obviously I'm not flying back from paradise just for your rotten birthday (which I know you'll ignore). Here is a great deal of money for you to fritter on obscure and alienating music. I miss you. You're in my thoughts, always.
Happy Birthday, little bruvva.
Maddy x

In my thoughts, always. And you in mine, sister – you in mine. I let the card slip from my fingers and drift and flip on the thermals. I lean out and let the whip of the wind take my breath away, and I spy on all the traffic below. I try to imagine what it'd look like if the vehicles had no structure. All those people set in a sitting position, flying around the roundabout. Madness, but that's the reality – lots of people in a sitting position are whizzing round the highways and byways, supported by structures of steel and aluminium. Only hours ago really, only yesterday, the four of us were inching down that very road – in a sitting position. Me and Adie hopped out of the car, right there.

Adie. What to make of him? He acquired the piercing yesterday, when we got back from Ben's. Big Bird and Petra carried on down to Jinty's parents' in the hire car, leaving us four chaps to dawdle back up north in Kurt. I felt sly on Simon. That whole ride back was a childish riot of giggling and tittering and he was as good as gold about it. Me, I was helpless. I haven't laughed like that in years. Whenever it seemed like my lungs and my guts just could not take any more of that shuddering, aching titillation, I'd look across at Simon's mad, half-shaven head with its clumps and tufts and I was off again – I just could not stop the tears from rolling down my face.

Off the Parkway and we hit gridlock. The city centre was gay with crowds and lights and Christmas clamour. Shoppers were on a mission to shop, traffic was bumper to bumper and Adie was still burning to party.

'C'mon! Ditch the motor, Si! Look at the flange out there! They can't get enough of it, man! They're fucking dying to meet a crew of guys like us!'

Ben raised an eyebrow.

'What? A crew of guys that hasn't had a wash in two days, still fucking trolleyed from last night?'

'Sure!'

'Whatever.'

'Simes?'

Simon was absolutely not up for it. He was on a mission of his own. Ditch the tormentors, then it was straight to Scott's to get his barnet sorted and a dash back to Baslow to face the music with his girlfriend. That's what he always calls her – 'm'girlfriend'.

'She might like bald men,' I quipped.

'Yeah. She might actually let you shag her, you virgin!' shouted Dangerous. Simon pulled a you're-so-funny smirk and edged his car another three feet forward. Adie began finger-drumming on his seat.

'Pack that in, will you?' whined Ben.

'Jesus!'

'What?'

'I thought you guys were meant to be *mad*?'

'Mad?'

'Like, when I think of you guys, I always think: they'll be up for it. Those are three guys who know how to have a good time.'

'Aye, well, some of us need a little breather every now and then – know what I'm saying to you?'

'Yes. I do. Jesus.'

The finger-drumming started again. He managed to stay quiet for less than a minute.

'Tiny bit disappointed, guys. You'd never make the BBC with that kind of attitude.'

'Sorry, Adie mate. You've lost us, there. BBC?'

'The Beer Belly Crew.'

Stunned silence. Ben looked at Simon. I stared doggedly out of the window, giggles rising again. Adie jutted out his jaw, pouring disdain upon his weak and fallible fellow-travellers.

'The BBC. Different-calibre men, I can tell you.'

I've been fortunate not to have had to endure too much pain in my small life, but silent cackling is well up there among the more arduous. I sat back and bit down hard on my lip and took stock of Adrian's dumb, affronted face. For the very first time since the very first time I clapped eyes on that bland face, I felt a real empathy with Adrian Dangerous. More than that – I felt as though I wanted to get to know him.

'Si?'

'Mmmm?'

'OK if we just jump out here?'

'Whatever, man.'

Adie and I piled out. We scampered across the roundabout and over the weir.

'I hope you know where you're fucking going, Hannah?'

'That, sir, I do!'

We were still in the Riverside when darkness fell. Adie, for one so overtly beery, was done for. He was happy-drunk as opposed to the objectionable goon he can become in the company of other gym jockies, and he'd dropped the macho act, too. He slumped back in the deep sofa, letting one idea run into another and another.

'Dunno, mate. Dunno what to do. Parents have as good as told me they'll have zero to do with me if I fuck this up. And guess what, mate? I'm fucking it up. Big time. Fucking nightmare. Haven't told a soul. Shan't tell them, of course. Never hear the end of it. Just have to get my head down and keep at it. Fuck it, hey? It's Christmas!'

'You've only just started though, mate. How d'you know it won't just click?'

He snorts a hollow laugh.

'Knew that after one week, bud. If I'd had any neck at all I'd have just gone straight to the Dean and said: Look – this is all wrong. What I'd really like is to read philosophy.'

Please oh please, do not let the giggles start up again, I pleaded with the innermost controlling me, as images of Polo-Neck Adie grappling with existentialism sprang up in frames all over the walls of the bar.

'Serious? You really want to do that?'

'Sure. Well, yes and no. I mean, that's where my academic interest lies, yeah. But emotionally, what I really *want to do* is write.'

The jaw's out again, anticipating some slight or challenge. None is offered. He lowers his voice, almost apologetic.

'I write poetry.'

I have to allow myself some small congratulation. How I kept it together I really do not know. It's not that there's anything intrinsically funny about Liaison living a double life as a secret, and unlikely, poet – it was just the situation. The gravitas, the surroundings, the drink and, if I'm completely honest, Adie's face all led inexorably towards hilarity. I did – I wanted to laugh in his face. But instead, I put my arm round his shoulder, gave him a very brief squeeze and said: 'Fuck, man – what you going to do?'

He shrugged, eyes glued to the beer mat he was shredding to bits.

'What I've been doing all along, I guess. Drink. Ignore it. Stick my fucking head in the sand and spend money I don't have, pretending that all is well.' He looks up and locks his eyes into me. 'What else *can* I do?'

I'm disappointed that no hookers lurk as we totter out into the early-evening darkness. I'm just as disappointed that I fail to persuade the sodden Adie to rethink the piercing thing when he's sober. He'll hear none of it. He won't even have it somewhere discreet like a tongue or an eyebrow or some-thing – it's going to go precisely one inch under his bottom lip and that's that. I can't reason with him.

The drinking continued. My recollection of events between the hours of six and midnight takes the form of time-lapse photography. I know we were in the Scream singing along to 'Last Christmas' and 'Simply Having a Wonderful Christmas Time' with a big gang of Tapton girls. And we were – we were having a fine time. Those hours, however long they lasted, were perhaps as close as I've come to being a Student (© my mum) in all the weeks I've been here. It was careless. It was fun. I didn't feel ridiculous at all.

I know we were in O'Neill's later on and I *think* we were in the Place – I think that's where Adie got into a scuffle with some lads and I'd *like* to think I was instrumental in breaking the nonsense up. Certainly, I have a recurring image of my slight frame stood between two monsters, shouting: 'Come on, lads – it's Christmas!'

We fared no better in O'Neill's. Adie went round the pub approaching big lads and challenging them to wrestle. *Wrestle*, for fuck's sake! That says everything about Dangerous that's hateful. He's a proper porkhead, really he is. I can't be doing with him when he's all sleeves rolled up and chest puffed out like that. He's belligerent – it's like he *wants* to get duffed up. That didn't quite happen last night, but one kid poured a pint of lager over his head and all his mates stood back waiting for fireworks. I was done with him. No way was I stepping into the breach again. Obviously, I'm no streetfighter myself. I'd do anything to avoid trouble, to the extent that I have next to no experience of fisticuffs, but my distinct impression was they didn't actually want to fight at all. They were standing right into each other, foreheads touching and really giving it the evil eye, but the other lad, the one that poured the pint on him, he just seemed to be laughing. He was wanting one of them to say:

'This is silly.'

Eventually, Adie did, in a way. He goes: 'Either hit me, or fuck off! Don't fanny around throwing beer at people!'

The lad goes: '*You* hit *me*!'

I was bracing myself, guilty by association and ready to get battered by his compadres, when Adie started laughing his head off. He put on a kid's voice and goes: '*You started it!*'

And then all the other lads start laughing and before you know it they're shaking hands and offering to buy each other drinks. Adrian, a man's man, was all for claiming his spoils of war. I had another agenda. I had not eaten since Wolverhampton.

The Manzil is where my recall becomes all too focused again. Adie, by anybody's standards, was out of the game by now. He was all over the fucking place. My sole objective was to get us out of there without any more trouble. If I couldn't do that though, I'd settle for getting Adie to talk a decibel or two quieter.

'I wanna be like you guys, man! I wanna be cool!'

'Adie man, listen! Shut up!'

'No, no – I fucking mean it! You guys are fucking too much! You're the best, man!'

'We're twats.'

'I mean, like, the music and the . . .'

He starts laughing madly. He's cross-eyed – literally cross-eyed with drunken sincerity. He taps his nose ostentatiously.

'I mean, fuck! The guys I know, right, all the guys from *vloorenserne* . . .'

Forced to bet, I'd wager he's saying 'The Law and so on'.

'They'd *love* to score. You know? You know? They'd like *love* to score.'

In his pickled mind there was doubtless some deft segue into his next onslaught – but I'm fucked if I could figure it out. All I know is that he smoothed out a napkin, produced a Biro and stuck that telescopic chin out halfway across the table.

'You know? I mean – the *music* you guys are into! It's *awesome*! I mean – gimme some of that stuff. I've *got* to get some of that stuff!'

Half an hour later, as we stood up to leave with Mandy and Dolita, the two girls who'd been throwing paper darts at us from the next table, I picked up his abandoned napkin. His Hip List read as follows:

Cigar Ross
The Eighties Twins
Bored of Canada

Scrawled along the bottom in parentheses was *Tattoo?* It was unclear whether this referred to the Faux Foo duo from

Moscow, or just a note to himself to add more bodily decor as a matter of priority.

It was also unclear how I was going to get out of this mess with the tipsy dart-thrower. The idea of trying to get down to rudities in the knowledge that King Dong was at work six inches away was of limited appeal. So was my prospective companion. I mean, she was an attractive girl in many ways – and she was bang up for it. But that, for me, was the most unattractive thing about her. I don't know – there's something shattering for me about the way a girl can give the whole thing up with just one glance too far. I can't explain it. There needs to be more mystery. I don't want girls just looking me in the eye and telling me it's all there for the taking. It's just – it's disappointing, is all.

As it transpired, Adrian dragged his quarry off to Ranmoor for a *liaison dangereuse* while Mandy and I walked slowly up the hill towards Tapton. Every step of the way I plotted my way out of the inevitable farce. It was easy in the end. Petra and Jinty saved me.

Mandy nipped off to the kitchen to make coffee. I sat on her bed, arguing with myself.

'Just *do* it!' said the Real Me – the Me that wanted sex.

'Don't be mad – you *know* what'll happen!' said Controlling Me, the Me that made my mind up.

'But it might *not* happen, this time!'

'Don't talk tommyrot – it *always* happens!'

'But this might be The Time! This could be the one where it all comes right . . .'

Controlling Me had to have a good old think about that one. He came back with straight aces.

'Why risk it?'

Why, indeed? I left her a note:

Mandy, as you can see I've got cold feet and hopped it. Please don't feel mad at me or bad at yourself. You're fucking gorgeous. I must be demented to back out like this. Truth is, I'm sitting here in a girl's room and all I can think about is my girlfriend – and who knows, maybe she's cheating on me out there somewhere – but I just can't do it. If you're smarting and you hate me, just try and think what you'd want *your* boyfriend to do, hey? Adrian was so loud, I didn't even get a chance to tell you anything about myself. I'm sorry.

K x

I left it on her duvet and sneaked out and sneaked back to Ranmoor, loathing every cell of my sly and furtive Self. The punishment didn't stop there though. Creeping down the corridor, dreading the groans and sighs of delight that would seep from Adie's room, I had an altogether more stunning blow. That's how it was. I stood there, shocked, uncomprehending. There, ahead of me, letting himself into his room was Dumbledore. Dumbledore is a shaggy, scraggy, wizened hippie from Mansfield. He's a dickhead. No other way of dressing it up – he has a long, thin beard, he walks around Ranmoor in bare feet and he calls himself (and would have you call him) Dumbledore. He's a tit. And he was letting himself into his room with a really cute, *really* cute, giggly girl draped around him and they were going to do it. Dumbledore was about to get sex! This slayed me. The notion that a human being so lacking in verve and allure that he dresses like a pixie and names himself after a fictional wizard was a successful and functional sexual entity just floored me. I only just made it back to my room.

I lay there defeated, beaten by myself, awaiting the onslaught of passion from next door. There was movement and bumping and fumbling, and some of the old dependables from the lexicon of love. There was 'mmmm, yeah!' and 'fuck me!' – and then there was Adie's voice booming through the walls, as strident and loud as ever. What surprised me more than his words was the joviality with which he shouted them.

'Investors are advised that penises can go down as well as up! Sorry!'

Jesus. Can you just *say* that? Can you go through a humiliating sexual malfunction and just laugh it off as One of Those Things?

The sun is white and molten behind the old church below. I watch the cars buzz round the roundabout. I hope that, wherever those people are going, they're glad when they get there. I push myself up off the railings and make my way back down. I decide that, if Jinty and me go to the Ranmoor Inn this evening I'm going to be upfront with her.

Jinty and Petra came in for last orders, and for a split second Jinty's eyes bore into me. I couldn't work out whether she felt let down that I'd brought the lads to our pub, or whether it was something else. I think it was something else. She smiled at me, very fleetingly, and it wasn't a happy smile. Still – better than a punch in the mouth. We were blootered by then. Adie had come a-knocking around six, as apologetic as I've ever seen the great dunce.

'Yesterday. Bad show. *Really* sorry.'

Having dispensed with the gruesome business of remorse, he tried his hand at sensitivity.

'Listen. Old Simes. Saw him slink over the bridge before – looked *bloody* awful!'

'Always does, mate – it's called "a twat of a haircut".'

'Seriously.'

'You sure?'

'Pretty damn sure . . .'

'Come on then . . .'

I know there's still some residual nastiness lurking in me about Simon. I can't help it. I *know* he's a good, good lad and I know we should be friends. I just hate to see him making such a prick of himself. He's become hell-bent on being The

Kid Who Knows, you know, and it's just fucking pathetic. He
wasn't like that before. He was normal – more or less. Still,
it was me who persisted until he caved in and came out with
us. At first he was making like he wasn't in. I even saw the
light go out under his door. Adie was just like, fuck it – let's
go on the batter. That's what he calls it. You don't go for a
drink, you go On The Batter. But once he'd planted the
idea that maybe all was not well in beady Simon's noggin,
I couldn't let it go.

'Simone de Baswell – desist from this folly! Your friends
are thirsty and they require your company!'

No answer.

'Ah, come on, Si! We all get lowies, man! Don't just lie
there, nursing it. Come on out and obliterate the fucker!'

No answer. I put my mouth right up to the gap under his
door.

'Ooooh! I'm sooooo depressssssed!'

That did the trick. The door opened and there he was,
shaven-headed and feigning sleep.

'What time is it?'

'Time you got the ale in, you tight-fisted yokel sheep-
shagging twat!'

He's lovely when he smiles.

So we sat there, the three of us – genuinely no sign of Ben
at all since yesterday – and, I don't know, it was just nice. It
was good. Inevitably, Adriano got the subject round to sex
and, this time, I felt all right about it. I felt like these were
friends – a revelation that took me aback, somewhat. But I
told, anyway. They asked about losing my virginity and I
thought about Maddy's card and I told.

She used to babysit for us. Her and her friends used to sit
in for little Emma and me, but more often than not it was
just her and this one girl, Paula Lane. Paula was one of those
girls that always looked like a woman. From the day Maddy
first brought Paula back to ours, I thought of her as a woman.

She had a broad face, quite hard yet quite pretty, with a wide, flat nose and very green, very slit eyes. She had little dints in her cheekbones, like she'd been screwing her eyes up. She was always looking at me, even when Mum was there, saying 'Isn't he cute' and stuff like that.

Going back, before Emma was born, Mum used to have my hair long and people used to stop us in the street and those who didn't ask 'How old is she?' would comment on how pretty I was. It was nothing to me. I was used to it. But Maddy hated me for it and, even years later when I had my hair short, she'd call me *Kitrina* and be quite mean to me. Her girlfriend Paula took it all to a different level, though.

Maddy was always threatening me, blackmailing me that she'd tell my mates I still wet the bed. I was eleven, nearly twelve. I didn't tell Si and Adie this bit, but what I had to do was just shut up and sit there while they put lipstick on me, put eyeliner on me, messed about with my hair. I'd sit there and let it happen not so much because I was scared of Maddy snitching, but because I didn't mind. I didn't mind Paula's big breasts in my face as she coaxed blusher into my cheekbones with her thumbs. I'd sit there and look down her top and I'd ogle her big tits pushed together as she went to work. That's where the trouble started.

She was straddled across me one night, putting lippy on me and telling me what a pretty boy I was. Maddy was upstairs putting Emma to bed, and Paula just hitched up her skirt and pinned me to the sofa.

'Gotcha now, haven't I?' she laughed. But I don't think she meant anything sexual. She was just telling me I couldn't run away and she could do whatever she wanted to me. It was really uncomfortable. She was quite a big girl, Paula, and even though she was leaning forward with her tits in my face, most of her weight was pushing down on my hips. I was trying not to look down her cleavage, but I couldn't help it. I'd already been wanking a few months by then, and all I ever thought about was Paula's big tits. I'd go into Maddy's bedroom and feel the alien sheen of her purple and crimson and jet-black bras, but nothing could get my cock shuddering like the image of big Paula's deep white cleavage. And that night, she wasn't wearing a bra. I could see everything. I looked down her V-neck top and stared and stared at those smooth, mysterious breasts and I came in my pants. She was too fat to feel my hard-on, but she saw my face and smelt the aftermath. She was straight up the stairs to Maddy.

They came back down with their hands on their hips.

'What are we going to do with him?'

'I really don't know.'

'He's a dirty, dirty, dirty boy!'

Paula turned to Madeleine, eyes gleaming.

'We should wash him! We should cleanse the little wretch . . .'

They brought through a bowl of warm water and I had to lie down and let them take my things off. They held their noses and made noises, but they were excited. It was obvious. They were washing down my cock and balls with a face-cloth and they were saying: 'Naughty, naughty Kit!'

Then Paula started licking me. She was kneeling down and licking my balls and it was just the most fantastic feeling. I was biting my lip, desperate not to make any noise that might make her stop what she was doing to me. My cock got *really* hard. That's the part I remember most – my knob was so hard that it hurt. The rest, I don't know. I try not to think about it too much. Paula took my hand and put it down her top and let me feel her tits as much as I wanted. And she rolled to one side and pulled her knickers down. And I was feeling her there, too. She was really wet, and she was rubbing herself hard against my fingers, grabbing my hand and hissing: 'Dirty boy! Dirty little boy!'

But then they rolled me over. They rolled me over and it

was Maddy – Maddy was on top, looking down at me. I was in her, it felt nice, but she wasn't bucking and panting like fat Paula. She was holding my wrists, holding me down and looking right into my eyes. I turned my head to the side so I didn't have to look at her.

It was only ever mentioned once. In the days that followed I would trail around behind Maddy like a puppy. She was never usually nice anyway, but during those days she was vicious.

'What are you looking like that for!'

'Like what?'

'With those eyes, you pervert!'

I didn't know what a pervert was. I looked it up. It didn't sound like me. The weekend came, Mum and Dad were going out and I was nearly exploding. No matter how horrible Madeleine was, I just adored her. On the Saturday afternoon, I asked her.

'Are we going to do it again?'

She stepped back three whole paces in scorn. Her eyes were glinting with contempt.

'What?'

'Are you and me going to fuck again?'

She leapt forward and cracked me hard on the side of the mouth.

'Shut up! We didn't do that!'

I was more confused than hurt.

'We *did*!'

'We did not!'

She came right up close to me and spoke into my ear.

'How could we? It's not even physically possible with a dick that small!'

That was it. We existed in the same house until she left for Florida, but we hardly spoke. Mum thought nothing of it. It was just the usual adolescent teething pains. Every now and then, especially in the months before she went, I'd see her looking at me sadly. But she's never said anything. I've never thought about it that much, either. I mean, it was nothing, really. That's what I want to tell her. I don't mind.

In the version I tell Adie and Si, Paula is the buxom slut who rapes the adolescent me. Simon is unsure how to react. He sits there, shaking his head and looking at me in a humble, uncomprehending way. Adie, on the other hand, is clenching his fists tight.

'Fuck! Fuck! That is *such* a horny story! I mean – how big were her baps, man? Were they, like, *rilly* huge?'

Dear Adrian. Who ever would have thought I'd befriend a guy like him? As we're leaving, Jinty comes up behind me and pinches my bum.

'I've missed you,' she says.

That night my dreaming is so powerfully erotic that I'm devastated, properly floored, when noise out on the corridor brings it all to an end. In one dream, I walk out of the Riverside Bar and Jinty is leaning against a wall. She's wearing boots and fishnets. She asks me if I need anything and I tell her I'm dirty. She leads me down to the river and washes my cock. She takes ages. Then I'm fucking Paula Lane from behind. Her tits are flying everywhere. They're so heavy that they clash into each other. Maddy comes over smiling, and holds Paula's tits still while I finish her off. Maddy is just about to say something to me when a slamming door and the word 'fuck', shouted twice, drags me from my fantasy. It's Monday. Another week.

Week 10: Day 6
Weather: Like a Summer's Day
Soundtrack: Banco de Gaia – 'Desert Wind'

I've dealt with the birthday thing well, I think. Tonight's the night I was meant to have my 'official' eighteenth, but I've managed to get Mum on my side. For all that she's the one who pushed me into this whole university thing, really, she's also now missing me like fuck. Her letters and phone messages and emails have taken on a slightly desperate tone. It's gone beyond that thing where she just wanted to be involved. She'll take anything, now. She just wants contact with me, her only son. I haven't wanted to think about it too much. I don't want to think about her finally being stuck there with Dad and finding she's bored by him. I know that Emma brings her a lot of joy, but I guess that sons are different. Mothers need their sons. By the same token, though, I've lasted this long and it really has become pathologically important to me to see out this first stint without running back home. People can use all kinds of excuses – get their washing done, sister's birthday, see some band or go to some club – but it all comes down to the same thing. They're homesick. If you deprive yourself of anything, though, you come not to depend upon it. It's a good discipline. Home comforts are just like anything else. Put it to the back of your mind. Be big about it. That's what I've decided I'm doing and, eighteenth or no, I'm not going back to Twiss Green till Christmas.

I made Mum feel proud of me for being so independent. I explained it just like that. I told her I'd rather postpone the party until I get back, like a double celebration sort of thing. She came round to that idea and she quite liked the idea of me hacking out my own life, all by myself, in big, bad Sheffield – but not, it transpired, because that's what was good for me. I was, I'll come clean, mildly shocked but greatly pleased by what came next.

'You know Willie's dropped out, don't you?'

I didn't. I do now.

'*Willie?* Thought he was having the time of his life?'

The way she defends the beer-swilling clod, you'd think he was her own.

'Oh, he *was*! Absolutely *loved* it!'

She now puts on one of those mum voices that mums don't actually use, except in adverts for Vick's Sinex Nasal Spray and so on. I can picture her face, shuddering with righteousness.

'It was the course, darling. Wasn't right for him. They were going over things he'd done at Culcheth two years ago . . .'

Thick, weightlifting twat – I'm delighted. I am overjoyed. Couldn't hack it away from home, hey? Well, *I* can! I fucking well can! That's why, Mum – that's fucking *why*. That's why I hardly phone or email. That's why I've turned away, every time the voices call. That's why I haven't been home. Because I wouldn't come back here, that's why. Still, who'd have thought it? I hadn't ever imagined big, beery Willie Wilson giving in so easily. Despondency, it would seem, can penetrate the thickest skulls and the dullest souls. It stiffens my resolve to dig in, put up and make this new life work. No way, no way in the world am I going back for this stupid party now.

What I hadn't counted on was the big pause, and the words: 'Emma's going to be heartbroken.'

That cut me deep. So it came to pass that they drove over for the day, just the two of them, and I made a big fuss of Emma, showed her all the grown-up studenty places I go to, all the pubs and bars and late-night restaurants. I took them to Vittles for tea and showed them the table where I write my letters. We drove past Bed and Republic for Emma (fave album: Gatecrasher – *Disco-tech*, the one with 'Save the Whales' on it. Little does she know I have the new *Resident Transmission* box set for her, for Christmas) and we strolled around the Orchard Centre for Mum. To cap it all off, we drove out to Strines for an early supper. Emma absolutely fell in love with the place, and made me tell her the story about the Barren Beauty of the Moors. By the time they dropped me off by the Crosspool Tavern it was past eight bells. I told them I was meeting a big gang of mates in there so that a) they didn't have to drive all the way back to Ranmoor, b) they'd have no excuse to linger at said Ranmoor, and c) they'd think I was normal, meeting a crew of pals in the pub for a Saturday night out. I promised Emma she could come and stay the weekend and I'd take her to Gatecrasher for her sixteenth and, waving them off, I felt like I'd really achieved something. I did – I felt grown up.

Everyone was out when I got back to halls. They scrawled a note telling me they'd gone down to The Office party night at the Octagon, but I was bushed. All I wanted to do was nothing. I splayed myself out, quite content, and listened to the first disc of *Selected Ambient Works, Volume II* hearing nuances I'd never heard before. Far from relaxing me, the music troubled and inspired me in equal measure. I was restless. The call of Broomhill entranced me for a second, but I went the other way. The Ranmoor Inn on a Saturday night had a whole different appeal to me.

I saw her straight away, reading her book in the corner. I leant on the bar, supping my pint slowly and watching her. She's quite pretty, Alex – pretty like Dawn French is, or Alison Moyet. She has beautiful, clear skin and a mouth that'd prefer to smile. She mistreats that mouth, making it so angry all the time. I watched her turn the pages, certain she'd look up. The pub was more or less deserted – she'd *feel* she was being watched, sooner or later. But she didn't. She read on and on, only occasionally lifting her glass of Guinness to her lips. She was reading Sarah Orne Jewett's *Country of the Pointed Firs*, which could possibly be my most cherished collection of stories by anyone, anywhere. Nothing happens in these stories. What happens is – people accept their fate. They get on with their lot in life until something happens. I love that. I take a slug and walk over to her.

'Just tell me to get lost if I'm invading your quiet time,' I say.

'Get lost.'

'Not a problem.'

I turn to go back to the bar.

'I'm kidding, right?'

'Sure?'

'Sure.'

She pats the stool next to her and allows her full lips to smile. I nod to the book on the table.

'Beautiful stories.'

'She is just a *god* to me. She redefined gender.'

'I just like the world she offers us, and the characters.'

'Sure. But that's a very simplistic way to read her.'

'I like simple,' I say, and smile at her. She's not sure whether I'm playing with her.

'That's so funny,' she says, in a way that implies that it, and I, are not funny at all. I give my pint an abstract glance.

'Wasn't meant to be. I just mean . . . I don't know. Things don't always have to have subtexts, do they?'

'No. They don't. But so often they *do* have a subtext.'

I don't know which way to steer this. The last thing I want is an intellectual workout. I came to the Ranmoor for peace, for quiet, for recreation. I look her in the eye.

'You know what you told us that night? At Strines?'

She looks me back with equal candour.

'Sure.'

'I, um . . . I'm really sorry.'

'Yep.'

She just says it, as a word. No added meanings, no self-pity – she just says *yep*.

'I mean, in a way, that's what I was getting at. No one gets abused in Sarah Orne Jewett, do they?'

At this, she flings her head back and laughs, raucously.

'Oh my God, Kit! You're precious! You're *priceless!*'

I stand my ground.

'But they *don't*. Old men go out in rowing boats. Four generations of one extended family travel from all around to have a picnic. People suppress their feelings. That's the whole point. They may well want sex, but they don't say so. They certainly don't get it off their daughters, do they? They're frustrated. That's how it is.'

She looks at me very carefully and takes a sip of Guinness. 'I was abused. Bad things happened to me.'

I lower my head. She lifts my chin with her finger.

'And I bet good money you were, too?'

'*Please!*'

'OK, no problem. People deal with this stuff in their own way . . .'

'Jeez, Alex – that's a bit rum! *Deal with this stuff!* That's like gays outing people cos they want everyone to join in the fun. It's not, like . . . it's not a *club*, you know? It's not something to *aspire* to!'

'Which is why those of us who are victims can look out for each other. I know about this stuff, honey. I *know* what to look for . . .' She sighs and ruffles my hair. 'And you *so* are damaged goods, baby.'

Back in my cold room I blink back tears of anger. No matter how many of Alex's voices come roaring or drifting into my head in however many guises, I shut her out. I don't want to hear it. I've been doing so well, lately. I put on my headphones and I shut it all out.

Week 11: Day 5

Weather: A Sting-Wind Like Only Sheffield
   Can Whip Up

Soundtrack: System 7 – 'Miracle'

Unusually, we all sit down to supper together. There is important business to be discussed. Christmas Nonsense is high on the agenda, and folk are taking votes. Jinty's in command.

'Look – can we just nail down the things we actually agree

upon, first? We're not doing the Ranmoor Ball on grounds of cost . . .'

'And penguin suits . . .'

'*Grazie, amore.* Now then – who's for Christmas Dinner?'

'At the Union?'

'Yep. It's five-fifty a head, but we really do need to book. Yeah?'

'That include wine?'

'What do *you* think, Ben?'

He looks up at the ceiling for inspiration as though he's Russell Crowe in *A Beautiful Mind.*

'I think it don't include wine.'

'Spiffing. Will I book for six, then?'

'Is there a veggie option?'

'Yes. *Yes!* Now for fuck's sake – we're going to be here all night at this rate . . .'

'Anyone up for FROUK tonight?'

'Look, you! Stick to the fucking subject! Ant 'n' Dec? Yes or no?'

'Do we get a proper close-up of their heads?'

'Yeah, fuck, just what *is* going down with their heads?'

'It's their foreheads, really. They're getting longer.'

'Ant's is way the longest. There's got to be room for a whole new head between his eyebrows and the start of his hairline.'

'There's enough room on Dec's for skilled and cunning Egyptologists to draw quite detailed instructions of how to get to Atlantis . . .'

Only after Jinty had thrown down her pen three times and handed the job to me twice did we get it all settled. It was Yes to the Ant 'n' Dec/Slade Christmas Party on the Friday and Yes to the Pop Tarts Doctors and Nurses bash on the Saturday. That was going to be the climax for all of us. No lectures, no exams, no nothing. Every single bar in the Union would be selling their stock off. It was going to be a riot – our last night before the big drift home for Christmas.

Simon was gutted we'd passed on the Fuzz Club's big party night. 'I don't care whether you dorks come or not. You'll be missing out on the cream of the Sheffield underground, man. It's going to be awesome!'

'Cream of the Sheffield fucking nu metal copyist scene . . .'

'There's some fantastic bands on . . .'

'What? Wisconsin Death Trip?'

'Wisconsin Death Trip *rock*!'

'Fuck off, Si! What's a Sheffield band doing calling themselves Wisconsin Death Trip, anyway? What's wrong with, like, Walkley Axe Butcher or something?'

'Kit? You're a prick!'

'Why? Cos I don't like metal? Thought the Fuzz Club was meant to be indie?'

'It *is* fucking indie.'

'Whatever.'

'Ah, fuck you, anyway! I'm going . . .'

Adie cleared his throat. 'I'll come.'

Simon looked shocked for a second – his small, gleaming eyeballs always made shock an option – then touched. He couldn't keep the surprise out of his voice. 'Thanks, mate. Cheers.'

Petra flashed a look over at me, gave it a second's thought, then she, too, piped up: 'I'd love to Simon, but it's going to be a question of dough for me. I'm really fucked. It's going to have to be one thing or the other. Maybe I'll bin the Christmas Dinner . . .'

'Ah, no, babe! That's the one thing we're all going to do together! We'll do the second sitting then just stay out all day. By the time Slade come on, we'll be mad for it!'

'Aye, well. Just saying. In the normal scheme of things I'd rather go the Fuzz Club than watch Slade going through the motions . . .'

Jinty stepped in sternly.

'Listen. We've taken a vote. That's that. We've agreed upon

the things we're going to throw ourselves into, yeah? As a gang, as *mates*, yeah? Let's just stick with the plan. Anyone wanting to dip into other stuff, that's up to them.'

Nodding all round. Jinty nudged Simon.

'Wisconsin Death Trip! Thought you were into electro-trance . . .'

Simon shook his head in real despair.

'You guys! You're so . . . *prescriptive!*'

There's only Petra and I didn't laugh at this. I caught her eye and she gave me the saddest smile. Fuck, but life is crap! This is a good girl, a great girl, a clever, witty, cool lady who happens to think something of me. And me? I'm not interested. Why can't I love her back?

A strange and haunting sound wakes me. It is the sound of Coldplay, emanating from Chez Dangerous. Yet it is not Coldplay themselves. It is something far, far worse. It's the brutal tones of Adrian himself, serenading some poor victim.

'*No-body said it was eee-zeh!*'

My God – can one long night get any worse? I gape for the green digital figures, which tell me it's 3.43 a.m. I've only been back in bed half an hour. Only just got back from Petra's. Shit. What a mess. What a lowlife I am.

For once, I'd let myself go, let myself enjoy the frippery of FROUK. It was OK, really. I didn't mind it, once I got up. We were all up dancing to the usual fromage – Abba, Wham, Take That, the Cheeky Girls – and then somehow it was just me and Petra, dancing together. I'm quite often afflicted by amnesia. Or, if it's not your full-blown amnesia then I sometimes remember things patchily, or not at all. But the snogging marathon with Petra I can recall all too fully. It just happened. Maybe the drink wore down our inhibitions, maybe it stoked up the fires. Whatever, we were slumped down on the floor by the servery for what seemed like hours, necking and groping and eating each other's face off. Petra was really going for it, like I'd rubbed the lamp and unleashed some fearsome – and very randy – genie. She was far and away the dominant one, pushing me down and forcing the pace – which was avid. I was aware of people coming and going, tripping over us, apologising and cursing. There were all the predictable shouts of encouragement:

'Go on, my son!'

'Are you getting anywhere?'

'Attaboy!'

I recall Jinty's voice soaring around us.

'You lovebirds coming for a curry? Or are you happy where you are?'

I was feeling Petra's breasts quite aggressively at the time and I'm conscious of feeling gratified that Jinty had seen me in all my masculine pride, as well as thinking: Are you happy now? Is this what you wanted?

It ended up that we were among the last to be kicked out of there, and I made every effort to act the bashful new lover as we dawdled up Glossop Road, arms around each other's shoulders. She was gone, Petra. She'd jumped right in, head first, and she was looking at me with those huge brown eyes and all I could see was adoration. For about a minute I felt wonderful – wonderful that someone could feel this way about me, that I could inspire such big feelings in a girl. I felt glad, too, that I was delivering. I was happy that I was making Petra happy, and I thought that maybe it wouldn't be too bad if I kept it going.

As we got towards Broomhill, reality started to snap. Fifteen minutes away lay Ranmoor and, whichever way it came, disaster. Disaster if I told Petra it was just the drink, it was all a big mistake. Disaster if I tried the line that it might ruin our special friendship if we were to have sex. But the biggest disaster of all would come if we went to bed together. No matter what, I was going to have to make sure that did not happen. But how, without breaking her? How?

Again, I found myself cursing Kit Hannah. Me. *This* was why I couldn't stay and chat with Colette that night. This was why I hid in toilets, and sneaked out of rooms and sloped home early, every time. I run away, because it will always end up like this – me on the verge of a shag and trying everything possible to avert it. We passed the little police shack and, in desperation, I turned to Petra.

'I just want to talk to you.'

She leant her head on my shoulder.

'Good. Me too.'

And with the burden lifted, just like that, it suddenly seemed not impossible that perhaps this time it might be different.

I don't know why I did it. I *do* know – I *understand* – but I still don't know what drove me on. Part of it was the sudden realisation that Petra was inexperienced, probably had not slept with anyone, and was taking it that a guy like me must have had lots of women. I did nothing to dispel that supposition. On the contrary, I started pushing it – giving her the impression that I was accustomed to girls just diving on me and that, by her reticence, she was disappointing me. It was nothing major. We were sitting on her bed sipping tea from *Simpsons* mugs, holding hands, and I was just being a bit of a tit, really. I was being horribly leery, saying stuff like: 'Is that all we're going to do? Hold hands?'

I cringe, just thinking about it, now. My face must've been trying to be seductive. I know I lowered my voice and slid down the wall a bit. Thing is, I *knew* she didn't want to do it and all I was doing was bigging myself up to Jinty. That's what it was – I knew they'd be round each other's rooms first thing, wanting to spill the beans. And Petra would have to tell Jinty: 'Ach, Kit was all over me trying to screw me, but what does he take me for? Some kind of slapper?'

So I wasn't quite prepared for it when she met my leery gaze and said: 'OK. Why don't we just get into bed and see what happens?'

Fuck. *Fuck!*

She gave me a long kiss and looked terrified and said: 'Just nipping down the corridor.'

So I got into bed and, I swear, I was shaking. I was panic-stricken. This time, there was going to be no way out. And even though she was a great girl, Petra, as lovely and warm and humane a girl as you could meet, she'd have to tell someone. She'd have to tell Jinty, everything that went on – good or bad.

Piglet saved me. I could hear Petra padding barefoot back down the corridor, and I braced myself. Maybe I'd be all right. I didn't feel remotely like a kid who was about to do sex, but who could say? Maybe I'd be all right. The door opened, and in came Petra, wearing a Piglet nightie. Had that been Nell McAndrew and had I been supercharged with testosterone, there'd still be no way I could make love to a girl in a Piglet nightie.

She put out the light and got in beside me. She, too, was shaking. The whole thing was taking on the tone of a ritual neither of us wanted to go through with. Sobered by the wind and the walk back, our kissing had none of the hunger of before. Petra clawed at the back of my neck, started trying to go for it again but it was fake, all fake. Still, I kissed her back and tried not to think of Piglet, but as I kissed her I tasted the salt of her tears. That was enough, for me. That was far enough. I got out and sat on the side of the bed and held my head in my hands.

'I can't do this,' I said.

She stayed under the duvet, stroking my back, stifling her sobs.

'I know,' she whispered. I turned to her and kissed her lightly on the head.

'I should go.'

'Yes.'

As I dressed, I could feel her eyes on me. I turned to let myself out. As I closed her door behind me, I could hear

Petra's howl of anguish. All I could think of was how awful it was going to be when we next saw each other.

It seems weird to think how quickly and easily I must have fallen asleep. For me, sleep comes in layers and, most of the times, I'll drift through each level before hitting a sandy bed of deep sleep, deep at the bottom of the ocean. Tonight, though, it was bang! Lights out. Voyage to the bottom of the sea. Music has come into my dreams though, and music has awoken me. I've been asleep for less than an hour, yet it was real, untroubled sleep. Petra will be awake. Over there, now, just across that bridge, poor Petra will be lying in a sleepless hotbed of blame and regret. If I'm certain of anything, it's that Petra won't sleep a wink all night. She'll agonise over everything that's happened tonight and she'll blame herself. I can't let her.

'In my place, in my place, were lines that I couldn't change . . .'

As I lie here, listening to Dangerous slaughtering Coldplay, I'm determined I'm going to take little Petra out – maybe not tomorrow, but soon – and I'm going to tell her how nothing that's happened is down to her. It's me. It is – it's all me.

The singing has stopped. I can hear Adie's blunt and lecherous voice, weaving its spell.

'Fuck! I've fancied you since the moment I first clapped eyes on you!'

My, but he's a silver-tongued fox! I can see now how impossible it must be for girls to resist. His latest flame quips back.

'I wish I could return the compliment. Fact of the matter is, I badly need fucking and you just so happen to fit the bill . . .'

No. Please, no, not her. Not Jinty.

Week 11: Day 6
Weather: Freezing Fog
Soundtrack: Sigur Rós – *Ny Batteri*

I lie there and I listen to them fucking again. My one desperate plea was that she'd wake up and hate herself and flee the scene, never to look him in the eye again. But no, they're fucking again. *Fucking.* The thing that disappointed me most about last night, about Jinty – no, be honest, the thing that *scared* me, the thing that totally alienated me and made me know, for sure, that I will never, never be a normal, mature, sexually active grown-up like they are – is the way she said: '*I badly need fucking.*'

She said that like it was the most normal thing in the world – like it's something you just *say*. Even that word, *fucking* – it scares me. Fucking, fucked, fuck – it's a word for a world they're in on. I'm not. I don't think I ever will be. I think of Petra, vulnerable, clever, trapped Petra, lying there in her Piglet nightie, crying. She's just a girl, Petra. She'll be fine. She's only just growing up. I've been like this since I was twelve – and it's fucking destroying me.

Week 12: Day 1
Weather: Cold Enough to Hang a Jacket On
Soundtrack: Aim – 'The Girl Who Fell Through Ice'

I didn't move all day Saturday, only to change the record or hide my head under the pillow or rush to the bin. Four times, four different times, there were knocks at the door. One of them was Jinty. She knows. She knows I know. I lay there and I didn't move and I was blissfully forlorn. I lay flat out and embraced the reality of Me. This is me, this is how it is, this is how it's going to be. Expect nothing except that things will happen to you that you cannot help. That's your lot, Kit. That's what is going to be.

I listened to *Agaetis Byrjun* and it was perfect. More so than Górecki, this is the soundtrack to my life. A nauseous brew of diarrhoea ripped through me, but still I lay still. Whenever the moment came, I fell out of bed sideways and squatted over the bin. The room was rank with the stench of my decay, but I was helpless. A dull buzz droned under my scalp and I could not scratch it, I could not stop it. I could not move. A stone, two stones thudded against my window, but the curtain stayed pulled. There was no one home.

I drifted in and out of sleep. I awoke yesterday at five thirty and I knew I wouldn't sleep again. Up and out, wrapped warm in layers of fleece and scarf and parka, I marched out and on, desperate for the crunch of the moors. By daylight, real light, I'd reached Bradfield and by nine I was well on the pathway to the Derwent Reservoir. Way, way, way up in the clean white sky a beady bird of prey scanned its terrain. Black and magnificent against the cold sun, it held high, stayed still and remote and potent, hardly moving its wings.

It was hard going. Way below me the magnificent thunder of Slippery Stones waterfall pummelled the slick slate chute. It stunned me still. I watched the torrent hammer down between the two silent watchtowers, felt its lure. If ever I were to jump, it would be here. It'd be perfect.

The swoop of the hawk snapped me to, and I tried to get my bearings. In hazy, hyper-real slow motion the distant wisp of chimney smoke singled out a lone pub, way below. I'd wandered right off course and now the folly of the thing struck hard. I might easily have stumbled on until dark, fallen, anything. No one was to know I was here. The best plan now was to take my time in getting down to the pub below and, maybe, call a taxi from there.

Sitting by the great open fire waiting for the cab to arrive – might be an hour, they'd said. Have to find a driver – I fastened on to a way ahead. There was nothing clear-cut, but there were things I had to put right. Petra, for one – as soon as I could, I would take Petra aside and give her an idea what's going on. I don't feel any need to unburden myself – I'm OK with it, and there's nothing anyone can do, anyway. Why weigh them down with it when all they can do is look sorry for me, maybe even exchange 'I told you so' glances? What I *can* do is start all over with her, as a pal, as a real, good friend and somehow be part of something good with her.

And then there's Jinty. That's a whole different set of problems. In many ways, I'd be better off without Jinty. I don't know. Maybe I'll suggest we don't see each other. All I know is, this Christmas break can't come soon enough. Until then, I'll do my best. I'm not the best pretender, but I'll try.

I needn't have agonised over Petra. When I tapped, nervous, bashful at her door and she welcomed me in, she was all eyes at my stuttering apologies.

'Did you not get my note?' she teased.

I found the note later, when we got back from the *pob*. Petra's note, which to my considerable shame I swept up off the floor yesterday at around three p.m. and used to wipe myself, said:

Kit, you're a honey. Thanks for being so lovely about last night. Let's be friends.
Petra x

We went to the Ranmoor, just the three of us – me, Jinty and Petra. I'm lucky to have two friends like these – girls who are cool without trying to be cool. Girls who seem to think I'm all right, too. We had such a good laugh. I mean, Petra's very serious. She wants to talk about Iraq, Bush, the oil conspiracy, Blair's slick Tory fraud and the heinous debt she's amassing every day she stays here. But she and Jinty balance each other beautifully. Maybe it's her age, maybe she's just *graceful*, but Jinty doesn't rise to anything. She listens, she nods, she takes in contrary points of view and she *always* manages to sound . . . I don't know – in *control*.

'God, Petra, that's so shitty. I mean, I've got to say, I can't sit here and make out I'm going through anything *like* that. I'm boringly stable. My parents are *really* old and quite well off and the fact of it is, they'll never see me short? Like, I don't ask them for *anything*. I still have some money saved from work. But debt, God – I don't know if I'd go through with it, you know? You must really love your course . . .'

'Love it? Nah. Sometimes I get that ace, you know – that buzzy sense of wonder about all the stuff you don't know, all the things you can learn. But I wouldn't say I'm *committed* in any way.'

Jinty tells us about how she wants to be a child psychologist. She's got a thing that we in Britain are still stupidly wary of therapy and analysis and that – shrinks. She thinks it's the way ahead. Everyone can benefit from an hour a fortnight, just talking about what's going on in their lives.

'Like, everyone says they're depressed – but nobody thinks they have depression.'

'There's a difference?'

'Of *course* there's a difference!'

'Go on, then . . .'

'Fuck, where do I start? OK, in the baldest terms, the thing you call depressed is a temporary state of low motivation, often the direct result of chemical or alcoholic excess. But that's not depression. Depression is a general and ongoing lowering of seratonin levels in the brain. This causes mood swings and is most commonly manifested by such things as lethargy, anxiety, obsession, sleeplessness and a basic inability to participate and enjoy.'

'Fuck! Kids can get *that*?'

She gives a half-smile that's telling us the subject is too big to get into on a Sunday night.

'D'you think that's what's going on with Ben?' says Petra.

'How d'you mean?'

'Well, like, his whole *thing*. I mean . . . it's scary. The poor boy's spending a fucking fortune pretending to be a drug dealer from the ghetto!'

I nearly choke on my beer.

'Erm, 'scuse me – people *know* that?'

'Know what?'

'I mean, is that common knowledge? That Ben's a total blag merchant?'

The two of them are in fits.

'Fuck, Kit – what do *you* think?'

'I think . . .' I laugh into my pint glass and take a swig. 'I thought I was the only one who's on to it.'

They exchange sly glances.

'Well, you might be. Maybe you are. Only, when we left youse that morning, yeah? Know we had to get up dead early to get down to Jinty's folks?'

I nod hard, a ticklish swell rising in my spleen.

'Well . . .'

She breaks off. She can't carry on. Jinty takes over.

'There was this *really* manky guy hanging round outside with a *disgusting* scabby old dog and he saw us coming out and he was *really* unpleasant, yeah?'

'*Stank!* Absolutely stank of piss!'

'And he goes, right: Is he going to be much longer in there? One night, he said. One fucking night!'

The pair of them fall about laughing and we indulge ourselves in that most evil and delicious diversion. We rip someone else to pieces – someone who's not there to defend himself, and it feels terrific – in a nasty sort of way.

While Petra's in the bog, Jinty leans into me.

'We have to talk.'

I'm in such a great mood now, I just don't want to think about her and Dangerous. I don't even mind, any more.

'Forget it, hey? It's up to you who you choose to . . .' I can't quite say it. *Fuck.*

'What?'

'I'm just saying. I'm not arsed about it. Really.'

It takes her a moment to get my drift and then Petra's on her way back and it's gone. We carry on ripping Ben and I try to throw in a few things about Adie's tortuous attempts to grunge up his clean-cut look. Jinty just raises her eyebrows at me. I could really fall hard for that girl – if I knew how to.

Lying there last night, it was as still and quiet as I've ever known it at Ranmoor. No matter what time, there's always some noise from somewhere. I lay still and listened and thought of Jinty – her smile, her tiny teeth, her *knowing* everything. I thought about her in her school uniform but I couldn't even get a wanking hard-on. I ate the remainder of a pot of Maltesers, pissed in the sink and tried to sleep, but rest would not come to me.

So this is it. The final week starts here. I'm walking down to lectures and, while I'm not exactly ecstatic, there's a certain sense of fulfilment soaking through me. I'm still here. I'm more than handling the coursework. I'm getting by. The more I think about it, just getting by is an achievement in itself. I pass Vittles without even thinking of bunking off lectures.

Week 12: Day 5

Weather: Sleet

Soundtrack: Photek – 'Terminus'

Good grief! I never thought I'd feel that tingle of thrill again but, crossing the concourse to start our day of Yule lunacy, I'm smitten with a titillating, puerile excitement. It's

Christmas! There's a choir outside the Union harmonising 'The Holly and the Ivy', and the gentlest drift of melting snow is starting to slick the floor and I've finished the very last lecture of the year and I just feel . . . *high*. I'm light-headed, free, complete, full of joy – and it's fucking Christmas! *Waaaaaaagh!* A dead-fit girl in a Santa outfit offers me a glass of mulled wine and I very nearly tell her I love her. I'm almost in bits, here. I've *got* to find the others. I hand my ticket in, get my wristband and I'm in there! We're off!

Adrian is pissed already. He hasn't been in classes all week, he knows he's in the shit and he doesn't give a fuck. He's standing at the bar with a paper crown on his head, tinsel round his neck and a four-pint jug of Stella in his hand. He spots me.

'Kit! My man! Fucking come here, you lovely little cunt! Fuckinell! I *love* you!'

He takes a huge long slug of beer and raises his other hand, in which he clasps a shrivelled sprig of mistletoe.

'C'mere, you!' He drags me closer and plants a harsh, stubbly kiss on my lips. 'Happy fucking Christmas!' He turns to the girl behind the bar. 'Hey! Darling!'

She gives him a patient smile.

'Yes, darling?'

'Ooh, fuck! I didn't realise how fucking gorgeous you are. Hey –'

'The answer's no. D'you need a drink or shall I attend to the other two hundred parched dipsomaniacs first?'

'Ooooh! Fiery! I love a girl with fire in her belly! Don't I, Kit?'

I try to raise the appropriate empathetic face for her. She smiles back.

'What's on offer, again? What's cheap?'

'Screamers? Pound all day?'

'Fuck – YES! Yes please! We'll have four. No – *eight*! Gimme eight Screamers, darling.'

She stops and sighs as though she's about to lecture him, but she obviously thinks fuck it – sooner he's sloshed the sooner he'll take the knock.

By the time we sit down to lunch, Adie is actually hilariously drunk. I've never seen him like this before. He's *monged*. He gets up on the table, falls over, gets back to his feet and stamps on the table for quiet. Incredibly, people shut up and listen.

'Calling occupants of interplanetary craft! News just in! Santa is alive and well and will be encouraging all helpers to snog the face off any earthling in possession of one of *these . . .*' He holds up his mistletoe to rampant cheering. Everybody loves him. 'Merry Christmas, yah bastards! Let's get fucked!'

Tumultuous din of approval. I catch Jinty's eye and she smiles and rolls her eyeballs. I wink at her and the look she gives me back, wow! It's something else. I'm swooning, big time. I'm just . . . *overcome*. First opportunity, I'm going to drag her to one side, tell her the pros and cons and ask her if she'll give it a crack, with me. I know she'll say yes. I know she will.

Back in Bar One, as Adie sleeps it off under a growing pile of jackets and parkas, dire rumours sweep the company: Ant 'n' Dec will not now be appearing. The story is that they were never confirmed, but the bottom line is that good old PJ and Duncan will not be hosting this evening's festivities.

'Fuck it!' shouts Simon, well on his way to joining Adie under the Pile of Shame.

'Aye,' says Ben. 'We're only here for Slade, anyway!'

From under the coats comes a terrible, if muffled, roar. 'IT'S CHRIIIIIIIST-MASSSS!!!'

The atmosphere in the Octagon is bacchanalian. Wild scenes of dancing and groping and snogging threaten to spill out of control at any moment. The appearance of Terry Christian on stage ensures this happens sooner rather later. A barrage of debris rains down on him as he greets the revellers with his trademark grin. A chant goes up.

'Who the fuck? Who the fuck? Who the fuckinell are YOU?'

He shrugs gamely. Another chant from the back of the arena.

'Where the fuck? Where the fuck? Where the fuck are Ant and Dec?'

He's a pro, though. He waits for it all to die down a bit and, finding his moment, quips back with: 'I'm sorry Gaz Topp couldn't be here with you tonight . . .'

As I stagger to the bog it strikes me there are worse ways to make a few bob.

Trying to find my way back to the gang, a harsh prod jabs my ribs. I'm stunned still for a moment. I'm thinking it's Colette. I turn round and there's Jinty, troubled. She's not looking at me as she speaks, she's looking around and behind her.

'Listen, just say no if you don't fancy it, but I really don't want to stay in here.'

'Know what you mean.'

Now she looks me in the eye.

'Rose Royce are on in the Foundry.'

'Who?'

She smiles. 'OK. I probably asked for that.'

She takes a big deep breath and looks right into me. 'Or we could go back to mine. Or yours.'

My face must betray a thousand demons. She's back at me straight away.

'Just for a smoke and that.' She looks round at the cavorting, rocking, fantastic crowd and tenses her face. 'Just a bit fed up with all this, you know? Can't hear yourself think.'

Who wants to think? I'm thinking. But I steel myself. I force myself.

'Sure,' I smile. 'I'd like that.'

'Good.'

But she doesn't look too thrilled, I must say.

All the way back up the hill I try to envisage her in that gymslip, or in her tight jeans, or in her bra. She's an absolute divinity, this girl. This is a privilege that's being laid before me. I should just breathe deep, start to relax and enjoy my blessed good luck. But I can't, of course. I'm fixated first by all the sex she must have had, all those lovers, all those *men*. She must be so expert by now. She must expect fantastic sex. She's adept at *fucking* and she's going to find me out and let me go, let me down lightly. Then, as we get up to the Broomhill Tavern, I can't stop my mind wandering to Adie. He had her, the bastard! He *had* you.

Her morose frame of mind isn't helping, either. She's hardly talking, but she seems comfortable with the silence. In the end, I figure attack may be the best form of defence.

'You angry with me, babe?'

She stops dead. 'God, no! No! Whatever . . . ?'

I shrug. 'Dunno. Just a feeling, like. You're hardly yourself though, are you?'

She picks up her feet again, scuffs along slowly.

'Ah, no, I don't know. I just . . . maybe it's this course, hey? All this insight into the mind and the mood and that . . .' She kicks a stone. 'That thing, too.'

'What thing?'

She jerks her head back in the direction we've come.

'All that. I dunno. I felt so *old.*'

'You *are* old, darling.'

This gets a reluctant chuckle.

'I mean it. They were all so fucking *happy*. They were having the time of their lives, you know?'

I nod.

'And I'm, like – have I *had* mine? When did that happen, again?'

She gives another big long sigh and puts her arm round me.

'I think I wasted my best years on Pete. What the *fuck* was I thinking, hey, Kittycat? What a fool! Right until the night before I left, you know, he still thought I'd come around. All that bullshit when I was slogging my guts out in night school and running the house for him, all that time he was saying, you know, great, fantastic, support you all the way, baby, and guess what? Dumps me. Bastard dumps my sorry arse when it dawns on him I actually want to *do* this.'

I snuggle into her.

'*I* think you've got a lovely arse.'

She looks straight ahead.

'Don't, baby.'

'Don't what?'

'Don't.'

I let it go. I know that, if I follow it through, tell her I mean it, there really will be no turning back. I still don't know if I can do this. I give her a clumsy little tug towards me and try to sound playful, try to jolly her round.

'Well, let me tell you, *Virginia* – we are what we are. I mean, me, Petra, everyone – we fucking *adore* you. How d'you know you'd be so . . . *you* if you hadn't been through all that? D'you know what I mean? Would you have that special thing that makes you Jinty if you hadn't lived the life you've lived?'

She says nothing. I give her a little punch.

'Or is that just bollocks?'

She snorts a little laugh.

'No, darling. It's not bollocks. It's very *not* bollocks.'

She turns and stops and looks down at me.

'Listen.'

Oh. Fuck. Here we go.

'Can we be together? Tonight?'

I knew it.

'I mean . . . God! Fuck! I just don't know . . .' She looks

at the pavement, jerks her head up and looks me in the eye. 'I don't know if I can fuck you, Kit.'

Yes! Yes! Oh my God, this is just too good to be true.

'I mean . . . I really do not know what's going with you and I think I'm about to fall very deeply and hugely in love with you and I don't know if that's right and I don't know if it's good and I *really* don't know if having sex is just going to tear us apart, you know?'

I nod sagely, trying not to betray my heartfelt relief. This is just . . . *perfect*.

'Oh, Kit, baby.'

She leans down and hugs me close. I'm starting to get hard.

'I'm sorry. I so don't want to fuck you up.'

She steps back and bites down on her lip. Her eyes are glistening.

'I love you.'

And suddenly, with that, it's over. She runs off, runs *really* fast down one of the side roads down towards the other halls. I go after her, but there's no sign. She's gone.

Week 12: Day 6
Weather: Dazzling Distant Sun
Soundtrack: Joy Division – 'New Dawn Fades'

The train pulls into Warrington and it's not even nine yet. Once I'd accepted that I wouldn't get back to sleep, I started to pack. I took the Walkman, a few CDs and enough clothes to get me through the next few days, shut the door and went. Outside, the gardens were strewn with bog roll and beer cans and the detritus of a high old time. My tree, stripped bare by winter, has been newly adorned with condoms and tinsel. I pushed out into the morning and flicked a glance over the tree and surprised myself with sensations of warmth and nostalgia, and

I knew I was doing right in going home. Enough, for now. Tonight, the big, last bender, the big farewell to all the crew – I just don't want it any more. I've done my time and I want out. I want some space, some peace, some quiet. I left most of my things there. I can come back with Mum sometime, pick up my stuff, but for now it just feels right that I'm back here, job done.

All the way back I cowered against the cold in a deserted carriage. All the way back I thought of Jinty. She loves me. She said she loves me. Eek! What do I do next? I know somehow it's best for her and best for me that we didn't have to clash today. I know her well enough by now to know she's useless the day after, useless with the awkwardness and the uncertainty. But I'm sure, too, that we shouldn't just leave this as it is. Maybe she'll call me. Maybe I'll email her. I don't know. I'm so happy she likes me, like that.

As the train slows into Warrington the sun flares up wild and high behind the cable factory. Shoppers are already amassing for one last riot, but the sunshine casts a weird shimmer over town. I snag a taxi and I start to smile as I picture Emma's face when I walk through the door.

2. Home

Weather: Molten Winter Sun
Soundtrack: Low – 'Blue Christmas'

No one's in. I knew Dad would be at the brewery – he properly loves his Saturday-morning shift down there, regardless of the extra dough. If Wires are at home he'll go along with his pals, one of the very few things I know he looks forward to. He truly is the Quiet Man, my pater. Mum and Em, though – I must say, I'm gutted they're not here. I would've rung, but I wanted to rush them. They'll be out down the Trafford Centre, those two will, getting each other hyper over Christmas. So it goes. I'll still be here when they get back.

I dump my bag and pop my head into each of the small rooms. Emma's gauche friezes and decorations hang alongside the arrangements of cards Mum methodically strings on cotton from ceiling to floor, every year. On a whim, I switch on the Christmas lights and snaffle a chocolate miniature. I amble up to my bedroom and, again, I'm shot through with that queer sense of achievement I had this morning, looking up at my tree. It's only a few months I've been away and it's not like I've been in a POW camp having my eyelids sliced off, but I don't know – I've come on, somehow. I don't feel so scared of everything – not today at least, anyway. Every now and then I get this sense of calm that just descends on me and that's how it feels right now. Fuck it, man – I'm *chilled*! I dredge through my bag for the Walkman and the *Christmas* CD and I lie back and let Low's beautiful desolation wash over me.

I splay out on my bed and I run it all around my mind, all the things that have happened since I last lay here. And the thing that keeps coming back to me is the image of Maddy's card flipping and spinning out of sight. Mimi Parker's heartbroken vocals seep through me and all through it, all through the tender howl of 'Blue Christmas' I see that card spinning, spinning away.

I pull the headphones off. I get up and walk to her bedroom. I hesitate by the door, push it open and stand there without going in. It's Emma's room, now – something else altogether. Where Madeleine's chest of drawers stood – her treasure chest, her Pandora's box of mystical satin and lace – there's a work-station with PC, scanner, printer. No trace at all of my tortured adolescence. I would sit in here and adore her, no matter what. For years and years I locked it all up inside, crushed any such thoughts and reminiscences at first sap. I shut the door again and, in doing that, I sense that others might be about to open.

NEW MAIL!

I don't think I'll ever get over the thrill of logging on and finding I have emails waiting to be opened. I love it, love it all – the funny little Information symbol, the exclamation mark, the anticipation and, best of all, just those words: You Have New Mail!

I have four new messages, but it's the third of those that is leaping out at me and, in so doing, making my heart leap, too. Jinty. My wrist is trembling so badly as I try to man-oeuvre the mouse, I can barely click her message into life. What's she going to say? Sorry, I was drunk. Sorry, I was teasing you. Sorry, it all got out of hand. Whatever, I know she'll be saying sorry.

3. Back

Exam Week: Day 1
Weather: A Blizzard
Soundtrack: Lamb – 'Lullaby'

My good heart carried on more or less throughout the holi-
day. I found myself subconsciously lurching – and that *was*
the subconscious – when some cavernous recess of my
animus tried to drift me back towards Sheffield, Ranmoor,
exams and all that. But this time, the reality bite was that,
not only did I not mind, I was quite glad to be going back.
I mean, Jinty's email threw me. It really did rock me back
on my feet – I had no idea. And I'm scared, too. No two
ways about it, she's got me thinking, thinking, thinking –
much more deeply than I'm used to – and it's serious shit,
too. But none of it has crushed me. Quite the opposite. As
ridiculous as it sounds whenever I allow myself to think it,
she really is right about me. Last night, with Alex, I was
immense. I'm a kid, right, I know fucking nothing, I've *done*
nothing. But Jinty's right. I have something to offer. I'm . . .
in fact, nah, it really *is* silly.

Point is though, I haven't slumped over any of this. True
enough, while the mere thought of Ranmoor can still dull
my heart, I no longer find it daunting. I'm not in awe of the
great concrete maze and I'm not hiding away from it. So
much so indeed, that I've come back early. I'm skidding down
to the library, trying to keep to the parts that have been grit-
ted and I can still taste the ale on my breath. I'm back, and
I've been back since Saturday. OK, there's circumstantial –
there was a major blizzard warning for the weekend that might
have seen the Snake Pass closed to traffic. Plus Mum tends to
like to have Sunday evenings free to start prepping her week's
work. And, last but not least, I have the small matter of a gang

of little tests that have to be negotiated. But I'm back. I came back before I had to.

Saturday night was weird. I didn't know for certain whether anyone'd be here, but I just didn't want to leave my room. I had stage fright. What if it was all back to square one again? What if they'd all been talking about me, all along? Somehow, my guiding principle was just to stay in, stay warm, stay quiet. I lay on my bed and mulled over the torn printout again.

Dear Kit,

This is really, really cowardly and I'll probably delete it anyway, but I somehow have to get down the jumble of thoughts and conflicts in my head – for you, if not for me. I know I shouldn't write all this in an email. I should be there to hold your hand and talk it through with you. There's never a chance, though. I can never get you on your own.

Here we go, then.

(I've read this email a hundred times. I still shit myself at that bit – the 'here we go then' bit.)

I'm so sorry to have run off on you like that.

(So I was right about that bit. I knew it was going to be sorry.)

I'm desperate not to make a mess of this, honey. Above all else, I think you are a very special, intense and unique boy and I don't want to do or say anything that stops you being you. So where to start, if at all? I suppose I should just say everything I want to say, in whatever order it comes out, hey? Like I say – I'm far too much of a coward to send this, anyway.

So let me start with the big thing, the biggest thing, maybe the only thing. I am utterly and wholly in love with you, Kit. That's about as good as it gets though, because I know that as much as I adore you and as absolutely as I think I am the one girl who could make you happy, I also should own up that I'm the last girl you should get involved with. You're so precious, and I'm scared I'd break you. Firstly, I'm not a girl. I'm a woman. I hate myself for it, I wish I were still a girl but that's all gone, now. I'm Big. By anybody's standards, I'm grown up. And yes, it makes me angry that a lady of my age can't contemplate a life or even a fling with a boy as young as you. When I allow myself to dream of course, it's perfect. It's right. Men have a predictably shabby habit of dying way before their lovely wives. If I nab a boy who's young enough we may stand a chance of seeing the whole thing out together, hey? But that's for dreams. Even if you were as grown up emotionally as you are psychologically, it's still not a relationship that could happen. I'm too old for you and that's that. The second Stop Sign is that I come with baggage. I have endured so many wretched and destructive relationships that I think I now approach affairs as a missionary. Quite sincerely, Kit, I have a need to give that is overpowering. I know how to make it work for me – or how not to let it make me unhappy – but you? I think I would smother you.

And you're not a boy who should be smothered. This brings me on to the other big thing, the thing that makes a girl like me, who fucking adores you, run away into the night and hide in wet bushes until I know you've gone, rather than even kiss you. This is *really* hard, Kit, and this is the thing I've tried to open up with you so many times. I just chicken out, in case I'm wrong. I'm a few weeks into a course – what the fuck do I know? Except that I think I do know. I think I'm right. I think I can help you understand why you feel so great one day, then go and do or say such unkind things the next. Up, down, up, down, any little thing can trigger either elation or despair. You've told me so many times, told about your lethargy, your anxiety, your irrational fears and doubts. What can I tell you? I've learnt a lot about this stuff and I've learnt so I can help you, with or without me. I'd love to talk about this properly, if you think that would help. You're special – special to me but, much more than that, you have it in you to do amazing things. I want you to be free to go and do all that – do it all.

More than any other thing though, Kit, you cannot shut me out. Please, please, please don't be awkward with me, don't hide from me. I've opened up my soul to you here, I *am* going to push this button and send these thoughts and feelings and, whatever you think, I've sent them with love.

Ever yours,

Jinty

I was still shaking ten minutes after I read it the first time, and it gives me goose pimples now. I did a remarkable thing – for me – once I'd composed myself. I called her. I dialled once and chickened out, started writing a text instead. But then I did it. I cleared the screen, sat out in the car, taking big deep gulps of air like they do in films – and I called her. If only I'd let her get past 'hello' – but nerves got the better of me. The fact is, at age eighteen and two weeks, I was telephoning a girl for the very first time. It's quite a moment in time. I fucked it up fantastically.

'Hey you, you nutter!'

That's what actually came out. What I was going to say was:

'Jinty, I'm overwhelmed. I don't know if I can say all I want to say now, on the phone. Can we meet?'

But I heard her voice, heard that nervous and affectionate quiver in her one small 'hello' and I didn't know how to handle it. I thought it'd be best to make a joke of it – let her see I wasn't feeling weird about anything. Wrong call.

'Kit!'

She said it on a down note – warning, anxious, embarrassed and a tiny bit angry all in that one small word. Shit. Whatever I said next, it was going to have to be good.

'Bit rich eh, *you* calling *me* a nutjob!'

The remainder of the call was a) brief, and b) polite. It was a bit tricky for her to talk, she said. She was at lunch with her mum and dad, but she was looking forward to catching up properly back in Sheffield. Fuck off, in other words. I've opened up my veins to you, and you're laughing at me. But I wasn't though. I wasn't laughing.

I reached over and tucked the printout under my keyboard and lay there, my clasped hands supporting my head. I can't wait to see her. There's so many things I want to tell her, so much I want to ask. One thing I want to ask is: if you feel that way about me, how come you boned Adrian fucking Dangerous? And who else has had you, hey? I tried to quell my jealous mind with visions of the amazing achievements Jinty's so convinced lie ahead for me. I'm *special*. I'd want to think so, too, if it weren't so laughable. I drifted into a shallow sleep dreaming of an exhausted and sweat-drenched Kit

Hannah receiving a *Blue Peter* badge from Adrian Dangerous for breaking the All-Halls Pogo-Stick Endurance Record by a massive thirty-five minutes. As Adrian pinned the badge, Jinty looked on, besotted with pride and mouthing the words: 'You're special.'

Adrian winked at me and said: 'Me too.'

I woke up wet with the perspiration of nightmares, shivering. My duvet was on the floor, my window, apart from the top right-hand corner, a white-out. Even with the heating on, the room was an icebox. I looked at my watch. Shit. Only eight twenty and I was wide awake, no chance whatever of sinking back to the bottom of the ocean. I hauled the duvet round my shoulders and padded to the window. Snowstorm. Outside, everything but everything was suffocated by the fat white spread. My tree, skeletal without leaves, was heavy with the snowdrift. One set of footprints punctured a hollow path down towards the bus stop. There was going to be no leaving Ranmoor today.

I got dressed, too cold to brave the showers, and skulked along to breakfast. In the canteen, every single table was deserted except one. All alone, cocooned and content with his coffee and his sausages and his *Observer*, sat Ratboy. Conscious of my arrival, his head craned half a turn before his controls caught up with him and took him back to his newspaper, back to splendid isolation. How odd to be him. I know those were his footprints in the snow. He, Ratboy, has got up and his inner self has motivated him to put clothes on, to walk outside in the scything cold and purchase a Sunday newspaper. This has been his choice, his taste. The shoes, the newspaper, the coffee, the sausages – these are the decisions Ratboy has made in his life, today. Head down, I went over to the hatch, picked up mushrooms and tomatoes and toast, tea and orange juice and hesitated there, too many tables to know which to pick. Would Ratboy expect me to sit with him? What would *I* want? No doubt about it, *anybody* sitting alone with their newspaper wants to remain just like that – alone. I waved brightly as I passed by though, just in case he should look up again, and I felt that, this time, he was the one in charge.

Regardless of the unsurpassed opportunity to get stuck right into my exam strategy without distraction, I couldn't settle to anything. Every twenty minutes or so I'd get up, check the status of the snow outside, toy with the idea of trudging over the bridge to see if anyone was back yet, without actually leaving my room. By five o'clock I'd built up not so much of a hunger but a substantial enough ennui to head off over for Sunday dinner and a change of scenery. I was surprised to see Alex heading down the passage towards me. I was doubly surprised at my heartfelt pleasure in seeing her – and not just to help kill the boredom.

'Hey! Magnifico! The very man!'

I pointed at myself in some lame attempt at self-deprecation – not a thing that comes naturally to my good self. She ran up and smothered me with a tight bearhug.

'Happy New Year, you psycho!'

My immediate and overpowering thought was: Who's been talking? But my second, and much better thought was: It's Sunday – let's go to the Ranmoor Inn.

And we had a great time in there. I mean, no, it wasn't actually *a great time*, something one will remember for the rest of one's born days, but it was good. She's a good woman, Alex – spiky, very easy to misunderstand, and indeed, I put it to her that she *likes* to get an adverse reaction. She laughed, pointed to her latest deranged Castro outfit.

'I go out like this and I don't want a reaction, right?'

'*Adverse* reaction, darling. You want people to pick fights with you.'

'I so do *not*!'

225

'OK, OK – maybe not that extreme. But you know what I mean.'

'No. Please tell me. Like, I'm me? I have a hunch that maybe *I* know what's going on in here?'

'Go on, then.'

'Which is all pretty simple.'

She took a big pause, looked at me like she really was not sure whether she could trust me. Then she went for it.

'I want peace and love for all mankind.' She paused again, took a sip of her Guinness. 'Which may sound somewhat trite. But it happens to be what I stand for, OK?'

And it *doesn't* sound trite, not the way she said it. I mean, I'm not the world's keenest when it comes to current affairs – worse than that, I genuinely believe that most of the kids I see around here *pretend* to be interested. I mean it. I think the majority are at this university to increase their chances of getting a really well-paid job so's they can purchase many a McDonald's and many a pair of sweatshop Nikes. They may not *know* it know it, but they know it. Their interest in the World Bank, Human Rights, the Oil War and so on will last as long as their student loan. Compared to that, I'd have to say I *am* truly interested in, like, bin Laden for example. Not in a mad, swotty, History Channel Bore sort of way, but I can't help wondering: what the fuck made him *do* that? That's what I said to Alex last night. Why d'you think it happened? Isn't your country massively to blame?

'Well, fuck, yeah, show me a war that didn't start with one small nation nursing a grievance . . .'

'Now that *is* trite . . .'

'No, no, hear me out, hear me out. Don't forget you've just asked me whether my own country is responsible for some nut flying a gang of planes through the side of the World Trade Center, huh?'

I held my hands up in surrender. She told me, with some reluctance, I feel, that the US could have done more to spot the growing anti-Americanism and, if only for its own sake, made some moves towards appeasement. But she doesn't truly believe that anything the US has done historically could have led directly to that very anti-Americanism and I know she's not for the persuading, either. I went down a different route.

'I just can't help thinking the US lost a truly enormous opportunity for historical greatness. Moments like that – they come along once a century. Maybe less. And what it is, I think, is the opportunity just to say: this ends now . . .'

'*Very* idealistic . . .'

I wasn't angry. Usually, I'm slightly bug-eyed when people are refusing to catch my drift, but last night with Alex I was perfectly calm. I knew what I wanted to say to her. It was a bit of a gushing tirade, but I still think I was right.

'Maybe, maybe . . . you say that as though idealism is a bad thing. Maybe it's anti-American, hey?'

'Touché.'

I took a big long slug on my pint and wiped my mouth with the back of my hand.

'No, what I mean is – you're right. The guys who flew those planes into the towers were driven men. They're men with hate in their hearts. So are the small boys and girls in Afghanistan who saw their towns and villages blown apart. Already, you have another generation of assassins in the making. What I'm trying to say is, *that's* the cycle of war. You did this to us so we're going to do that to you. It's playground stuff on a huge, huge scale . . .'

I looked her in the eye and went for the kill. Boys. Blame the boys.

'It's men showing how tough they are. If they don't fight back, they're cissies. I just think America had the chance on September 12th to say, fuck all that. We're not interested in getting you back. We're appalled that the world has come to this, that men will commit such an atrocity. We want to know why. We want to know how we stop this from ever happening

227

again, here or anywhere else. We propose a summit, right now, where we address all these issues and we do not leave until we've reached a resolution. That, for me, is the mark of greatness. And your country let it slip through its oil-stained fingers.'

She was silent. I was stunned. She was thinking about what I'd said. She was actually thinking about it and allowing doubt to seep into her head. I'd never see Alex so . . . *unsure* of herself. We didn't mention the Middle East again until the crusty trudge back through the snow. She put an arm round me and said: 'So we can count on your presence at the Stop the War demo next week, Foreign Secretary?'

'Ooh, fuck that, no way!'

She stopped in her tracks.

'Why the fuck not?'

'I don't do demos.'

'Well, you fucking well should, Kit! You shouldn't just *do* them − you should *be* them. *You* should be up there on that platform rallying the youth, not some lame dick banging the same old hippie drum . . .'

'Exactly!'

'Exactly *what?*'

I gave it thought. I did what Alex did and I ran the whole thing round my head, gave it a good old look to see if maybe there was something I'd been missing. *Why* do I not want to join my fellow students on a demonstration against something I probably do feel strongly about? Partly, it's the fellow-student thing. I'm getting better, but I still can't feel like I'm one of them − someone who's just been for a few beers. But there's something else. There's a really big obstacle, for me. It's the placards. It's those commands. Grants Not Loans. Stop the War. That's what it is − it's the sheer stupidity of the stop signs. I looked her in the eye and I told her.

'You can stop traffic with a lollipop stick. You can't stop a war, though.'

This time I put my arm round her and guided us on.

'Sick,' she said. 'You're a very, very sick man.'

'Boy,' I said, and she didn't argue.

I have to steady myself on a traffic light as I try to turn into Glossop Road. I'll be seeing her today. I'll see Jinty and it'll all be fine.

The Morning After the Last Day of Exams
Weather: Low Flat Sky
Soundtrack: Pink Floyd – 'Us and Them'

Here I lie in this stale, sexless, wanker's bed thinking of what might have been and might yet be – if only I could get over this thing. But I cannot get over this thing. I cannot get over it because I don't know what it is and, like Jinty said, perhaps I don't really want to find out. I screw my eyes tight shut to try and blot out the faces and voices. Jinty. Just think of Jinty. If she'd known that the last thing she should do is probe me like that, she'd have left well alone, I'm sure.

She's been great, Jinty has. I know that. I'm lying here and I am fucking bad. I'm not at all sure I'll make it through the day. This is as bad as I've been for a long time. I've hit the bottom now, and it can get no worse. Yet through it all, through all these awful, awful noises and voices I know that Jinty is my salvation. I think of her and I am clear. There is a way. If I come through this one, I'm straight round to her, this time. I'll tell her everything. I'll tell it all and, fuck, it will be so *good* to tell. It'll be good to tell her.

She came straight round to see me first night back – well, *her* first night back, which turned out to be Tuesday, as the weather transpired. She pointed to Adie's wall and made a shhh gesture with her finger over her lip. She grinned that beautiful smile of hers and her eyes were twinkling and I knew it, I just knew that if I kissed her there and then it would be all right. More than all right – it'd be wonderful. But of course that's what I didn't do. I looked her in the eye and did my very best to give off an 'I'm confused' vibe, a 'what d'you want me to do' sort of thing, and that in turn seemed to make up her mind for her. The tiniest, tiniest flicker of regret came over her, then she forced another big grin, took my hand and led me out.

We sat in the Ranmoor Inn and we talked a little bit about her feelings for me and how she'd spent the Christmas break convincing herself that, as much as she herself thought she could make it work, it was probably doomed. She took both my hands and looked into me and said: 'I'd take this any day, rather than nothing.'

'What?'

'This. Just being here with you, being your mate. If you and me fuck it up, then we fuck it up for ever. We could never go back to just being pals again.'

I hung my head and I'm such a craven, snivelling wretch I went through the whole thing of acting hurt and troubled and bruised – but the truth is I was relieved. I mean, yeah, of course I'd love to be in bed with her now, those long, long legs curled around me. But what if I can't do it again? What if I made a fool of myself? Would she still feel the same then? No – of course she fucking wouldn't! She wants a lad who knows what he's doing. She wants someone who knows what she wants.

So we drank and made jokes about things she'd thought about me (gay) and things I'd thought about her (tall). We tittered about Ben's fibs and Simon's ongoing odyssey of cool and Adie's drastic new goth-skater look. We were completely at our ease and it was just lovely. I really did start to think that, in any case, she was probably right – we probably are better as friends. And then I had to throw the spanner into the works again, didn't I? Mention of Adrian gave me an itch that, after a few pints, I had to scratch.

'What about him, though?'

'Who? Pete?'

'*Nah!*' I fixed my eyes right into her, a tiny bit furious through the drink but not really cross at all – just acting hurt, because I felt like it. '*You* know who I mean . . .'

She lowered her eyeline. I shouldn't have brought that up. There was no need.

'I had sex with Adie, yeah. That's all it was.'

I can let it go now. I should leave it.

'But why *did* you have sex with him?'

She sighed out loud. She addressed her pint as she was talking.

'I wanted sex, Kit. I hadn't had sex for a very long time. It doesn't make . . .'

'But why *him*?'

'Dunno.'

'Next door to *me*?'

This was the bit I *really* was sorry about. She threw her head up, eyes glittering with pain and hurt and, more than anything, with some kind of hatred of me. Maybe not hatred – but she was letting it all out, all the stuff she'd been trying to gloss over. She let it all out with one sentence.

'Well, I didn't think *you'd* be *there*, did I?'

And she stares me out until it all comes back to me. Petra. It was the night of Petra. Shit. We'd been doing so well, me and Jinty. We'd got this thing back on to an even keel, we were friends, best friends, real, deep, loving, caring friends. And I'd just turned her into a threat again. With that one stupid and self-pitying remark I'd plunged her back face to face with her true feelings about all this. Fuck.

But she's a different kind of woman, Jinty. She, truly, *is* special. I mean, she's a woman, for starters – she's grown up and she knows things and she's done things I can only know about through books. And she dealt with me beautifully. She made it all fine. She just . . . well, what she did was, I think, she just put a lid on the whole thing of me and her and she went to the bar and she came back and didn't, wouldn't, refer to it again. She looked me over carefully, delved into her handbag and gave me a leaflet. It was about Depression.

'This is what I was going on about. In my email? When I was saying it's dead normal and *loads* of people suffer from it?'

I just laughed. 'Me? Depressed?'

She looked hurt. I pulled a sad clown face and put on a sort of comedy American accent and tried to make a joke of it.

'I can do depressed!'

She smiled into her pint. 'Well, like I said – I'm no expert. Read it, anyway.' She looked up and caught me full on in her laser beams. 'For me?'

So I did. I read the leaflet and, yes, no doubt I display some of the symptoms listed in it. But fuck, who wouldn't? Which young person who works hard, drinks, takes drugs, stays out late, eats a bad diet and doesn't get their full quota of sleep does not display symptoms of listlessness, low motivation, anxiety and so on? Mood swings? I don't have mood swings. I screwed up the leaflet and chucked it at the bin. It missed.

After that, I threw myself into my exams – which, I have to say, I kind of enjoyed. I mean, when I'm into it, I'm fucking good at this stuff. I don't know – I just don't see it as *work*. I can't approach a written examination with that formulaic practical-criticism mindset. If I'm writing about something then I'm passionate about it, whether I love it or hate it. It's hard for me to go through the motions. Whatever, I was still elated when it was all over, for now, yesterday. I know I've done OK and I raced up to Broomhill with a real eager need to drink, drink hard and let my shoulders loose.

★　★　★

I met Jinty in O'Neill's for happy hour. She gave me a big squeeze, asked me how I'd done and got the drinks in. She sat back, watched me slurp my pint, smiled and said it, calmly.

'Drink.'

'What?'

'Alcohol. You and me need to have a small conversation about the grog.'

'We do?'

She nods and does almost a 180-degree turn in her seat, so her whole body is facing me.

'We've just started covering it . . .'

'What?'

'Drink. The many and various effects of alcohol on the human psyche.'

'And?'

'*And*, dear boy, *I* need to ask *you* some questions . . .'

She's beaming at me. She's devoutly radiant and jovial, like Satanic Matt when he finally pins down some miscreant who'll succumb to being preached at.

'It's simple, really. Or it *may* be. I hope.'

She takes a deep breath.

'Does your depression –'

'I'm *not* depressed!'

She holds her hands up.

'Right. Let me put this another way. Do you have certain times when you're more likely to, um, *relish* life, yeah? Are there times when you like your life better than other times?'

I stare at her, dumbfounded.

'Yes. Course there are.'

'OK, OK, good. So, like, are there times, therefore, when you're more likely to, you know . . . ?'

I raise my eyebrows at her.

'You know what I'm wanting to ask you, Kit. Are there times when you're more liable to feel sad?'

'I hardly ever feel sad.'

She sighs out hard in exasperation. 'OK. Whatever.'

I flick her hand with my middle finger.

'That's a really lame way to conclude an argument.'

'What is?'

'Using the crap catch-all phrase "whatever". Ever.'

'I wasn't aware we were arguing.'

'We are now.'

'Look. All I'm trying to suggest is that you have a certain disposition, right? Everyone has a governing disposition. Yours leans towards melancholia – as does that of many, many, *many* people.' She frowns at me. 'And those with a melancholic disposition are infinitely more sensitive to the effects of alcohol.'

'You're telling me I shouldn't drink now?'

'No. I'm not.' She slaps her hands down on the table. 'Yes. I am, if you want the truth. It's my belief you have an acute bipolar disorder and you need counselling. But that's just a matter of opinion. What is a matter of fact is that *none* of us needs to drink anything like the amount we do.'

She reaches for my hand. I let her take it, but don't squeeze back. My hand lies limp in hers as she struggles for the right way of putting it.

'But you, Kit . . .' She lowers her head, then comes back up to lock stares with me. 'It's fucking you up. I'm sure of it.'

I hold her gaze. For a time, we just sit there looking at one another. I relent first. I'm a bit drunk and a bit irritable, but overriding that is a deep and satisfying understanding that I'm sitting here with someone who gives a fuck about me. I give her a tiny smile.

'Thanks, honey. But I'm sure it's not, you know.'

She almost hisses her reply.

'So what's wrong with you, then?'

Thankfully, I'm getting that same calm-over, similar to the war debate with Alex. The drink is levelling me out, but I'm sure of myself, too. I'm sure enough to listen to what she's saying and give it room. I look her in the eye, but take a slug of drink as I do it.

'I don't know what's wrong with me.'

'*Are* you gay?'

'No. I'm not gay.'

'How can you be sure?'

'Take my word for it.'

She fiddles with the beer mat, shreds it in her fingers.

'Are you happy?'

'Sometimes yes, sometimes no.'

She's getting vexed with me. She can't tell whether I'm playing her or not. I'm not. She leans right across the little table.

'Do you find me attractive?'

'Yes.'

'Why don't you do anything about it?'

Now that, interestingly, sums it all up. Just the way she put that particular question – *Why don't you do anything about it?* – says everything about what I find, not just intimidating but, when it comes to it, debilitating in the presence of sexually knowing women. She's putting the onus on me. She's implying that she expects a man to do manly things, to be a hunter, a predator, one who gets his way. In that short sentence, she's giving me a glimpse of what she expects from me – and I know I can never match up. With that, she's told me that we can never get it together, me and Jinty. My sea of calm is deserting me. My throat is starting to tighten and my palate is drying up. I take a nervy swig of ale. I'm probably blushing.

'We've been over it, beautiful. We both know why.'

'No. We don't. *You* don't.'

Now she's looking at me desperately, with tears in her eyes.

'Maybe you don't *want* to know . . .'

And the truth of it is, I hadn't been unhappy for a while.

Just for a moment, I thought I was special. She wasn't to know that. Now, I lie here in my tosser's pit, a miserable dribble of spunk drying on my belly and I am fucked. Absolutely flattened. Snatches of distant, discordant voices haunt me.

Why don't you do anything about it?

Fuck, fuck, if only. If only I could. Visions, apparitions, faces I don't know taunt me, talk about me, look at me in that way that says they know. They all know. I pull the sheets tight around me and prepare myself again. I don't see myself getting up for a long, long time. What would be the point?

4. Second Semester

Week 1: Day 7
Weather: Bright Sun, Bitter Wind
Soundtrack: Radiohead – 'Lucky'

It's like I can't trust my happiness. I can't even trust myself
when I'm merely so-so. I have a tripwire. I reach a certain
point of saturation and it's inevitable – what goes up must
come down. And this is no standard Sunday malaise, either.
This is something I am quite simply learning to live with.
This Is Me.

In many respects, it'd been like starting all over again after
the O'Neill's thing with Jinty. It really set me back, truth be
known. For a day or two, I was back to that timorous little
fart who hid away in his cell rather than face the music. I
still am that boy, but there's a difference. I don't know if I'm
starting to understand it, whatever it is – but I'm ready to
accept it. Like I say, this is me. I'm getting used to what that
really entails and, if I have a few good days and a big black
slammer comes and levels me, I'm sort of expecting it. But
today is going to take some getting through. Today is definitely one for getting out, just me, leave it all behind.

Friday started out such a good day, too. I've never been
one for Valentine's Day – obviously. I didn't exactly *dread* it,
but it's fair to say I wasn't someone who was up before the
postman. A few years ago, I think I was just fifteen, Mum sent
a really badly made-up, horribly pink card with gaudy, swirly,
laughably girly handwriting – all hearts over the 'i's and little
smiley faces, from A Secret Admirer. I mean, really! *A Secret
Admirer.* Even with a bogus valentine card she couldn't quite
bring herself to just make something up. What'd be wrong
with writing, like: *Gotcha in me sights, sexbomb! Oodles of love
and kisses from Big Michelle, the Culcheth Bike (you're next, big*

boy!) xxx? At least that'd be something I could have a wank over. But she didn't. She made it obvious and it was horrid – an all-time low.

So it was with a brand-new sense of intrigue and fear and, yes, dammit, puerile excitement that I rolled myself out of bed Friday morning to find two envelopes pushed under the door. Now, my plan, a whole eight hours earlier when I rocked through Ranmoor, drunk and nasty after six pints with Nick Cave lookalike a.d. (as Dangerous now wishes to be known) at the Fuzz Club, was to set my alarm and get up and swipe every single pink envelope from the mail racks – strictly for the good of mankind, of course. Observers with very little else to do in the Taptonville Road locale around Thursday teatime might have witnessed Hannah, K., arm buried up to his elbow in the postbox, trying to fish out yet more of the offending pink billets-doux. And there I was, Sheffield's, nay, *the world's* number-one defender against envelopes sealed with teddy-bear stickers, staring down at two cards – one pink, one sealed with a Piglet sticker. I had a fair idea who'd sent them.

And there's more. Passing through reception on little more than an idle whim, I'm stopped by a smiling George who points me in the direction of *two more cards*! I say, I say! One can all too easily knock this whole Valentine's malarkey as little more than a post-Christmas marketing blitz, but I'd have to venture that, when you're on the receiving end, it's sort of like . . . *nice* getting cards from secret admirers. Even if one of them has identical handwriting to that of a.d. Dangerous – that wag!

By the time I met Ben at the Interval, I was up to five. It was just there, in my bag, as I pulled out my pen and jotter before the lecture – one mercifully plain envelope with plain enough handwriting that said: *Boy with Bum (forget ya name!).* Opening it up, there's a pristine black and white of a peach or a heart or, most likely, a bottom. It's hard to be sure what it is. Underneath is a poem – if one could properly call such smut a poem – and a telephone number. Who the fuck's it *from*? In the finest traditions of Banacek, my all-time favourite afternoon detective, I apply the science of reduction. I reduce everything back to the last time I could be sure, absolutely sure, that the new card was not there. Ranmoor's main reception, when I stooped down to tuck the two new cards into my bag – I know for certain this 'bottom' card wasn't there then. That still left a lot of opportunity for somebody to drop a card in my bag. The likeliest spot was there in the Arts Tower, outside the lecture theatres. Quite seriously, hundreds of people would have been milling around, chatting, sipping coffee and jostling for position. I was pretty sure who'd sent the first four, but this latest – possibly last – is the titillating one. I plop it down in front of Ben, aiming for a tone of mild boredom in my voice.

'Handwriting? Anyone you know?'

He slides it towards himself, makes a point of scrutinising it. 'Nah, mate.' He puts it back down. 'No suspects?'

I pop my bottom lip out, try to look as clueless as possible, offer him a humble shrug. He picks the card up again, has another look, reads it, snorts loudly and chucks it back at me.

'Botty man!'

People at neighbouring tables are looking over. I'm starting to enjoy it. I'm a lad with a mystery admirer.

'Ain't got a scooby, mate. Anyway. Don't question it. Just think yourself lucky you *got* a soddin' card . . .'

I offer up my best sympathetic smile.

'Know what you mean, kidder. But I got to say – luck doesn't really come into it . . .'

He looks up. I am smiling. Even Ben recognises that I am taking the piss.

'You twat!'

'I know.'

'How many?'

'No. Nothing. Just the one.'

'Go on! How many?'

I hold up one hand.

'Five? Fuck off! You never got five valentine cards!'

Now *everybody* is looking, and I don't dig the attention any more. Ben is staring at me, truly *flabbergasted*. He's shocked and stunned. He picks up the card, sneering now, and flicks it open with disdain. He scans it, shakes his head and reads it out loud.

'To Boy With Nicer Bum Than Mine
I send this humble valentine
Please call me on my mobile line
Cos you're a ten and I'm a nine.'

He laughs his jagged laugh – a little forcefully, I can't help thinking. People only turn round to look for a second, but I can feel my ears going red. I slide low in my chair and try digging into my baked potato again. They *know* I like them soft here, so what happens? They see me coming and single me out for the rock-hard bastard, every time. I'm going to start eating meat. That's what I'm going to do. Ben's still staring at me. I'm not rising to it. That subject is now closed.

'Still going to FROUK, then?'

'May as well, hey? Not much else on. Might be a laugh, hey?'

He gives a weary nod.

'You got a ticket?'

'Nah. Pay on the door.'

'I'd get a ticket, you know. Going to sell out. Nice arse or not!'

This slays him for some considerable time, giving me ample opportunity to tackle and, ultimately, abandon my baked potato. He takes a deep breath.

'Seriously though, mate. Valentine's Day? FROUK? Be

surprised if there's any tickets left, you know. Be *very* fucking surprised . . .'

I give this some thought. I'm a chap who likes to avoid as many things as possible until the last possible moment, but this suggestion of Benny's does actually make sense.

'Come on, then. Let's get 'em while we're down here.'

He gives a bit of a huffy sigh.

'What? What's up?'

He shrugs. 'Think I'll have to give it a miss.'

'Why, man? You were bang up for it . . .'

He makes a gesture with his thumb and forefinger. Money. 'Skint?'

He nods.

'Fuck, man. Already?'

He nods again. I get up and put my hand on his shoulder.

'Come on. I'll sort you out.'

'Nah, mate.'

'*Yes*, mate! Amount of times *you've* sorted *me* out, hey?'

He smiles up at me, wet teeth doing little to promote a vision of happiness or gratitude.

'Lovely of you, man, but I need to sort this out myself. I'm flat broke. I mean it. I am absolutely on my fucking arse. It's all down to me and I need to fucking do something about it. Staying in more's a start, like, but . . .'

Blimey. This is not the Ben I've come to know (and border-line quite like – ish) talking here, like this. This is bad.

'You, er – you knocked all the other stuff on the head?'

'Dealing?'

I nod. He sighs even deeper.

'Weren't really doing much of that.'

I don't push it. He knows we all know, and it's best left well alone.

FROUK is FROUK. We get almighty wankered on Screamers, Reef and good old jugs of Stella. We dance ironically – that is, we dance like knobs – to the blistering sounds of Tatu, Abba and Justin Timberlake. We positively smoulder with tongue-in-cheek saucy goodtime fun, and we positively hug Simon (hair gelled madly with tiny, new-grown spikes) when he suggests we slope off for a curry. On the way out, five of us doing a conga to the coat check, I feel a nip to my bottom. I turn around and find myself face to face with a pink, pretty, provocative face. Colette.

'Still got that arse, then?'

All sorts of bells clang at once, but I have no time to damp them. Here she is, right here, now, waiting for a cute answer from the cute arse. I'm palpitating, properly – my heart is jolting through my ribcage. I make a pathetic thing of trying to crane round and check my backside, but she puts me out of my misery with a kiss. Fuck! Rockets rip through my guts, stars and comets scintillate in my head. This is a kiss like no other. I can feel her trying to pull back for air, but I lean deeper and deeper into her, probing with my tongue, feeling for the love. She pushes me back, gasping, and looks me full on, eyes flashing.

'Take it you got me card, then?'

I give it a comedy slap on the forehead – it was *you*, sort of thing. She just looks straight at me, those green eyes taunt-ing, goading.

'Yeah. Ta. I got it.'

'So?'

I make a terrible attempt at looking confused. She just cocks her head to one side. The tip of her tongue darts out for a second. She jerks her head back, looks me full on.

'What you going to do about it?'

And with that, all the spunk, all the guts, all the soul drains from me. I'm empty, emptied out in front of her. I fight my throat against gulping. I throw all of my consciousness into gulp-prevention measures. I gulp, hard. I strain for a cocksure tone.

'I, er . . .'

That's a squeak. That was nothing other than a mouse's squeak. I try again.

'I've got your number.'

And then I do something plain abysmal. I hate myself for this. What I do is, I fire a pretend anxious look over to the coat check, where I can see Jinty handing the tickets in. I do this in such a seedy, furtive way that I know it can only lead Colette's eyeline over, forcing the penny to drop. And she does. She catches my fake-frantic glance over at Jinty and she puts it all together.

'Oh. Fuck. I see . . .' she goes. And she sounds properly gutted. I shouldn't feel so bad. Last time I saw her, she was all over some rugger-bugger in Flares. But I *do* feel bad. I feel crap. I want just to walk off with her, start the whole thing up – but I can't. I won't. Colette gives me an embarrassed shrink of the shoulders.

'How silly do I feel . . .'

'Don't . . .'

'Shit. Listen . . .'

She pulls a speck of fluff off my shirt. She can't look me in the eye.

'Don't, erm . . .'

Fleetingly, she flits her eyes up to me – and she is done for. She really does look bruised. She lets her hand drift from my shoulder, turns and hurries away. I can't help looking at her bottom as she goes.

'Who was that?'

It's Jinty, looking tall and suspicious and very sexy indeed in her red satin sheath dress. I watch Colette disappear into the crowd.

'Dunno. Secret admirer.'

I end up back in Simon's room smoking skunk, talking shit and listening to Radiohead. That track 'Lucky' is just perfect

– for me and, it would seem, for him. For Si. Sad Si is stoned, twatted, completely out of it and all he wants to do is talk.

'Saint Valentine, man . . . some fucking saint, eh? Must've been looking the other way when I was fucking born. Wind must've changed direction . . .'

He stumbles over and turns the music up and slumps on to his bed, facing the ceiling. From where I sit on the floor, I can see how bulky and how bulging his eyeballs are. He must look mad without his specs. He starts singing.

'*I'm on a roll . . . I'm on a roll, this time . . .*'

As he sings his voice starts to falter.

'*I feel my luck could change . . .*'

And he's crying. He's sobbing silently but convulsively, his head and throat and shoulders shuddering as he weeps. I don't know what to do. If he were Emma or Petra, I'd stroke his head and try to shush him. I kneel by the bedside.

'Hey? Si, man – what is it? What's up, buddy?'

He lolls his head sideways so he's facing me, snot running down his mouth and chin. He shakes his head. His mini spikes look absurd.

'Don't . . . know . . .' he manages, before the sobbing starts again. Fuck it. I stroke his head and try to balance my unease with forced humour.

'Hey now, Baswell. You may well have piggy wee eyes and a crap haircut, but you do compensate in other ways . . .'

He sits up, glaring.

'Do I?' He's not crying now. 'Name one.'

I shrug and try to get a smile out of him. 'Actually, fucked if I can think of anything . . .'

He forces a smile. 'It's all right for you, man. *You're* normal . . .'

And before I can take this in, before the acute shock of being accused of that most prized and elusive quality *normality* properly hits home, he goes into one. No girlfriend. Ever. That whole thing about going back to Baslow to see his girlfriend?

246

Poppycock. Never even entered my head he'd make that up, actually. Ben, yes — from the very first, he came across as a scammer. But old Si, *Cymon* the scenemaker . . . he's the sort of lad that's driven me to the point of topping myself. For the longest time I've sat on the top deck looking out at the girls'-school bus stop where spotty boys, boys with glasses, boys like Simon stand for hours necking with girls like it's their natural born right and heritage. They are always tall, geeky, unprepossessing lads who really ought to be hiding themselves away in shame, but no — not only do they seem oblivious to their own design faults, they seem to think they have something to offer. They're confident. They're functional. They're living. That's the sort of lad I had Simon down for. Fuck.

'I mean, I thought it'd all be easy when I came here. I thought, like . . .'

It's too much for him to finish his drift. He's off into his soundless, pitiful cries of despair again. And I *do* pity him. I could say so much, now, to bring him comfort. But then he'd know — and I couldn't be doing with that. I pat him on the head.

'Listen, mate. Give it time. Just give it time, yeah?'

Oh, you fucking sage, Kit. He'll be just as right as rain now, won't he — now you've said that. I do the only decent thing remaining and I get up and get out of there.

The bad thing, the thing I genuinely do find hard to justify, is that yesterday I was on top of the world. I'm not going to try and deny it. I was on a high because of what Simon told me. His confidence has made such a difference — or it did for a day. I spent yesterday on the buses of Sheffield, hopping from place to place, looking, watching, taking it all in and *feeling good*. I felt good about me, about *being* me — and I felt good about life. So it's really no surprise at all that I've woken today with the talons of faceless dread clawing me back down under. I should have been expecting a knock any day now, and there it is. There we are. I'm going down again.

I could do some good. Instead of just lying here, waiting for it to go away, I could go out and do some real good. I could go call on Simon, help make it better for him. He'll be mortified, poor lad. He'll be doing everything to avoid me after what he's told me there. He'll have woken up and it'll be – Fuck! What did I say to Kit? What did I *tell* him! I could at least reassure him that I wouldn't say a thing to anyone – and I won't. I really could be doing more to help him through this – but in doing that, I'd only end up hurting myself.

I give myself a big mad sigh and force myself to get up and do the one simple, positive thing my psyche will allow. It's been bugging me, and I can do something about it. That leaflet Jinty gave me – the thing about depression. It's been wedged between the bin and my bed since I flicked it there, ages ago. I just haven't been arsed to get down on my knees and put it in the bin properly. I crawl over and prise it out and, instead of binning it, I straighten it out and sit with my back to the wall and read it again.

Week 6: Day 1
Weather: Bright Spring Breeze
Soundtrack: PJ Harvey – 'To Bring You My Love'

I very nearly didn't open his mail. Not only does Erk not write any more (he says he can't afford stamps, for fuck's sake), he has become an arch Web pest, carelessly bouncing on any mouldy spam titillation that comes his way, and in particular those whose immense download times are in inverse proportion to their fun rating. An email from Erk these days comes hand in hand with a weary sigh and a mutter of 'What's that nuisance want?' So it was with equal measures of surprise and chagrin that I read his terse adieu.

Kit, mate – getting off. Bank hawks closing in after Sheffberter blitz. Beak won't gimme another chance after the shoplift palaver. And Blunkett's latest loan scam is just bogwank. It's this simple – I cannot afford to be here, whether they railroad the new scheme through or not. I'm better off biting the bullet now and finding me a job while I'm still young enough to work my way up. Depressed? Me? Oh yes! Oh very yes indeedy, me old Chinaroon . . .
Bon chance,
Erk

Crikey! Another one bites the dust. Like, I wasn't *completely* shocked and stunned when old Willie Wilson jacked the whole thing in last year, but Erk's made of much sterner stuff. For all that he wasn't having the best of times in Birmingham, you always had a feeling that Erk *liked* that isolation. Over the Christmas break, he seemed to revel in how truly awful his existence was down there.

'I'd sum it up as follows, Mrs Hannah. Withnail or I. That is, it's like *Withnail and I* – but without the meths. Or anyone to drink it with.'

That's what he said when Mum bobbed her busy head into the room and asked him how he was liking Brum. Usually with Mum, any question to Erk is a very poorly dressed entrée to a good old nose about me, if not an out-and-out excuse to ignore his answer and change the subject with neither guile, tact nor shame to Hannah, Kit: Comparisons With Less Gifted Contemporaries. But this time she gave every indication she'd both heard and digested what he'd said – or at least that's how I read her brief and frenzied blinking, followed by the brusque withdrawal of the surveillance head with no further questions.

I spank out a very quick reply.

Bad one, man. You absolutely sure? Look before you
leap, hey? Give me a number and I'll call you.
Kit

But the truth is he won't send a number and I most likely would not have called anyway, because Erk and I are not how we used to be. It was weird at Christmas. I know it was for him, too. We'd sit there at mine or his and cover the same, solid Erk and Kit ground:

Life's so shit.

Where's the point?

Nothing really matters.

How do we know we're really alive?

And – of course – how come girls aren't interested in us?

That was the weirdest one. When we used to say it, we did – we *celebrated* our abject lack of success with girls. It was a joke. We'd sit there and moan about how pitifully low our expectations were, but we'd be laughing about it – laughing at ourselves, our sad, sad, sad predicament. But this time when the subject came up, Erk was different. He was different because, in his heart of hearts, he was *terrified* I might have copped. He didn't want to ask, he didn't want to hear things he may not like to know – but he just could not help himself. He *had* to know. He cranked his head sideways, like he does, and went: 'So, erm – anything of interest?'

I was dead tempted to make something up, but I didn't. I just grinned back at him and said: 'What do *you* think?'

But he still wasn't sure. His eyes gave it all away – he was scared I might have met someone. I don't think he wants bad things for me, like – I don't think he wants me to *fail* as such. It's just that, so long as I'm as crap as he is then no one's really counting, are they? It's just business as usual. That's the way I see it. He's quite all right with being Erk the Jerk, so long as I'm there by his side, the loyal and hapless fellow div. I think he'd be quite content for us to sit there being depressed for ever.

But he's clever, Erk. He's *so* fucking sharp, and I'm sure he knew things had changed between us. The worst thing is I don't feel any twinge of pain in letting it slip away. If I was fucking him off, letting him down, blacking him out, then yeah, I'd feel a twat about it. But this is more like we've both just got a bit bored with the act but neither of us really wants the weirdness of talking about it. I know we'll be friends again one day. I'd like to think so.

The other reason I really *can't* sit and wallow in a long and thought-through response to Erk's plight is that we're looking at houses again today. And it's St Patrick's Day, too. Not that I have, to my knowledge, even a loose thread of lineage with Ireland – but everyone's been looking forward to it like mad. Even Adie, who I distinctly recall not so very long ago refer-ring to natives of the Republic as 'your Paddy', is virtually lick-ing his lips at the first real party occasion since we got back. St Patrick's was always a huge thing in Warrington. Way, way, way before all the old pubs no one wanted to drink in put in a long wooden table and renamed themselves O'Reilly's or MacNamara's, Warrington had a wild and convivial St Patrick's celebration. Dad's best friend Heesh (his name was Mr Rourke but he always told the kids in the road to 'heesh' the noise) used to play in a band and he'd always invite us to the party at the Irish Centre. I can't see the student version of St Patrick's being much more than an orgy of red-faced drunks gorging green-dyed Guinness – but it's something to do. I've told them I'd prefer to avoid the promotional leprechaun hats and the toy shillelaghs down the Union, but if that's what they want to do, I'm not going to the wall over it.

★   ★   ★

I sit outside the Nursery, waiting for them. Ben and Adie just don't care, they'll live anywhere, but this really matters to me. Especially in light of Ranmoor, I need to feel sort of, like, *at home* in my next place. For the last month that's been the big thing, really – finalising the crew you want to get a house with and making your swoop before a) all the best places have gone, and b) you upset anyone who might subsequently emotionally blackmail you into sharing a house with them. Every twat has become obsessed with getting a deposit down on a fucking house or, more to the point, not getting left on their own. I, to my real joy and quite genuine surprise, have been approached by several different groupings. To my slight dismay though, none of these cliques comprises the core trio I'd prefer – Petra, Jinty, and, yes, Adrian O'Dangerous. I've thought it through and, as unlikely as it may have seemed six months ago, the bovine a.d. has calmed down so much that he is, truly, a different person. I mean, I can live with Sad Simon very easily. I could kick along with Ben, at a push. But given any kind of dream scenario, the ideal foursome would have to include two gals and two guys, I tend to think. Given that Petra can't *stand* Adie, though, it's looking more and more like I'll end up in a house of boys.

The place we're looking at today is a small terrace in the marvellously named Stalker Lees Road. I've taken a peek from the outside and the gaff is wee, but the neighbourhood is very fine indeed. The street is tucked just behind Eccleshall Road, where be pubs, cafés, restaurants galore, all kinds of everything a small student could want. It's great. I like it already. I've had a good fucking wander about and I can really see myself getting homey round here. There's a rambling, moody cemetery just the other side of the brook, the Botanic Gardens are a stroll away, the art school is just up the road – good bar, interesting and entirely different class of pretenders – and the Nursery Tavern is quite literally over the road. I'm sat here and they're almost late and, the more it looks as though they ain't showing, the more I want us to get this house. I'll meet the landlord on my own if I have to.

Week 6: Day 2
Weather: Still Bright, Getting Milder
Soundtrack: Durutti Column – 'Sketch For Dawn I'

The Dog & Partridge was fantastic. My mistake was in congratu-lating Ben for dragging us down there. His red face glowed with self-regard. He puffed out his well-covered chest – upper body still sheathed in ever tighter Italia top – and proceeded to speak in a monstrously poor Irish accent.

'Shure oim Oirish, arrr'nt oi? Me farder's from Dooblin and me mam's from Dannergaaal . . .'

I must have stood there stunned, just looking at him.

'What?' he goes. 'What's up?'

'Nothing.'

He poked me in the chest, getting into his role nicely.

'No. You drink in *moy* pub wid *moy* people, you tell me what's on your moind.'

I studied my glass nervously.

'Your mum and dad, Ben . . .' I looked up from the Guinness. 'They're dead.'

This knocked him back for less than a second.

'Aye, so they are, shure enough. What's your point?'

I went back to scrutinising my pint glass for signs of alien life forms – or a word or two from beyond the grave.

'Nothing,' I muttered.

I wasn't prepared for what happened next. He belly-bumped me hard, stuck his face into mine and screamed.

'WHAT'S YOUR FORCKEN POINT, YOU ENGLISH BASTARD!!'

Old men with grey cauliflower ears, blousy wives with deep

cleavages and fleshly necks, everyone in the pub turned to
see what all the commotion was about. I wanted none of it.
And in a trice, just like that, I decided it wasn't fair – on Ben,
not me – to let him carry on like that. I put my arm around
him and walked him to the door.

'C'mon, kidder. We need a word.'

Outside, it was cool but not cold. What there was of the
wind was mellow, almost warm. I faced up to Ben.

'Ben, mate. You've got to stop all this.'

'All what?'

I gave a deep, reluctant sigh.

'All the bullshit, mate. I'm not saying everyone's on to you
– but they will be, soon, if you carry on telling all these mad
porkies.'

He stepped back, made a fist, came at me – and slumped
on my shoulder, crying. Or laughing – I'm still not sure
which. He just stood there, face buried, giving the occasional
twitch and shudder. We must have looked an odd couple
indeed, standing outside an Irish pub, he with his head on
my shoulder, me trying for all the world to look as though
I wasn't there.

Back inside the pub a.d., Alex and Petra were singing rebel
songs. Later, at Sheik's, I tried to make fun of them, accusing
them of buying up Wolfe Tones CDs and swotting up on all
the best songs just for Paddy's Night. Alex turned this into a
row about racism. I was having none of it.

'Look – having a mild appreciation of the country you're
brought up in does not make you racist!'

'All patriotism is racism.'

'Fucking . . . *bollocks*!'

I could feel my eyeballs bulging, Simon stylee. Alex raised
her eyebrows at Petra.

'*This* is the voice of reason?'

I leant over, tapped her hand. 'Hey, I'm just making a
point, yeah? All that Irish bollocks – the Irish in New York

slaughtered 30,000 immigrants from Africa in 1876. They've got as much blood on their hands as anybody. There's nothing fucking noble or romantic about attaching yourself to their . . . *cause!*'

I turned to Petra. '*You* . . .' I pointed in her face . . . 'are British.'

'Scot.'

I twisted my face at Alex. 'And *you* are American.'

'Appalachian-Dutch.'

I took a deep breath, looked at Ben, looked at them all. '*None* of you is Irish. That's just racism of a different sort.'

''Scuse *me*! I am not and never have been *remotely* race-prejudiced!'

'Get lost, Alex! Show me *one* person – black, white, yellow, brown – who isn't racially prejudiced.'

'Nuh-uh. Not me.'

'So, like . . . you've never looked at the credits to, like, *Sex and the City* and wondered how come they all have Jewish surnames?'

'Dangerous *territory*, Kitty boy . . .'

'No. It's not. I know exactly what I'm saying here. I'm saying we make inert value judgements based on accumulated attitudes to race. It's not racial hatred. It's not racism. I'm asking you to admit that you have made and will make assumptions on that basis.'

'Never have. Never will.'

'What? You see a group of young black men walking towards you at night and you don't think: fuck!'

'I'm from Memphis, Kit. We have none of this tragic fear of the black man in Memphis.'

'Oh don't you? You from fucking *east* Memphis, by any chance?'

I'd read an article in the *Observer* about White Flight – how the moneyed old Memphis families and their yuppie progeny are upping and legging it to the suburbs, so paranoid are they about the rate of growth of the black population in the city. Alex's face colours slightly – but not for long.

'Yes, I'm from east Memphis. My family always has lived in that part of the city. I have no reason to feel ashamed of that.'

'Bet you had slaves.'

'You fucking racist piece of shit! How dare you assume that home help is black help!'

You could still hear my laughter on West Street ten minutes later.

She took her stick well, though. All the way back she had to endure Petra shouting 'Thomas!' like the maid in *Tom & Jerry*. She had me asking whether her granddaddy had paid off Little Richard and Chuck Berry yet, and whether she'd recommend we buy or sell cotton. She gave us a game shrug of the shoulders and said: 'See? What'd I tell you? Racist pieces of shit, all of you! Later.'

We gave her a rousing blues bass line all the way down Ashdell Road, until she was out of sight. Ben pulled me over.

'Listen. I need to ask you about something.'

And that's what this is about. We're sat in Vittles and he's got a plan. There are bombs over Bagdhad, but Ben's Shock and Awe campaign has a slightly more D.I.Y. sensibility.

'Ben, mate – is this kosher?'

'Straight up, man. I swear on me mother's life . . .'

Our eyes meet in appreciation of the irony.

'It's true, mate – me cousin works in sales there. It's not even a scam, man. She can just get a bostin' group rate for the opening weekend . . .'

Me, I'm not one for mass-participation, regimented fun, so the global lure of funfairs has tended to pass me by thus far. Ben's plan – his money-making scheme, to help reduce his burgeoning debt – is to organise an outing to the grand reopening of Alton Towers. He seems to think my endorsement will send students scurrying to book. I bet he says that to all the boys. But I don't mind. I'll help him if I can.

'How much you thinking of charging?'

'Well, you know – even if I just make a fiver a head, I can clear two ton on a fifty-seater coach. How long'd it take to earn that in McDonald's?'

I nod as sagely as I can.

'Fair dinkum.'

'So what d'you say?'

I do my best approximation of his Black Country accent.

'Ah say ah.'

'You're in?'

I nod. 'When is it?'

'First weekend in April.'

'You're on.'

His face lights up. It does, he is *beaming* and, for once, I'm glad that I've been able to do some minuscule thing for someone else. It feels good, it does – no matter how easy it was to give it. Ben takes a good slug of his English Breakfast tea – racist twat – and carries on grinning.

Week 8: Day 6
Weather: Warm, Cloudy, Fine
Soundtrack: Morrissey – 'Seasick, Yet Still Docked'

a.d. has been very quiet these last few weeks, so it was a treat, really, to see him throw himself into the rides. He was much more like his old self – but in a good way. I wouldn't say the rent thing was a turning point – he's been changing, slowly, for the better, too, ever since he got here. Physically, too – he's so much thinner and I can't help thinking he looks better for it. Still don't like the piercings, though – especially that fucking stud beneath his bottom lip. But that whole thing with his deposit cheque has definitely taken its toll on him. If he doesn't come up with the money before we break up for Easter next week, they'll force us to find someone else. And if we don't find someone else, we'll lose the fucking house. Bad one, all round.

All the way down to Staffordshire, he sat on his own, reading poetry. Bit rude, I thought, in light of everything. That's all he does, these days. He sits there and wears black and reads Sylvia Plath and fucking Rimbaud. Any twat can wear black and read Rimbaud, for fuck's sake! I mean, it was me persuaded Ben to give him the discount and me, really, who convinced him to come along in the first place. He was going to just stay in all weekend, try and not spend money. I basically put it to him that he'd crumble about six o'clock and end up drinking twelve pints on his own and going down the Union and spunking every last penny. At least Ben's trip'd be all-inclusive, more or less.

As soon as he dived off the coach though – and this was Adie back to being Adrian Dangerous – he was bang into it. He was like a kid. Every fucking ride – Air, the Ripsaw, Black Hole, Nemesis, Oblivion – he was on it, and the scarier the better. He was whooping and hollering, letting everyone know he was here.

'Look at him,' said Jinty. 'He's reliving his childhood.'

'If he ever had one,' said Petra.

Petra's wearing the 'Stop War, Blair Out' sweatshirt she picked up at Menwith Hill. I don't know if she's getting more cynical, Petra, or whether she's just growing up. She's not such a laugh, these days.

'Waaaaaay – oh!' Adie was leaning right out of the Ripsaw, arms out like wings.

We all stood back and watched him show the world how fearless he was. It was good to see him like that. He was Dangerous.

The three of us spent a fucking mint on one of those cheesy Euro-dance machines. It was just like a mini-FROUK. You stand on the mat, select your tune (knowing looks from

Jinty when I put Tatu on) and the footlights take you through your moves. All you have to do is hop, skip and jump where the lights tell you to, throw your hands around a bit and give a half-hearted clap every now and then – make a tit of yourself in front of people, fundamentally – but it was harmless. It was a hoot.

Round three o'clock the sun broke through properly – you could really feel it on your scalp. I couldn't recall the last time I'd had that balmy ease of the sun warm all my cares away. We found ourselves in the woods over by McDonald's.

'I'm starving,' I said.

'Me too.'

All eyes were on Petra. She twigged.

'Oh no – no way, kids! No *way* are we setting foot in *there*!'

'I only want a portion of fries.'

'See? *Fries!*' She turned to Jinty for support. 'They've already stolen his soul . . .'

We didn't go to McDonald's. We went instead to the old derelict mansion house, where they have the supernatural trip, *Hex*. I loved it. The end bit where the benches tip you into the bowels of hell . . . I just thought it was brilliant. Jinty reckoned it was a pale rip-off of *The Blair Witch Project* but the whole thing absolutely scared Petra shitless. So much so that, instead of feasting on Ronald McDonald's fine potato fries, we spent the remainder of the day in the Merrie Englande pub, drinking on an empty stomach. I was bollixed by the third pint, sat outside in the melting April sun. Everything around me felt remote, yet part of my world, my life. I was aware of birdsong and distant laughter, but also vaguely conscious of a gradual slowing down. The call of birds grew more plaintive as the heat drained out of the day. All around us, people were flooding for the exits, eager to beat the big push out from the car parks. Petra stood up, woozy.

'I'm spannered, guys. I'm going to have to take a wee stroll or that's me boaking all over the coach. Coming?'

I shook my weary head.

'Nah, mate. Couldn't walk as far as the bog just now.'

So it was just me and Jinty, and it was fine. The beer and the sun and the slow, tender drag of the afternoon had me beguiled. Jinty finished her pint, smiled at me with real fondness and tapped her glass.

''Nother one?'

I looked down at mine.

'Thought you were meant to be weaning me off it?'

She covered her eyebrow with her hand and squinted against what remained of the sun.

'Come on. Let's walk. Just down to the gardens.'

'You serious?'

'I'm serious. I want to talk to you.'

'So this little Micheline minx? Did she tell everyone?'

I had my legs parted, hands clasped, forearms resting on my thighs and I was watching the ants around my feet. I didn't know ants came out this early.

'That's the thing I really do owe her for. She stayed up there with me for ages. And when she came down, she didn't say a thing. Everyone thought we'd done it.'

She shook her head, lost in wonder. We sat on the bench and watched the goldfish glide under the surface. Jinty was still holding my hand, tight. She took another deep breath, still coming to terms with it.

'So your big fear is what? Being unable to have sex? Or no longer being attracted to women as a result of all this?'

I couldn't believe it was me talking. Not just that I was so calm, so matter-of-fact, so precise – but that I was, finally, talking about this, unhindered. I told her everything. How, after the thing with Paula and Maddy, I'd hung around them and let them say whatever they wanted to me in the hope that we'd do the same thing again. I didn't understand quite enough to fully appreciate what had taken place – but I knew that it felt fantastic and it made *me* feel fantastic and I wanted them to do it to me again. They didn't though. Paula and Maddy soon stopped being friends. Maddy ridiculed me about everything – my dick, my size, my disgusting, dirty mind – and chased me away whenever I came near.

I started going out with the lads at school, out to parties in each other's houses, things like that – and there were opportunities for sex. Each time though, I couldn't do it. The last time was when I was fifteen. The girl, Micheline Roberts, was one of the hottest girls round our way. Everyone wanted to go out with her, even the hard lads from Orford and Bewsey who used to come and hang round the girls'-school gates at hometime. But she liked me. There was a period when I used to be a lot funnier than I am now and one of the few things my dad's ever said that has stuck is that people like to be with people who can make them laugh. If I'd have known it'd lead to sexual disaster with Micheline Roberts, I'd have kept my fucking quips to myself. She came up to me at Barry McFadden's party. I was, of course, in the kitchen. She was wearing a light blue cropped vest top and a denim miniskirt and she asked me upstairs in front of everyone. I had to go. After we'd been kissing for twenty minutes and I hadn't made a move, she stood up and smiled at me.

'I wore this to make it easier for you,' she said.

Even now, I can taste my terror.

'Easier to get at me.'

She made it all sound so simple. She stretched up, showing yet more of her slim tummy, and pulled off her top. My dick twitched a bit. I thought I might be OK. But once we got under the sheets and I got on top, where I thought I should, I just couldn't get it to go in. It was neither hard nor soft. It was just small, and useless. I was useless. I didn't try again after that. I hung around with Erk and made jokes at his and my expense. Our favourite words were *success* and *normal*.

I looked up at Jinty. 'Know what my sister said to me?'

She smiled sadly and shook her head. 'What?'

'It isn't physically possible with a dick that small . . .'

That rocked her for a second. She caught her breath and leant over and grinned and gave me the gentlest peck on the cheek.

'I really don't think you need to worry about that, baby. Not from what I've seen.' I was almost swooning. She stood up and faced me. 'I'm so glad you told me this, Kit. Really, baby. It's all going to be fine.'

And I was glad I'd told her, too.

Week 9: Day 6

Weather: Easter Sleet

Soundtrack: Low – 'I Don't Understand'

I'm sure Mum was quietly relieved when I told her I wasn't coming with them. She'd be pleased I was taking my work seriously of course, but she could really do without the expense of another airfare. And as great as Miami sounds, I can do without a tearful reunion with my sister right now – as I'm sure she can do without the strife of having me there. Best all round, I tend to think.

So this is it. I'm going to start on the tablets and immerse myself in some of this fucking reading I have to do. And it's not like it's all *work*, you know. There's stuff here I'm *dying* to get into. Steinbeck, Fante, Dos Passos – that whole tradition of realism that the Yanks just *do* so beautifully. All those bastards were depressed, anyway. It's nothing. It's nothing once you say its name, anyway. I might not start on the tablets, yet. Maybe I'll leave that till summer – give it my full concentration, no distractions, no exams, no nothing. Maybe I won't start on them at all. Not fucking Seroxat at least, anyway. If Kit Hannah's going that route it's Lithium or nothing. It may well be nothing. As Dr Leather said, just making the appointment with him was the biggest step of all.

Breakfast is pretty well deserted. Fucking Dumbledore is casting his pixie spell over yet another poor innocent.

'Uh-uh. No way, Jose. It's one or the other and you have to decide which camp you're in. Are you *Harry Potter* or *Lord of the Rings*? Make-your-mind-up time . . .'

I feel strangely grown up as I sweep past him aloof and full of disdain. Fucking kid.

I'm cutting the crust off my last piece of toast trying to debate whether to have marmalade or honey on it, when someone plonks themselves down next to me. Now, this can only be bad news. Any gesture from me, any upward glance or facial twitch might invite a tumult of unwanted conversation. Yet I'm dying to see who it is.

'Finished with the marmy?'

It's Ratboy. It's fucking Ratboy. What in God's name is *he* doing intimidating me like that?

'Sure. There you go.'

I slide it to him, still not looking up.

'How's it going?'

How's *what* going? I think. My breakfast? Fine until you came along. My course? My life? What do you *want*?

'Yeah, OK ta. Not bad.'

'Good.'

Now I feel rude. It's just plain bad manners not to reciprocate. Sighing, but so quietly, so inwardly that I don't even know I've sighed myself, I look up and face him. God, but he's ugly!

'What about yourself?'

I might have known this'd invite a treatise of Darwinian proportions.

'Well, you know, I'd hoped to have made some friends by now.'

Pause. Looks me *right* in the eye.

'But that's not to be.'

He takes a munch on his toast, observes the unchomped remainder as though clues to his unpopularity lurk within.

'But, you know – that's just a thing. It's a fact. It's what *is*. As things stand, now, today, I have no friends, no better means of passing my time. That doesn't mean I won't have a friend tomorrow. Does that make sense?'

So long as you're not pinning your hopes on me, it can make as much sense as you like, matey.

'Mmmm. Yeah. Think so, yeah.'

He shifts round in his seat. Shit. He's warming to his theory.

'I mean, take girls, right? You don't have a girlfriend yet?'

Jesus! What does he do with his time? *Watch* people?

'Erm, well, no – not as such, anyway. I . . .'

'But you will have. It's an absolute fact. Statistically, scientifically, probably, you *will* have a girlfriend at some point.'

'It's not really a question of science, is it?'

'Well, yes, actually. That's exactly what it is. It's just fact. There's somebody for everybody.'

I'm stunned. Not by how sure he is of himself, this blinking, odd, ferret-like lad – but by how right he is. Of course he's right. He smiles his crooked smile.

'It will happen. It *will* happen.'

'But shouldn't you take steps towards it?'

'I don't know what you mean.'

'Shouldn't you help bring it towards you, like? Shouldn't you *make* it happen.'

His flaky eyelids flutter open and shut, open and shut.

'No. Things don't really happen like that. Not in the natural scheme of it, anyway.'

He crams one large corner of toast into his mouth and pushes himself up from the table. He holds out his hand. He shakes; I just sort of leave my hand there while he waggles it up and down.

'Good talking to you, anyway, erm . . .'

'Oh. Kit. Yeah, Kit.'

'Kit. John. Bye.'

He picks up his funny little bag and marches off on splayed, flat feet.

Week 11: Day 4
Weather: Blissful, Balmy Sunshine
Soundtrack: Beth Orton – 'Central Reservation'

At least Adie won't talk about fucking exams. It's all any twat can think about at the moment. Like, we're at university – you *have* exams. You're probably going to pass them, you know? It's all going to be just fine. Talk about something else, for fuck's sake! Mind you, Adie's not much better. The Man in Black is a man possessed. I push open his door and he's on me immediately.

'You're still coming, aren't you?'

'Still coming, amigo. Nothing's changed since breakfast.'

'What about the others?'

'*Relax*, man. We're coming. We're all coming. We'll be there for you.'

He takes deep, significant breaths and paces around the cell. 'Good. Good.'

It's taking everything in his power to keep him level. You can feel the fear and the energy – he's shitting himself. What's happening is there's an open mic for poets down at Muse. It's meant to be all right – not as teeth-gratingly awful as you'd expect. They've had some good people down there, too. This whole thing with Adie started after he heard Paul Farley's reading. He's done nothing but lock himself away writing – apart from *talk* about his writing. He's started going on about his 'voice' and, worryingly, his 'plainsong'. Uh-oh. But we're

265

coming, anyway. He's doing his first reading tonight and it's fair to say there's only been Si try to have a little dig at him.

I shuffle through the crap on his desk, like I always do. There's some Chomsky conspiracy theory, a volume of Philip Larkin, a battered Catullus for fuck's sake – and there are lots and lots and lots of credit-card bills. It's too late to pretend I haven't seen them. There's fucking *loads* – Marbles, Capital One, egg, RBS. There's Visas, Mastercards, American Express, everything. I try to slide the Chomsky back on top of the pile, but too late. A black speedball flies across the room and slams me on to the bed. He jumps on top of me and pins me down, ramming his knee into the small of my back.

'You fuck! You fucking fuck! What the fuck you doing looking at that!'

I can hardly raise a croak. 'At what?'

He sticks his knee in harder and pulls my arms up behind my back. It hurts.

'My things! My fucking things, you nosy fuck! Hey!'

'Adie, I swear to you – I didn't see anything. I was looking at the book.'

He relaxes his grip a bit. He gives my arm a warning jerk.

'Well, *don't*! Don't fucking look at *anything*!'

I step back, rubbing my coccyx reflexively and hoping his poetry is fucking shit.

Which is a matter of opinion. Personally, I was cringing for him. I mean, Muse is a really nice bar. It's pretty nondescript from the outside – no name, grey paint, very understated – but inside it's all leather sofas and a nice, gently buzzy ambience. There's a good crowd in there, too. It's mainly students and youngeroonies, but there's a few older types – fellas with Chicano beards and their glassy-eyed, wine-slamming companions. The thing is, they're all there for the poets. Nobody so much as murmured when Adie got up.

He was terrified, clearly. He got up and looked out across

the room, his thick black eyeliner making his face deranged as well as scared. He stood there and chewed on his lip and seemed to talk to himself. Maybe he was trying to master his nerves, maybe the audience, but that was really the last and only time he lifted his head up. From the moment he cleared his throat, he was bent over his papers, awkward and acutely embarrassed.

'Erm, thanks. I'm, ah, a.d. Thanks. The, ah . . . well, let's just start, shall we?'

Supportive if muted applause from Jinty and a few others. I joined in just as they were stopping.

'"Mini Me". This one's called "Mini Me".'

He cleared his throat again and started. I had a life-flashing-before-me experience, but it's all images of Adie. Adie in his rugby shirts, sleeves pulled up to his wrists. Adie bursting my door down and flinging himself on to my bed. Adie's amusing badges and his *Be Prepared* belt. Adie getting his under-lip pierced. It all flickered in front of me as Adie opened his mouth and began to recite poetry.

> *He laughs at what he hears*
> *And sees*
> *His little boy, his little me*
> *Is starting to take notice*
>
> *He sits up when a girl goes past*
> *He meets with nameless friends*
> *He speaks up with his breaking voice*
> *And says he's going out*
>
> *It's just the same when he was me*
> *And he could see the girl go by*
>
> *But still he laughs at what he hears . . .*

There was a brief pause while people clicked that the poem was finished. Sporadic and somewhat robotic applause seemed to give a.d. courage. He wiped his top lip, allowed himself a brief smile and ducked down to the lectern once again. He gulped hard and took a deep breath.

'OK. Right. Thanks. Yeah. That one, I mean . . . well, let's see. This one's also, erm . . . I mean, this one's called "Father".

> *Love me.*
> *Love me.*
> *Love me.*
> *Please.*
>
> *Say you care.*
> *Say you will.*
> *Tell me I don't let you down . . .*

I tried to look anywhere but at him, yet that strange fascination that makes us ogle at car wreckage drew me back towards his face. His demented eyes were wet with tears. It was excruciating. I couldn't, could not physically stand there and listen. Yet, if I were to move off, he'd see. The polite thing to do, the thing a friend would do, is wait for him to finish that poem then slip off to the loo. No, really, what a *friend* would do – a friend would stick it out. A friend would stand tall, stand solid and support him come what may. For me, though – I'm his friend, for sure. But all I could think was: What happened? Who is this *poet* person? Where did Adrian Dangerous go? And it was *bad* poetry. I didn't want to stand there and listen to my friend spouting bad poetry in front of an audience. I spied a possible harbour, a little cranny out to the left of the bar. As I melted further and further back and edged closer to safety, I could hear a.d.'s voice quivering with raw emotion as 'Father' reached its climax. He was almost shouting.

Love me.
Love me.
Love me.
PLEASE!!

And I'll be damned if the crowd didn't absolutely *love* it! There was that same shocked silence at the end, then, almost in unison, a torrent of applause. There was cheering. One plummy voice shouted, '*Bravo!*' But I couldn't go back in there. It was dreadful.

Afterwards, we all piled into Pizza Volante and toasted him and congratulated him, but he seemed drained by the whole thing. He smiled and said thanks, but he was withdrawn – far away and unreachable. Conversation completely dried up. People started making excuses about exams as pudding orders were cancelled. And in the bustle of not being last to leave, we missed Adie. He just went. One minute he was there, next thing he was gone. A twenty-pound note lay at his place. Me and Jinty walked back up towards Broomhill together.

'Beautiful night, isn't it?'

'Gorgeous.'

'So mild. I love nights like this.'

'Me too.'

Jinty stopped. 'Listen.'

I listened. 'What?'

'You can still hear birds singing.'

I listened again. There they were. Sleepless with the thrill of new life, new season, birds chattered and called. There was something in the damp night air. Mixed up with the elusive fragrances of spring was an atmosphere, a spirit – something just poured through me like never before. It was a childlike excitement like I haven't had for fucking ages, but it was more than that. I had a sense of something marvellous, something joyous about life's possibilities. Instead of my standard, innate sensation of dread, I was overwhelmed by a conviction that

I was standing on the cusp of something good. Jinty started walking again.

'They don't want the day to end.'

'Who would, hey?'

She was dragging her long legs slowly, like she was trudging off the beach after a long day in the sun.

'Got some grass, if you want?'

'Not skunk, is it?'

'I've *got* skunk. But I've got something a lot milder. You want?'

'I want.'

Week 11: Day 5
Weather: Gentle May Showers
Soundtrack: Sigur Rós – ()

The first thing I wanted to do was see Adie. a.d. Not for any of that macho shit – no way in the world would I go boasting and bragging and dishing the dirt. It's just that, I don't know – I see him differently, again. I feel I can know him better, now. I can be a real friend to him, now we're both on the same side. But more than anything, he's part of what happened. That whole magical thing – it really would not have been the same if it hadn't started with his (still frightful) poetry reading.

Me and Jinty wandered back to hers. Softly, softly, it started to rain. As soon as we got inside, she started knocking up.

'Stick something on,' she said.

I had a forage through her CDs. It was coming down to a choice between Beth Gibbons and Sigur Rós. The thing with that Beth Gibbons album, right – too much wobbliser. That Low/Mercury Rev wobbliser, the bowed-saw/wailing-banshee thing that's always there in the background – maybe it's a Steve Albini stamp or something, but it's getting every-where. I can't really be doing with too much wobbliser on a track. She passed me the badboy and from the first toke it had to be Sigur Rós. The soothing wash of the piano fused with the smoke and sent me under. I lay back on the floor and closed my eyes and let the sweet sinsemilla fill me up.

If the time did not stand still, it hardly moved. The plan-gent call of Sigur Rós soaked through me, soothed my heart, my soul, my groin. More and more, I came aware of my balls, my tingling balls and the pulse of my dick. More and more my mind subsided and my throbbing balls yearned. I took another deep drag and groaned to myself and shifted my arse on the floor, jutted my hips out. Then she was beside me.

'Let me,' she said.

I didn't stop her. I let her. She put the ball of her hand between my legs and rubbed slowly, rubbed my cock until it stiffened under the denim. I closed my eyes and let her. The music changed to a celestial keyboard refrain, growing in intensity. She unzipped me and carefully, delicately, she pulled it free and slowly, deeply, began to suck me. I've played the track, the third track, again and again today and I can't get the feeling back. But it happened. Once, just hours ago, it happened and I celebrate that. I can never forget it. She was beautiful, my Big Bird. She was perfect. She leant me back, and she did it all, and, when she was on top of me, she gripped my wrists and dug her nails into me and bit down hard on her lip. The guitar track started and she was rocking hard with it, faster than the music, lost to everything.

When she was finished she opened her eyes and looked down on me and smiled so beautifully. She was sweating hard, panting, and she was perfect. She laid her hand on my head and gave a breathless little laugh and said: 'Well, then?'

I could not have loved anybody any more, ever.

I knocked on Adie's door, but no answer. He'll be revising, poor lad. Out of all of us, he is absolutely cacking it about his exams. I'll leave him alone. I can try again later.

Week 12: Day 5
Weather: Early Showers, Brightening Up
Soundtrack: David Gray – 'Sail Away'

Jinty and I walk away from the graveside, hand in hand. Throughout the ceremony she's been just about clinging on, I can feel it. I was hardly there, myself. I couldn't help drifting back to his last night. More than the poetry reading, more than the birdsong and the sex with Jinty, it's the Sigur Rós soundtrack that takes me away. I can hear it, every plaintive knell.

'You stand alone.'

And I see Adie. Poor Adie, all alone. He must have made his mind up long before he left the pizza place. Could we have done anything? Of course we could. Right up until the jump, he would have let any of us talk him out of it, if only we'd looked closely enough. To try and blame yourself is a useful tool of grief, but in Adie's case I know we could all have done more for him. He walked out of Pizza Volante, strolled up to Sorby Hall, took himself to the very top floor and jumped. No note, that we know of. Poor bastard.

Jinty sits down on a still-damp bench. Her face is pained, pinched with sorrow. She turns to me tries to smile.

'Remember him at Alton Towers?' she says.

I nod.

'Remember what we said?'

'Something about him being back on form?'

'Well, sort of. We said he was reliving his childhood, didn't we?'

I hang my head. Fuck. Everything about him, everything from way back, it all adds up. It all adds up to this.

'Well, he wasn't. He was saying goodbye to it.'

Her eyes well up and this time she can't hold back. I put my arm around her and hope she doesn't cry for long. I can't stand crying.

On the drive back to Sheffield, Jinty tells me we're not going to date. Every time she looks across at me, I think she's going to start crying again, but she doesn't – her eyes are moist but she's smiling at me. She takes my hand.

'Ah, Kitty baby – I feel all gooey when I look at you . . .'

'So why you dumping me, then?'

'I'm not *dumping* you . . .'

'So? What, then?'

'I'm . . . I'm just . . .' She gives a big sad sigh and shakes her head. 'You're just starting out, darling. You want to go to the States. I'd only hold you back.'

'Very noble.'

She does that sad smile again. 'You'll only break my heart.'

So that was that, really – snuffed out before we'd even begun. We're not going out, me and Jinty. What she says, right, what she wants is for us to be friends, *real* friends, life-long companions, supporters through life. Friends. I'm a bit saddened by it. I've been doing my level best not to play the smitten geek these last few weeks. It's only the thing with a.d. that's kept me straight. I'm mad on her, I am. I'm fucking mad on her. But I know it's for the best. How can a midget like me go out with a Big Bird? That's what she's saying, isn't it?

Last Day of Skool
Weather: Hotter Than July
Soundtrack: Coldplay – 'In My Place'

The Fox & Duck is rocking. Every fucking pub in Broomhill is rocking, but this is where we've been since four o'clock, since the last of the exams called time, since Petra shuffled in to squeals and hugs and a hundred offers of drinks. This is mad. I'm in the Dox, getting plastered with all sorts of Characters from all sorts of places. I'm a fucking student. Alex is chewing my ear off.

'But *why* do they have to be sympathetic? Tell me, please, because that I do not understand!'

'They don't, Alex. Characters do not have to be sympathetic.'

'*Whoa!* Rewind! You've been telling me you can't stand Arturo Bandini because he's unsympathetic . . .'

I haven't been saying that. I know I haven't been saying that because I plain don't believe in all that cant about rounded characters and sympathetic leads and story arcs – it's shite, but I can't be arsed debating the point. I turn my wobbly head to her.

'Alex?'

'What!'

'Come here and give us a hug!'

And she does it. Her face opens up into a big fat smile, all dimples and pearly-white teeth and she crushes the daylights out of me with a hug. Petra and Jinty are slumped over a corner table, consoling each other. They're well gone.

'Where did it go, though? Where did that year go? That was a year of our lives – gone. We'll never have that back now. Never.'

'I was just a wee girly when I pitched up here. God. All I wanted was to be a big girl like you. I wish I was still little. I wish I had it all ahead of me.'

'*You* fucking *do*, you daft moo! What about me?'

'Nah. No way. That's gone, now. All of that – we'll never have that again.'

I spot Nick Roland making merry with Jock and two girls off the course and I'm about to go over when a truly wonderful sight assails me. It's Ratboy. Ratboy comes walking into the pub . . . with a girl! I mean, she's doesn't conform to conventional notions of beauty by any means, but blimey – I have to congratulate the weird bastard. I barge my way through the crowds. It's only when I get there that I realise I've forgotten his name. Still, what the fuck, hey? He's with his new bird, he won't care what people call him. He'll just be chuffed that I'm saying howdy to him, bigging him up in front of her.

'Ratboy!'

He turns. He doesn't exactly seem overjoyed by the salutation. I nod to the girl.

'Looks like you were right, hey?'

'I beg your pardon,' he says, all puffed up and affronted. I wink at him and nod at his girlfriend again.

'Someone for everybody, hey?'

He closes his lizard's eyelids and rocks back on his feet. I'd swear he was counting to ten. The eyes flicker open again. I know who he looks like now. The spazz off *Road Trip*. The one whose car they requisition. Him.

'This is my sister, Ann. She's here to escape the delights of Ilkley and sample a student revel first-hand. Ann, this is Kit.'

It's one of those moments when I can picture perfectly how my face looks: awkward, grinning, foolish. I shake hands as warmly as possible in the circumstances.

'Ann. Hi. Lovely to meet you.'

And it's at that very moment that the door happens to swing open and Simon happens to stagger in, flushed and grinning and holding his hand up like a traffic cop.

'SCHTOPP!' he shouts. Nobody does, but Ann seems

tickled. For no good reason, I cup my hands around my mouth.

'Baswell!'

His eyes shine brightly behind his specs. I wave him over. 'Here a mo!'

He pushes his way through. He's already looking at Ann rather than me.

'I want you to meet Ann. Ann and, erm . . .'

'John,' says Ratboy. 'John Dowie.'

And with that, another skin is shed. John Dowie, from my first day here. How frightened I was. How very, very scared. And it was this, more than anything, that frightened me. Being here, in the Dox. Being normal. Being a Stude.

'John, right. This is Si. Lord Cymon of Baswell.'

I do a stupid little bow and start to edge away. I get to within an arm's reach of Prof. Roland when I feel a pinch on my bottom.